THE SALISH SEA

THE SALISH SEA SERIES: BOOK ONE

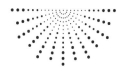

SUSAN LUND

CHAPTER ONE

REDWOOD BAY BOAT LAUNCH, Clallam County, Washington

March 2005

When she woke up, the room was still dark.

She slept on the floor beside the bed, her body tucked against the outside wall with the window on it. Before she fell asleep, her mother and Dennis had been yelling and her mother was crying, and she was afraid.

She always hid beside the bed when her mother's boyfriends came and played on the bed with her mother. She'd take her stuffed toys and a drinking box of juice, and she'd wait until they left. Then, Dennis would return, and she'd climb up onto the sofa to go to sleep under the worn wool blanket. By then, her mother and Dennis would be asleep and there'd be no more crying or yelling or hitting.

The hitting was the worst.

It scared her more than the yelling, because her mom got really quiet afterward.

That morning, after everyone woke up, Dennis went out for smokes. When he returned, they got dressed and went to the brown car parked in the space outside their motel room. It was still dark, and she was cold and sleepy, and her stomach grumbled.

"Mommy, I'm hungry," she whispered, careful not to talk too loudly.

"Quiet, sweetheart," her mother said. "We're going to get some money and then we'll eat, okay?"

She nodded and squeezed her stuffed doll more tightly, her stomach not satisfied with the drinking box that was all they had left from the groceries.

They drove for a long time, the streetlights casting shadows on the sidewalks and making the area along the coast look really scary. They pulled into a parking lot and her mom and Dennis got out.

When she tried to follow, her mother stopped her.

"You stay here, baby girl," she said. "We're going to get our money and then we'll be back."

That upset her. Her mother was going to leave her in the car. She cried, afraid to stay alone.

"I want to come," she whispered, trying to keep her voice down.

"You can't," her mother said. "You can't come with us. Stay in the car and you'll be safe."

"No!" she cried, panic filling her at being left alone in the dark parking lot. "Please, Mommy, take me with you..."

Finally, her mother relented and grabbed her by the hand, pulling her down the steep pathway to the beach below the parking lot. There was a small bay, sheltered by tall trees and dozens of old logs rotting in the surf.

"Stay here," her mother said and pointed to a spot on the sand between two large logs. "We're going to talk to the man on the boat and get our money. Then, we're going to IHOP for breakfast, okay? There's one on the way home."

She nodded, her stomach growling out loud.

"Good girl," her mother said. "Stay here. Keep your head down. I don't want the man to know you're here."

She ducked down, leaning against the big log, and held her stuffed doll against her chest. She peered above the log and watched as her mother and Dennis walked to the shore. Soon, a boat with a red roof drove into the cove and up to the beach. A bright light shone on the sand and then her mother and Dennis got onto the boat and the boat drove away.

She frowned and wanted to run after the boat, but it was gone and disappeared around the end of the bay. She told herself that they were going to get their money and then they would go to the IHOP and have pancakes. She liked hers with whipped cream and strawberries. Her mother liked eggs and bacon and toast and hash browns. She didn't know what Dennis liked because he was her mother's new friend, and they hadn't gone to IHOP yet.

She loved going to IHOP. It was the best part of the month.

After the boat drove away, she sat in the silent bay, the water lapping against the beach the only sound. She sat there for so long that she started to shiver. Then, the rain started falling. It was only a light drizzle, but it covered her face, and her teeth chattered. She wondered when her mother would come back.

She hoped it was soon.

She was so cold...

A long time later, she didn't know how long, after she had cried and then calmed down, and cried again, the sun rose and she glanced around at the rocks and trees, the sand and the

SUSAN LUND

fallen logs. Her mother still hadn't returned, and her stomach still grumbled, and her coat was wet from the rain.

A strange man came toward the beach on a path leading down from the parking lot, a large walking stick in his hand. He came over to her, but she tried hard not to look at him. She wasn't supposed to talk to strangers.

"Hello, there," the man said. "What are you doing here all by yourself? Where are your parents?"

She didn't respond at first, and kept looking out at the water, hoping the boat would come back.

"What's your name?"

She shook her head, not going to answer.

"My name's Derek. Where did your parents go?"

She pointed to the water, figuring it was okay to point because she wasn't saying words.

"Did they go in a boat?"

She nodded and kept staring straight ahead.

"How long have you been waiting?"

She shrugged, not knowing how long.

"Was it dark out or was the sun shining?"

"Dark," she said finally, her voice cracking from her throat being dry. She looked at him and he was smiling. He wore a black rain slicker with a hat. He seemed like a nice man.

"Is that your car in the parking lot? The brown car?"

She shook her head. It wasn't their car. It was a rental car. That much she did know.

"Did you *come* in that car?"

She nodded and wiped her nose. "It's a rental."

"What did the boat look like that your parents went in?"

"It had a red roof."

The man called Derek nodded and then he glanced around the beach. "You've been waiting here for quite a while if it was

4

still dark when you came here. You should come with me and wait in my car."

She shook her head. One thing her mother told her was to never go with a stranger. *Never.*

"Okay. I'll bring a blanket for you," Derek said. He disappeared up the path and then after a few moments, he returned. He held a brown blanket in his arms and had an umbrella in the other. "Put this around you and hold this to keep the rain off."

He had a cell phone and spoke into it for a while. Then, he sat on a log across from her and told her about himself.

"I have a daughter," he said. "Her name is Amber. She's all grown up now, but once upon a time, she was as old as you. How old are you? Three? Four?"

"Almost five," she said.

The man frowned like he was mad.

"You're awfully small for almost five."

He told her about their home nearby and how he went for a walk every day to look for sticks that he could polish to make walking sticks. He showed her his stick and talked about his wife and his sister, who were both teachers. He asked her questions about herself, but she didn't know much, and she didn't really want to talk.

In a while, two people in uniforms struggled down the cliff and came over to where she and Derek sat.

The lady spoke to Derek and then turned to her.

"Hello. My name is Deputy Gallagher. What's your name, sweetheart?"

"I don't know."

"You must have a name. What did your mother and father call you?"

She shook her head. "Baby. Sometimes Baby Girl."

"Where's your mother and father?"

"Mommy went with Dennis to get some money and then we're going to IHOP. My father is dead."

"They went in a boat?"

She nodded.

"What do you remember about how you got here?" Deputy Gallagher asked.

"We drove in the car."

Deputy Gallagher looked at her for a moment, her hands on her hips. "You need to come with us," she said. "It's cold and rainy. Someone will wait here in case your mom and Dennis come back, okay? They'll bring them to the Sheriff's Office to be with you, okay?"

She shook her head. "I don't want to go to foster care." She started to cry.

"Oh, sweetheart, no," the deputy said. "When your mom and Dennis come back to get you, you'll go with them. Right now, we need to get you out of the rain. You can come and sit in the car with me and dry off. I have a juice box that you can drink."

She was cold and wet. All she'd had was some toast with jelly the previous night, so she was hungry. The drinking box she had earlier wasn't much and she was thirsty. Another drinking box sounded really good -- good enough to tempt her into going with Deputy Gallagher.

"Okay," she said finally, wiping her eyes. "I'll go."

She took Deputy Gallagher's hand and walked with her up to a car, her doll tucked tightly beneath her other arm. They sat in the back and the other deputy gave her a dry blanket. Deputy Gallagher handed her the juice box. "Here," she said and sat beside her on the back seat. "That's a lot better, isn't it?" Deputy Gallagher said. "So. Can you tell me where you live?"

She shook her head. She didn't know where she lived. She

lived with her mother and sometimes with Dennis, but he wasn't always there.

"Do you live in Port Angeles?"

She shrugged. "I don't know."

"What's your mom's name? Do you remember Dennis calling her a name?"

She tried to think. *Charl.* That's what Dennis called her when he used a name.

"Dennis called her Charl."

"Charl," Deputy Gallagher repeated. "Short for Charlene?"

She shrugged, not sure.

"And your dad? Do you remember your dad's name?"

She shook her head. "Just Daddy."

"Do you remember what your mother called him? What's your last name?"

She tried to think but could come up with nothing other than "Daddy. Just Daddy."

"So, you got up this morning and had breakfast with your mom and Dennis, and then drove here."

"We didn't have breakfast. We're going to IHOP when my mommy gets her money."

"She was going to go on a boat and get her money?"

She nodded.

"Did it take a long time to get here or was it fast?"

"Fast."

"Do you live in a house or somewhere else?"

"I don't know." She was starting to get really upset. "We were staying at a motel."

Deputy Gallagher turned to the other deputy. "They could be staying at the Empire or at one of the bed and breakfasts. Contact them to see if a couple with a child registered."

The other deputy nodded and spoke into a cell.

Deputy Gallagher turned back to her. "So, you drove here

from the motel and your mom and Dennis were going for a boat ride to get her money. Was the boat here when you got here?"

She shook her head. "It came after. Dennis called on his phone."

Deputy Gallagher smiled. "You're doing really well. Really well. Did the boat come right up on the beach? Was it a big boat?"

She had seen really big boats before and thought it was small. "Small. It was white with red on the roof."

"Good job. So a white boat with red on the roof came here. Then, what happened? Did they get on the boat? Did you see the man who was driving the boat?"

She nodded. "He was tall."

"Did he have dark hair or light hair."

"He had a hat."

"Okay. What color was the hat? Was it white? Or dark?"

"Dark."

"Then your mom and Dennis got on the boat and it drove off?"

She nodded.

"Why didn't you go with them?"

"My mommy said I couldn't go. She said that the man couldn't see me and that they would come back and get me when it was time to leave. They said I shouldn't talk to anyone and to wait for them to come back."

She hugged her stuffed doll tightly, and took another drink from her juice box. Her mother sometimes left her alone for a long time, and she always watched TV and waited. Her mother always came back.

"Is that Dennis's car?" Deputy Gallagher asked, pointing to the brown car in the lot.

She shook her head.

"It's a rental," the other deputy said to Deputy Gallagher. "I called in the plates. It's registered to a car rental in Seattle."

She craned her neck to see over the front seat, but the bay wasn't visible from the parking lot. She was afraid the police would take her away and she'd never see her mother again.

Deputy Gallagher left the car and talked to the other deputy, glancing back at her while they talked. She knew they weren't happy from the way they were frowning.

Deputy Gallagher came back and opened the door, getting inside. "You're going to come with us, sweetie," she said and looked at her over the back seat. "We're going to take you to the Sheriff's Office where it's nice and warm."

"I don't want to leave," she said and started to cry. "Where's my mommy?" She rubbed her eyes with a fist.

But they took her anyway.

They drove for a long time, and she felt afraid that she'd never see her mother again. Finally, they arrived at a building and took her inside. It was warm and there were other deputies sitting at desks. Deputy Gallagher took her to a room in the back, and while it was nice and warm, and she had some hot chocolate and a donut with sprinkles, she was so scared, she didn't want to talk anymore.

She cried to herself, because she knew that this was what she always feared.

"Don't tell anyone or they'll take you from me and put you in foster care," her mother always said. "Then I won't get to see you ever again. Don't tell anyone. Not ever."

She hadn't meant to tell anyone ever, but she was cold and wet and scared.

Most of all, she'd worried where her mother and Dennis were. They should have come back to get her. At that moment, she was afraid she'd never see them again.

CHAPTER TWO

MYSTIC BEACH, Vancouver Island, Canada

February 2012

In the winter months, King Tides were larger than normal, hence the name.

Kathy Meadows took her Lab-shepherd mix Kirby out for a walk every day, no matter what the weather was like -- rain, shine, sleet or snow. Not that it snowed much on Vancouver Island, but it happened on occasion. On a snow day, she'd simply put on a warmer coat, for the snow on the Island was usually gone moments after it hit the ground. So different from her home back in Winnipeg, Manitoba where winter was one long deep freeze with temperatures more akin to Siberia than the rest of Canada.

Kathy, or Kath, as she was called by friends and family, moved to the Island with her late husband Chris, and had lived in Victoria for ten years while Chris worked for the City as a planner. They'd retired in nearby Jordan River and had lived there for the past six years in a rustic cottage overlooking the Salish Sea. Chris passed away the previous year and rather than move to Victoria or back to Manitoba and be closer to family, Kath decided to stay where she was. She had enough friends in the small town and in Victoria that she could spend the rest of her life there if she wanted.

During a King Tide, all manner of objects washed up on the shores of the Salish Sea -- fishing nets, buoys, plastic garbage -- anything that could float. That morning, there were signs the tide had been particularly high. A line of seaweed and sticks marked its apex, reaching almost up to the breakwater near the small parking lot where she'd parked her Volvo Station Wagon. Other than that, the beach looked the same as always. An old wooden dock stretched out into the small bay, which was sheltered by an outcropping of tall pines.

On that morning, she and Kirby walked the beach. Kirby loved the water and would rush in and grab sticks and other items from the surf. It was the Lab in him. Labs loved water, and Kirby loved it more than most.

Kirby seemed particularly interested in something he'd found between a couple of rotting logs.

"What have you got there, boy?" she asked, stepping over the logs and seaweed that collected on the sand. "Got a stick?"

She reached the spot where he was standing, his tail wagging furiously, his nose down between two logs. Something was wedged in the crevice between them.

She peered down between the wood and saw a running shoe.

"Just an old shoe," she said and reached down to grab it, intending to put it into the trash bin back near the parking lot. She made a point of cleaning up any litter she found on her daily walks. Some people were such litterbugs and didn't care about the beauty of the beach but not Kath.

When she lifted the shoe, she saw that there was a sock still in it -- one of those gym socks, and then...

"Oh, my God," she said and dropped the shoe in horror. There was a bone inside.

She'd read about shoes being found along the coastlines of British Columbia and Washington State. This shoe had to be one of them. Some poor soul, depressed and fed up with life, had likely jumped off one of the many bridges in the area. That, or an accidental drowning was the usual cause of the shoes washing up on the beaches.

Thinking it was a game, Kirby jumped over the log and tried to grab the shoe, but she stopped him, putting herself between him and the shoe.

"No, boy," she said. "Back!"

He was far too interested, and probably wanted to get the bones out of the shoe, so she put him back on his leash and led him away, fastening the leash to a post near the parking lot. Then, she went back to the shore where the foot was and looked at it more closely. It appeared to be a lady's running shoe by the size and color. Dark pink and grey, it must have belonged to a young woman. More than likely a young woman who'd taken her own life.

That made Kath sad.

Some poor soul had killed herself in despair, and the only proof was a foot trapped in a running shoe. Kath immediately thought about the girl's parents, family, and friends. Had they wondered about her for years, knowing she probably killed herself, but not having a body to show for it? For Kath, having Chris's ashes in an urn on the mantle over her fireplace was a comfort. Their own children, two girls who were now grown and married with kids of their own, had moved around the country to follow jobs and attend university, but she talked to them each week to hear their latest news. Going years without knowing how they were? That was too hard to imagine.

Not ever having a body to bury, or ashes to keep, would be terrible.

She glanced around and wondered what to do.

"I should call someone," she said out loud to herself. She'd taken to talking to Kirby, now that Chris was dead, or to herself. "Should I leave the shoe here or take it to the car?" She chewed her lip for a moment and then took out her cell phone. "I'll call the police."

She knew one of the constables working at the local RCMP detachment in Jordan River and so called him up. Pete Brady was the son of one of Chris's co-workers back in Victoria. He'd know what to do.

When he answered, she told him what happened.

"I was walking my dog at Mystic Beach and he found a running shoe stuck between two logs. There's a foot inside. I think it's one of those feet that washes up now and then along the coast. What should I do?"

"You did the right thing, Mrs. Meadows," Pete said. "I'll let the BC Coroner's Services office know about it. In the meantime, I'll make sure someone comes there to check it out."

"Thanks, Pete," Kath said. "I wasn't sure what to do. I'll wait until they get here."

"I appreciate that," he said.

"Say hello to your dad and mom for me, will you?"

"I will," he replied. "You take care."

"You, too," she said and ended the call. She went up to where Kirby was sitting like a good boy, waiting patiently for her to return.

"Well, Kirby, looks like we're here for a while until the RCMP come to take over."

She sat beside Kirby on a log and glanced up and down the beach. From what she'd read about the feet, the reason they turned up along the coast was due to the buoyancy of the new running shoes. When the body disintegrated in the water, the joints came apart and because the foot was protected inside the shoe, it would float to the surface and get carried on the currents.

In the winter, when the tides were especially high, they could be carried miles and miles from the place where the body initially came to rest.

Kath gave Kirby a good back rub and waited for the RCMP to arrive.

In about fifteen minutes, an RCMP vehicle drove up and parked in the lot next to Kath's Volvo. A young constable in uniform exited the sedan and came over to where she sat with Kirby, waiting. He looked to be around thirty, with a pleasant face, blond hair and blue eyes.

"Mrs. Meadows?"

"Yes, that's me," she said and stood, extending her hand. "Kathy Meadows. I called this in."

He shook her hand. "Nice to meet you," he said and smiled. "I'm Constable Towers. Constable Brady told me about the shoe."

"Yes," Kath said. "Terrible. Just terrible. Gave me a real fright, finding a shoe with a foot still in it. You know, I read about the Salish Sea feet, but never imagined I'd find one."

"Speaking of which, where is it?" he asked and glanced around the beach.

"I'll take you there," she said and left Kirby with his leash attached to the pole. "It's just down the beach, between some logs."

She led Constable Towers down the beach to the logs where she'd found the shoe and pointed to it.

"There," she said. "It's a lady's running shoe. There's a sock and some bones inside. My dog found it. I touched it, not even thinking that it was suspicious. There's so much junk washing up on the beach during the high tides. I never imagined."

"I guess you wouldn't," Constable Towers said. "I'll take it from here. Were you wearing your gloves when you picked it up?"

"Yes," she said and glanced down at her leather gloves. "I guess I was."

"That's good," he said. "You won't have any prints on it."

"Okay," she replied and watched while he put a small flag near the shoe and took a photo of it with a small portable camera. "What will happen next?"

He stood up and glanced around. "Where did you find it?"

"In between those logs. It must have floated in and when the tide went down, it got trapped between them."

He nodded and took a photo of the logs in question. "You can leave if you want. Thanks for your help."

"Don't mention it," she said. "It's my civic duty."

She gave Constable Towers a smile and then walked back to Kirby, who was waiting patiently, his tail wagging.

As she untied his leash and got him latched in on the back seat of her car, she wondered about this young woman. Who was she and where did she die? The closest bridge to jump off was up near Port Renfrew. Of course, the foot could have come from Victoria, or even across the Salish Sea in Washington State.

At least now, if the foot was identified using DNA, the family of the dead woman would finally know for sure.

It was a cold comfort, but a comfort, nonetheless.

CHAPTER THREE

Tess McClintock sat at the desk and watched out the window as the waves roared onto the beach a few dozen feet below the cabin.

After the attack, she and Michael rented the small cabin so that Tess could recover and they liked it so much, they decided to rent it for the entire year. They could escape on weekends whenever they felt a need to decompress. Located north of Seattle overlooking Skagit Bay, the cabin had been a haven for Tess while she nursed her wounds and tried to get over the trauma of almost dying when she'd gone to rescue Lisa Tate. Now that she was back to work, she still wanted to spend every weekend there.

Tess planned to stay at the cabin all week. The event still plagued her dreams and made sleep uncertain, so her boss, Kate, agreed that staying there for a week would be a good idea for what continued to ail her. Michael decided to commute to work each morning, since he didn't want her staying there alone. The drive didn't seem to bother him, so Tess agreed.

That morning, her mind wandered from what it should have been focused on — the most recent draft of her article for the *Sentinel* on the sex trafficking and serial murder cases she was still following up in Bellingham. On the wall beside her was a cork board with photos of various people involved in the cases — Eugene Kincaid, Richard Parkinson, and Rachel's father Thomas Gibson to name a few. A small map of the Pacific Northwest sat in the center of the board and red push-pins marked the location of bodies found over the years. Connections were drawn from one person to another in a maze of red lines. Most of the red pins were in Washington State, but they extended outside its boundaries from Idaho to Oregon to British Columbia, Canada.

The door to the room Tess and Michael shared as an office opened, and Michael entered. He'd taken an extra day off work to stay at the cabin for a long weekend, but the weekend was over, and he had to get back to the office. He came up behind her and took hold of her shoulders, bending down and kissing her on the cheek.

"You know that cork board makes you look like some kind of crazed private investigator or conspiracy theorist..."

Tess laughed and turned to face Michael, who sat on the stuffed chair beside the desk. "I know, I know," she said and sighed. "Just trying to figure it all out."

Michael was dressed in his office clothes, as he called them -- a pair of dark blue slacks, a button-down shirt and a casual jacket. With his neatly trimmed beard and reading glasses, he looked like a professor getting ready to teach a class, not an investigator with the DA's office.

Tess thought a professor of forensic psychology was exactly what Michael should be, and would be, once he did his PhD like he planned and started teaching forensic psychology and criminal profiling.

Michael gestured to her laptop and the document opened on the screen.

"How's the article coming? You going to meet your deadline?"

"Damn right I will," she said and glanced at the page. "I need something to show for the past weeks I've been here recuperating, or Kate will have my head."

"I'm sure she'd understand if you're late," Michael replied, his voice soft. "All things considered."

Tess knew what he meant by that. All things considered referred to the fact she was practically murdered by a serial killer who went by the name of Eugene Hammond aka Eugene Kincaid. She still had yellowing bruises on her cheek, hip and chest from where he'd kicked and beaten her. The broken ribs on her left side still ached. Cautious about opioid addiction, she'd avoided using anything stronger than Tylenol and Aleve to fight the pain.

"What's your conclusion?" Michael asked, rubbing his chin thoughtfully.

"Parkinson was involved, but only as a buyer," Tess replied, checking out the board. "Ericsson was the supplier and he tapped both Gibson and John Hammond for girls, and who knows how many others in the pipeline. That's your bailiwick. John Hammond and probably Daryl Kincaid must have picked girls up in various places over the years, and then sold them to Ericsson for the sex trade. Ericsson supplied them to Parkinson, if they were the right age and look. Once Parkinson was no longer interested, Ericsson would sell them to someone else in the pipeline."

"My thinking as well," Michael said. "You're really good at this. You should be an investigator."

She made a face but didn't voice her fears about going into the FBI. It no longer held the attraction it did before everything that happened up in the mountains. She'd been too close to a serial killer twice, and almost lost her life as a consequence. The nightmares she experienced from her first run in with Eugene in Paradise Hill hadn't declined. After her last run in, they were even worse.

"It shocked me to find so many connections," Tess said with a sigh. "I've been researching this for years, but it still surprises me. Rachel and Gibson, Hammond and Parkinson. Even Lisa. Eugene was linked to them all."

"The child porn and sex trade is pretty incestuous, and it's no surprise to me that there are connections between our suspects. And victims."

"I know," Tess said. "I should be more jaded by now, but it still makes me sick."

"It should," Michael said and stood up. "Don't let it get you too down, but don't get jaded either. We need people to know about this dirty underbelly or they'll never do anything to stop it."

Tess leaned back in her chair and took in a deep breath. "Do you really think there's anything we can do to stop this? I mean, truly? Isn't this just a product of our modern society? The anonymity of the big city, the power of money, the lack of support for children and families..."

"I have to believe that we can do something, even if only after the fact," Michael said and squeezed Tess's shoulder. "Or I'd never be able to do this work."

"You like working for Nick. Will you be able to leave and start classes next year?"

Michael shrugged. "I love working for Nick, but I was thinking the other day that what I really liked, when I worked with the FBI CARD team, was teaching."

"Really?"

Michael nodded. "I was responsible for teaching at the local offices for a while. I loved outlining the program, getting special agents up to speed with the latest files, and what they need to know to do their jobs better. Maybe I should have gone into teaching as soon as I started having nightmares, instead of denying it and trying to soldier through."

Tess shook her head. "You can't go back and change the past. It's good you're on the right track now. I'm sure Nick will miss having you around in September."

"I may still work for him on a part-time basis," Michael said and went to the door. "We'll see how it goes. This Investigator job," he said and shook his head. "Doing investigations after the fact is great. All the evidence and information, none of the risk."

"Maybe you can do both. Teach part-time and work for Nick part-time."

"We'll see." He blew a kiss to her and she smiled as he left the room, closing the door behind him.

With that, Tess turned back to her article, determined to finish it before the end of the day.

Later, Tess's cell rang, the chime forcing her out of her intense focus on a series of dates she was trying to link up.

She checked her call display to find that it was Kirsten, Michael's sister.

"Hey," she said when she answered the call. "How are you doing?"

"How am I doing? How are you doing? You're the one who was almost killed by my serial killer ex-husband."

Tess bit her bottom lip, knowing how hard it must have been for Kirsten to admit that. Tess couldn't imagine how she'd feel if she were in Kirsten's place.

"I'm fine," Tess said. "I've had some time to recover and I'm keeping busy, so my mind doesn't dwell too much on what happened."

"What are you working on?" Kirsten said, her tone doubtful. "Or do I need to ask? You're working on the case, right?"

Tess laughed. "Guilty as charged."

"Yeah, I know. I spoke with Michael just now and he said you had this crazy corkboard on the wall with all these lines and photos, linking people up together. You need to let yourself recover."

"I am. How are you and the boys handling things? You have more reason than I do to be upset at everything."

Kirsten sighed. "That's why I'm calling. Phil and I talked about it and we think we're moving to Seattle. It's big enough that people won't know the association between our names and what happened."

"When?" Tess asked, excited to have Kirsten in town. "Where will you live?"

"Phil has to speak with the district manager of the real estate company he wants to work for, but we should be moving by the end of the month. Sooner, if I can find us a place."

"That's pretty short notice," Tess said.

"We'll do an Airbnb for the first couple of months and then find a more permanent place once Phil has been working for a while. Besides, real estate agents know all the short-term rentals that are available. Phil's new manager is looking for something. It will be nice to be close to you and Michael."

"What will your mom do? She'll be lonely without you and the boys."

"She's moving, too. She said there's nothing left in Paradise Hill for her except bad memories. She'll live with us and help with the baby when I go to work."

"You're going to work?"

"Yes," Kirsten said. "We'll need the money. There's no way our house will sell for a while, so we'll be carrying the mortgage until it does. We'll try to rent, but big houses like ours are not that much in demand."

"I'm sorry," Tess said. "This has been really hard on you and the boys."

"It has," Kirsten said. "It's only my hatred that keeps me from crying my eyes out every day. I'm just so glad that Lisa killed the sonofabitch. I wish I'd been there to see it. That would have been sweet revenge, seeing the screwdriver slide into his neck. I'd have liked to watch the light go out in his eyes..."

"I understand," Tess said with a sigh. "I didn't get to see him when he was dead, but Michael did. He died flat on his stomach, his face in the dirt. When Lisa stabbed him with the screwdriver, it punctured his jugular vein and his trachea and so he coughed up blood. It wasn't pretty and he choked on blood before he died."

"Good. The sick bastard deserved to die more slowly, maybe while his balls were cut off and shoved down his throat."

"Kirsten!"

"Well, it's true. He should have suffered more, considering every person he murdered and what he probably did to them first. All the families of the missing girls... He deserved to be tortured first and then slowly killed."

Tess shook her head at Kirsten's malice. It was completely understandable, but at that point, Tess only felt exhausted by everything that happened. Her body was healing, but she still had nightmares. It would be good when she was able to forget it completely and move on to another case, but first, she had to finish writing her article on Eugene Hammond aka Eugene Kincaid, the Paradise Hill serial child killer.

"I'm actually excited about living in Seattle," Kirsten said.

"Some anonymity for a change will be really nice. I talked to Phil and he's hopeful that he can make some good money selling real estate in Seattle. Bigger market, more competition, but bigger rewards."

"Where will you work?"

"For the real estate company, in the office doing admin stuff," Kirsten replied, sounding excited. "I did some work for Phil and liked it. I don't have my high school diploma, but if he's the boss, he can hire me anyway."

"Perks of being the boss's wife, I guess," Tess said with a smile. "Call me when you get in town and we can meet for lunch or coffee. When the boys are in school. Just you and me."

"That sounds good," Kirsten replied and they ended the call.

It would be nice to have Kirsten close by. Although their lives had changed so much since Tess left Paradise Hill so many years earlier, there was still a bond they felt that time didn't seem to erase. Besides, it would be good for Michael to be able to spend time with his nephews, since he hardly got to see his own boys now that they lived in Tacoma. Maybe Mrs. Carter and Tess's mom would be able to rekindle their friendship.

Tess thought the move would be good all around.

She turned back to the list of names on the spreadsheet in front of her, determined to get the dates and times matched up as best she could.

Hopefully, that would help identify more of Parkinson's and the Pacific Northwest pedo ring's victims.

CHAPTER FOUR

Michael arrived at the DA's office just before nine and was sitting at his desk with a fresh cup of coffee when Nick called him.

"Can you come down to my office? I'd like an update on the Parkinson case."

"Be right there," Michael replied. He gathered up his files and made his way to Nick's office. Nick was on the phone but gestured to Michael to come in and take a seat. Michael did so and waited for Nick to finish his call.

He glanced outside the window at the street below, watching as cars drove by, their windshield wipers flapping against the rain, which had been steady for a few days. While he waited, his mind passed over the Parkinson file. Currently in the county jail, Parkinson was awaiting trial. He had been denied bail because of his flight risk. He owned a small jet and employed a pilot and could be out of the country in mere moments, if he wanted to run. Plus, he was clearly a predator, and there was evidence he had abused dozens of young girls over the years and maybe had one or more killed.

Michael wished the trial could be soon, but it would take months before it got under way. At least Parkinson couldn't hurt anyone else in the meantime.

"So, what have you got for me?" Nick asked, after he ended his call and turned to face Michael. "Tell me. I've been busy working on the fraud case that's been in the news. Catch me up."

For the next half hour, Michael reviewed the Parkinson case.

While Parkinson was in jail awaiting trial, the FBI and local police had done an extensive check of his property for evidence and had found a veritable truckload. Not only were there boxes and boxes of videos, both on old VHS tape and also digital on hard drives and memory cards, there were dozens of scrapbooks and photo albums detailing all of Parkinson's victims. He had an entire secret library deep in the bowels of the mansion dedicated to storing the evidence of his perversion and assaults.

He wasn't the only perpetrator. There were others involved. Several different men appeared in the images and recordings and the FBI was busy using its facial recognition software to ID them, but the camera angles had been such that it was nearly impossible to get a full-on image of any of the other men's faces. Instead, the techs spent their time trying to identify the men through other means, including tattoos or scars and matching them to police and FBI databases of suspects and any convicted in the past of sex crimes against children or otherwise.

"They've identified no one?" Nick asked, frowning in disappointment.

"Not yet, but they have a long list of names and addresses of businesses in the Sea-Tac area that worked with Parkinson or appeared in his business records. They've been trying to match up dates in Parkinson's meeting calendar with their travels to Bellingham. Some of them may be legit clients. Most are probably just consumers of Parkinson's porn. But a few, FBI suspect, are clients who visited the mansion and took part in the activities. There were at least seven different men on the videos. They're working on it, but it's slow going as you can imagine."

"I guess Parkinson was smart enough not to record their actual faces."

"Exactly. He's been doing this for two decades at least. God only knows how many girls he's raped and where they are now. Some, like Marcy, are probably dead, either because they tried to escape or because they got caught up in the trade and have died from overdoses, or suicide."

Nick shook his head in disgust. "In my not-so-secret fantasy, I've got my hands around Parkinson's neck and am choking the life out of him."

Michael nodded. It was a feeling he shared. No punishment, however cruel and unusual, was too much for men like Parkinson.

"I'm with you," Michael said in commiseration. "Hopefully, in front of some of his victims so at least they'd get the satisfaction of watching the lights go out. I hope we can nail him for Marcy's murder so at least he'll be put away for life with no chance of parole, due to special circumstances."

"That's my hope, too. Good work. Keep at it and keep me updated if anything materializes on the ID of these men. We'll charge as many of them as we can and try to shut down the network."

"Sounds good," Michael said and gathered up his files. He stood and was almost out of the office when Nick stopped him.

"How's Tess?"

Michael stopped at the door, his hand on the knob. "She's

doing better," he replied, thinking about the bruises that lingered on her body and how hard she was trying to ignore her trauma. "She's in denial about how hard it's been on her and is focused on writing her articles for the *Sentinel.*"

"Tell her not to push herself so hard so fast," Nick said. "This case is going to be around for a while. It'll take a year at least to make any real progress. She has time."

"I try to tell her that the wheels of justice grind on, even if too slowly for most people's taste."

Michael closed the door behind him and went back to his own office. Nick was right about Tess. She had to give herself time to recover from her experiences. It might take years. She hadn't fully recovered from her earlier run-in with Eugene so there was no way she was going to get over almost dying because of him for a while. While he was no longer a threat, she would have to deal with PTSD.

That, Michael knew all too well, was sometimes harder to escape.

Later that day, after Michael had finished a teleconference with the detectives in charge of the case from the Bellingham PD, he called Tess to see how she was doing

"How are you?" he asked, hearing fatigue in her voice. "Pain got the better of you? You sound really tired."

"I'm fine, just weary. I had a bad sleep last night."

"Have a nap," he said and closed the file in front of him, giving her his full attention. "You have the time. I'm sure Kate understands that you need to deal with the psychological as well as the physical wounds."

"I know, I know," she said but he could tell she didn't really know it. She was putting too many demands on herself too soon after the attack. Michael knew the feeling all too well.

He'd done the same after his own bout with PTSD.

"Talk to Kate. I'm sure she'll give you more time. This case is going to go on for a year or two before anything really significant happens. Parkinson is rich, and powerful, and will do everything his money can do to delay and cover up his crimes. He probably knows a lot of very powerful men, and maybe even has dirt on them and can use that to fight. Cut yourself some slack, okay? We're in this for the long haul."

"You're right," Tess said with a sigh. "I'll go talk to the therapist that Kate recommended. I know talking about what happened should help, but I just wish it would all go away, and I could get on with my life."

"You will," Michael said. "I'm living proof."

"You are," Tess said and he could hear the smile in her voice. It was mixed with clear affection. "Okay, Mr. Experienced. I'll be a good girl and take a break. You win. Oh, you spoke with Kirsten, right? She called me a while ago."

"Yes," Michael said. "She called to tell me she'd decided to move to Seattle. What do you think?"

"I'm happy about it," Tess said. "It's good for her and the boys to get away from any notoriety around their father being the serial killer everyone's talking about. I get my old best friend closer, my mom will be able to visit with your mom, and you get to be an uncle to the boys."

"We both win," he said firmly. "We'll be able to have big family dinners every Sunday."

"We will," Tess replied and she sounded really happy at the prospect.

"I love you, Tess. I want to make sure you recover from this and can move ahead with whatever you decide to do."

"I love you, too," she said. "I know you're right. I'll have a nap now and call the therapist later, okay?"

"Okay. See you for supper. I'll bring home some ribs. How does that sound?"

"Perfect."

They said goodbye and Michael put his cell away. Having Kirsten around might help distract Tess from everything and give her some better balance. Maybe she was finally realizing that if you ignored PTSD, it forced you to deal with it one way or another.

Before the end of the day, Michael got a call from Special Agent Mark Anderson, one of the Special Agents on the FBI task force working the Parkinson case.

"What's up, Mark?"

"Do you think John Hammond and Daryl Kincaid were involved in any other murders closer to Seattle?"

"Why?"

Michael could hear Anderson shuffling some papers. "We've just uncovered a couple of unidentified sets of remains along one of the routes Hammond and Kincaid both took from Paradise Hill to Seattle. The ME is there now, and based on what she's seen, she has the ages at between twelve and sixteen, both females."

"That's also ground Eugene Kincaid traveled," Michael said.

"Yes, I know. They could be his or just more from Ericsson. Once we get the scenes processed, we'll be doing DNA profiles, but there's a backlog and it's not priority given what we're dealing with up in Bellingham, so I thought you might have some ideas. If you want to come down, I'd appreciate another set of eyes."

Michael rubbed his chin. "I'll clear my desk and come down. Before I do, I'll check over my lists and see what I have that might match up. Send me the locations of the remains, and I'll drive right there."

"I'll send them right away. It will be good to have you here. Get a feel for the locations."

"That a good idea." He checked his watch. "I'll leave now and be there ASAP."

"Thanks for this, Michael. We're swamped right now trying to see who might be still out there with Parkinson's other clients, so we could use some help on the cases from someone who knows the details. I should have probably asked Nick if we could use you, but I figured he'd want you on this any way, so I called you directly."

"I'm sure Nick would be happy to farm me out to help you guys," Michael said.

"Great, it's one thing off my to-do list, so thanks."

"Glad to be of help," Michael said. He ended the call and checked his email. Sure enough, there was an email from Anderson with an attachment and a situation report on two sets of skeletal remains found and their location.

Michael would take a drive to the locations to see for himself where they were buried. He'd also look to see what potential victims were from those areas and then they'd all have to wait for the DNA results to come back.

Unless the crime lab prioritized those samples, the tests could take weeks -- or months.

Michael would have to work on Nick and see if he could pull some strings to get the results more quickly.

They could be Eugene's victims, or they could be John Hammond's and/or Daryl Kincaid's victims. For that matter, they could be Ericsson's. Unless there was some way to exclude any of them as potential perpetrators, it was impossible to know.

He cleared off his desk and grabbed his jacket. He wanted

to pop into Nick's office before he left just to pass the cases by him and ensure he was on the right track.

"Hey, boss," he said, popping his head in Nick's door. "You got a minute?"

"Come in," Nick said and waved Michael inside. "What's up?" He turned away from his computer screen, and leaned back in his chair, stretching his arms out above his head. "Something new on the Parkinson case?"

"I got a call from Mark Anderson on the FBI Task Force. Looks like they have a couple of sets of remains along the trucking route John Hammond and Daryl Kincaid drove from Paradise Hill to Seattle. One set is in Riverbend, and the other is in Bandera, near the Snoqualmie Pass. They think they might be part of that series of killings, either by Eugene or his dad. The more I read about Daryl, the more I think he might have been killing young women all the time."

"A father-son serial killer duo?"

Michael shrugged. "Not sure they were working together, but they might have both been killers working on their own. Daryl was one sick son of a bitch. He's the one who killed Patrice. I wouldn't doubt he'd killed before that and maybe after."

"It's worth a second look," Nick said. "Not that we'll be able to ever prosecute anyone for the murders, but we may be able to separate out who did what. If there's anyone operating now, we need to know and find them."

"Girls go missing every week somewhere in Washington State. If you add up all the missing girls and young women in the Pacific Northwest, there could be a half-dozen killers in the area."

Nick shook his head in disgust. "Glad I have boys," he said. "I don't think I'd let my girls go out the door without a bodyguard."

Michael nodded. "Me, too. It's still really *really* rare that a woman or girl is abducted by a stranger. Most of the assaults and rapes and murders are from people they know. Family. Significant others."

"That's right, but at least I know I wouldn't be one of the bad guys."

Michael stood and went to the door. "I'll keep you updated on what I learn. I'm going to take a drive and visit the sites, get a feel for them."

"Sounds good."

With that, Michael left, checking his watch. It would take quite some time to get to the locations, but he wanted to visit the sites before they were finished. He called Tess to let her know he would be working late and to go to bed without him, depending on how late he had to work.

He felt energized by the prospect of visiting a crime scene. Maybe they'd be able to clear up some old cold cases and even better, figure out who killed those young women.

CHAPTER FIVE

CLALLAM COUNTY SHERIFF'S *Office*

March 2005

After the deputy gave her a cup of hot cocoa and a donut, she
was asked questions while the deputies tried to figure out who
she was and where her parents were. It was all a blur to her,
and she felt afraid that this was what her mother always
promised her — if she didn't keep quiet, they would take her
away and put her in foster care. She'd never see her mother
again.

She tried not to cry, but she couldn't help it. The cocoa was
warm and the donut sweet, but she only wanted her mom to
come and get her, take her back to IHOP and go back home.

A nice lady named Leanne came to the Sheriff's Office and
bent down to speak with her.

"Well, aren't you just as pretty as a penny? What's your name?'

She shook her head. "I don't know."

"What do you mean, you don't know? What did your mom call you, sweetie?"

"Baby."

The woman nodded. "We have to call you something. How about Penny? That's what we'll call you. Penny. A pretty name for a very pretty girl."

She smiled, liking the name Penny.

Leanne asked her the same questions that the deputies had asked, but she really couldn't answer them.

She didn't know her name.

She didn't know her mom's last name.

She didn't know Dennis's last name.

She didn't know where she lived.

She didn't know her phone number.

She didn't know her grandma and grandpa's names.

She sat in her chair in the Sheriff's Office with a warm blanket wrapped around her and cried, her only comfort the stuffed doll she carried with her all the time.

"I want to go back," she said between the tears and sobs. "I want my mommy…"

"I know, Sweetheart," Leanne said, her voice soothing. "You have to stay here with us for now. There's a Sheriff's Deputy waiting at the bay for your mom and Dennis to come back. When they do, they'll come here, okay? Then, we'll get everything straightened out."

She nodded, and settled down in her chair, to drink the hot cocoa, which was now only warm, and eat the donut.

Her mom and Dennis didn't come for her.

She ate lunch at the Sheriff's Office, and read comics that one of the deputies brought to her, and watched television in a small room with a sofa. When late afternoon came, the Sheriff and Leanne talked alone in the Sheriff's big office. Leanne came and sat beside her on the sofa, her expression serious.

"Penny," she said and smiled. "Do you like that name?"

She nodded.

"How are you doing?"

"Good," she said. Despite being afraid, she was now more comfortable, watching television.

"It's getting late and I know you wanted to wait for your mommy and Dennis to come here and get you, but I have to take you to stay with a nice family until they do. Mr. and Mrs. Murphy have a bedroom for you, and you'll have a bath and some clean clothes and a nice meal. When your mom and Dennis come back, you can go with her, okay?"

She didn't know what else to do so she nodded. She would like a bath and supper and clean clothes.

"Okay," she whispered, but something told her that she was not going home with her mother that night.

She was going into foster care, just like Mommy always warned her if she didn't keep quiet. She started to cry once again, her fear that she was never going to see her mother again making her little body shake.

She went in the car with Leanne and they drove through the darkened streets until they got to Seattle. The entire time, Leanne talked to her, telling her stories about her own child-hood and how she had been in foster care, too. How she would only stay with the Murphy family until her mother came back. How they were really nice and had a family cat and a fish tank, and there were other kids in the neighborhood that she could play with.

She didn't respond.

This was her greatest fear, besides spiders.

Foster care...

The Murphys lived in a nice house with a yard and two stories. They greeted her and Leanne at the door and welcomed them inside. She said hello to Mr. and Mrs. Murphy. There was one other child there, an older boy, who said hello and then disappeared up the stairs. Jonah, his name was.

She sat on the floor with a collection of toys while Leanne talked to the Murphys and went over the story of how she was found. The three of them watched her and talked in quiet voices. She sat with her stuffed doll and examined the toys, but she really didn't feel like playing.

"Come with me, Penny dear," Mrs. Murphy said and took her hand. "I'll take you to your room. You can have a bath and get some clean clothes and then we'll give you some supper, okay?"

She nodded, still not used to the new name they gave her, and walked up the stairs with Mrs. Murphy.

The room she had for the night was small, with a tiny bed and a chest of drawers, and a big bin where all the toys were stored, but it was the first real bedroom she could remember. For most of her life, she remembered sleeping in the same room with her mother and Dennis. She either slept on the extra bed, the sofa, or on the floor, and she kept her toys on the sofa beside her, or under the bed against the wall.

She never ever had her own room.

She had a bath, and put on some new clothes that Mrs. Murphy picked out for her — some pajamas with leggings, a warm robe, some clean underwear, and socks. She went downstairs to sit at the kitchen table and was given a plate of spaghetti to eat with a single meatball on top and some garlic bread. She'd never eaten a meatball, but it was good.

She was hungry after a day only eating donuts and drinking hot cocoa.

"That's good, Penny," Leanne said, smiling. "Eat up. You must be really hungry. I'm going to go now, but you're in good hands with Mr. and Mrs. Murphy. They have kids stay with them all the time who have nowhere else to stay. We'll talk again tomorrow, okay?"

She didn't talk much to the Murphys. They didn't ask too many questions. Leanne had talked to them and so they already knew.

She went up to her bedroom after her meal was finished and crawled into bed, her stuffed doll still in her arm.

"If you need anything, you just come and knock on that door down the hallway, okay? John or I will be happy to help you. Good night, Penny. Things will be better tomorrow."

She nodded, but she didn't believe things would be better tomorrow.

She was afraid that her mother would never come for her and she would be in foster care forever.

The next day, she woke up early and lay in her bed, glancing around the room as the light from under the curtains slowly brightened. She almost didn't remember where she was, but the bed was really warm and soft, and she felt good and clean for the first time in a long time.

She got up and went to the door, opening it up to see what was happening. Mrs. Murphy came out of the bathroom and went down the stairs. She had to pee, so she went to the bathroom and then went downstairs.

Mr. Murphy was sitting at the kitchen table reading a

newspaper. Jonah was sitting at the table eating breakfast. Mr. Murphy glanced up from his newspaper when she arrived in the kitchen.

"Hey, Penny," Mr. Murphy said. "Sit down and have some breakfast. There's eggs and bacon and toast if you want it."

"Okay," she said and sat at the place Mr. Murphy pointed to. In the kitchen, Mrs. Murphy was cooking.

"How are you, Penny dear? Did you sleep well?"

She nodded.

"Do you want some eggs and bacon?"

She nodded again. "Yes, please."

Mrs. Murphy served her, and she ate her food, which was delicious. It was almost as good as IHOP, except without the pancakes and syrup.

The house was warm and nice and smelled good. Mr. and Mrs. Murphy and Jonah were nice and had soft voices.

But she still wanted her mother.

"When am I going to go with my mommy?" she asked, when Mrs. Murphy took her empty plate away and put it in the sink.

Mrs. Murphy shook her head. "As soon as the Sheriff's office finds her, honey. Until then, you'll stay with us, okay?"

She nodded, but she knew, deep down in her heart, that she wasn't going to see her mommy. Her mommy was going away, and she would stay in foster care.

Mr. and Mrs. Murphy were nice, and Jonah was nice, but she wanted to go home with her mother and Dennis, back to the motel room, and back to her space on the floor beside the wall.

Her eyes filled with tears and she sat at the table and cried, while the Murphys tried to console her.

"Don't worry, honey," Mrs. Murphy said and put an arm

around her shoulder. "We'll look after you until we find your mother, okay?"

She nodded, but she didn't say anything, fear and sadness making her unable to speak.

She stayed with the Murphys for a week, until Leanne found her a more permanent foster home with the Parkers, another older couple with two other foster children who lived with them. The two children were more her age, a sister and brother from a family that could no longer care for them, and the three of them had their own rooms in the big house with a yard and a dog.

Mrs. Parker, who she was to call Marnie, was older with white hair. Her husband was Bernie, and had whiskers on his face and a big smile.

"All our own children have grown up, so now we look after children who need a place to live. We love children," she said when they arrived at the Parker's house.

She looked at her new room, which had a single bed with a colorful quilt on it, a chest of drawers, a desk and a shelf unit with dozens of toys inside. The room was nice and had a closet where there were clothes of different sizes hanging up.

"It's all yours," Marnie said. "Your own room. I made the quilt myself. You have some new clothes we just bought from the exchange. And there's a bike in the garage for you, if you want to learn to ride it. It's pretty rainy out right now, but when it's dry, we live in a quiet neighborhood and you can ride your bike on the street around here. There's kindergarten you can go to as well."

"When will my mother come and get me?" she asked, although she was starting to believe that her mother would never come for her.

"When they find your mom, we'll talk, but right now, this is your home, okay?"

Marnie bent down and looked in her eyes. She seemed like such a nice woman.

She turned to look at her new bedroom.

It would be okay to stay here until her mother came back, but she was afraid that her mother never would.

She was right.

CHAPTER SIX

MICHAEL DROVE to the burial site at Riverbend. When he arrived, Dr. Keller was there, working away to uncover one of the sets of skeletal remains. She had on her usual set of white overalls, a protective face mask, gloves and boots and was intent on unearthing some bones. Overhead was a white tent to keep the rain off Dr. Keller while she worked.

She glanced up and saw him, then turned back to her work after a quick smile.

"Michael," she said. "I wondered when you'd turn up."

"I'm here, I'm here, let the bells ring out," he said with a laugh. "Can't keep me away."

"Guess not," Keller said.

"What have you got?" Michael asked, kneeling beside the shallow grave, careful not to disrupt the scene.

"Looks like a young female, age somewhere between puberty and maybe sixteen. On the short side, but based on everything, under eighteen for sure."

"No wisdom teeth?"

"No wisdom teeth," Keller replied. "I'd guess closer to twelve than sixteen, but I could be wrong. More tests will narrow it down. Of course, if we have a DNA match, we'll know for sure, but until then, that's the best I can do."

"That helps me narrow the search. Knowing the way the sex trafficking system works, she could be from anywhere and just dumped here."

Keller let out a disgusted sigh. "Monsters."

"You got that right," Michael said. "How long do you think you'll be?"

"Almost done," she said and sat up, her hands on her hips. "I want to get to the site down near Bandera before dark, but regardless, I'll be working late. You sticking around?"

"I'm here for the duration or until you kick me out."

Keller laughed. "Good. I could use some company. I'd like an update on the cases, too, if you don't mind."

"Sounds good. Is there anything I can do for you while I watch?"

Keller shook her head. "No, my assistants will be taking care of the real grunt work. Why don't you give me an update while I dig?"

"My pleasure."

For the next half hour while Dr. Keller finished her work on the skeletal remains, Michael updated her about the cases up in Bellingham and what police had been able to piece together about the sex trafficking ring operating out of the city.

"Based on what we know, Parkinson was one of Ericsson's clients, who ran the ring out of Seattle but had an office in Bellingham. They ran an escort service and matched up clients and girls based on particular criteria."

"What's the link to Paradise Hill?" she asked and glanced up at Michael. "That's where you're from, right? I read about the girl who went missing from there and who killed Kincaid. Lisa Tate. She was a friend, right?"

"She was," Michael said. "She was one of my charges the night she went missing and Kincaid was stalking the girls. So I always felt guilty about her disappearance."

"Poetic and real justice, if you ask me," Keller said. "I'm so glad everything worked out and there's one less serial killer alive. Although I would have liked to see him brought to justice in the system, it seems better that he was killed by one of his victims." She glanced up. "That's between you and me, of course."

"Of course," Michael said, understanding that she'd want her opinions to remain private. "I agree completely. Kincaid should have gone through the system, and we might have been able to find more victims, but it is what it is."

"That it is," Keller said. She sat upright and glanced around. "I wonder who this poor soul was? Some child who was in the wrong place at the wrong time and was taken or ran away. Sometimes, I don't want to know who the victims are. Their stories are too painful. Other times, it makes me feel better to know I've helped close a case, even if the family is traumatized. Especially if the evidence we find is able to stop a killer. Do you think this one is connected to Kincaid or the child porn ring?"

"Fits the MO. Young female dumped in a shallow grave in the forest just off a secondary highway along a major trucking route. Could be Kincaid's work, or it could be some other monster. The FBI estimates there are between twenty-five and fifty serial killers operating at any given time, responsible for at least three murders each. I've read estimates that are four times that high from some researchers in the field."

"What's your opinion? More than fifty or fewer?"

"More," Michael said with a sigh, watching as Keller took a photograph of the exposed skeletal remains. "Probably closer to two hundred. If so, there are probably several operating in Washington State and the Pacific Northwest."

"You're going to do your PhD in Forensic Psychology or Criminology?"

"Forensic Psychology," Michael replied.

"When will you start?"

"Probably next year. I want to follow this case through to the end with Nick."

"Understood," Keller said. "It's good we still have you working in law enforcement, even if you're not out catching bad guys and rescuing abducted kids. You're helping prosecute them, which is just as important as finding them. Nick's lucky to have you."

"I'm extremely happy to be working for him."

"Good. I'm extremely happy to be done here. I just have to store the bones and we can head down to Bandera."

While Keller finished collecting the bones and cataloguing them, Michael checked his email and read over a few from detectives working the various cases connected to Eugene Kincaid.

They took separate vehicles and drove south along the main highway between Riverbend and Bandera, and then took a side road to the location of the second set of skeletal remains, discovered by a landowner who tore down an old abandoned building on his property and found the remains when he started digging a new foundation.

The body had been buried under the floorboards, which reminded Michael of that first day he'd returned to Paradise Hill and the fire that exposed Melissa's remains, which had been inside the cellar beneath the cabin's floor.

"This remind you of anything?" he said when they finally arrived at the site and saw the hole that the landowner, Trent, had dug. "Like another body buried beneath floorboards of an abandoned building?"

"It does," Keller said, wrapping plastic tape around the cuff of her rubber gloves. She already had on the rest of her gear and was ready to descend into the pit. "I remember reading a report on that case in Paradise Hill, before we met."

"This building is off the beaten track, in a stand of trees. If Kincaid did this, he was taking a big risk. He must have done it at night, or else just took the risk of coming here and burying the body."

"Have you checked out the landowner's family?"

Michael nodded. "Yes," he replied. "He bought the place recently. We're looking at the old owners, but there have been several. Each one will have to be tracked down. When you have a better idea of when the body was buried, we can match up the dates to the owners, rule out the other owners and their family members."

When Keller finished preparing her protective clothing, she climbed down the ladder to the bottom of the hole and bent down, her case in hand. For the next hour, she meticulously exposed the skeletal remains further, until the entire skeleton had been uncovered. The individual, probably a young girl by the looks of the bones, had been lain on her side, her hands folded beneath her cheek. Her wrists were bound by duct tape, the remains of which were still present. The glue itself had disintegrated but the fibers were still evident, showing the pattern that Michael recognized from other burial sites.

Michael wondered who she was and what her story was. She was obviously murdered or died in captivity. Whatever the case, she was young, and she was buried in a deserted building in an effort to hide her death. It could be a simple case of a family member of one of the owners killing the girl and dumping her on familiar territory. This far from civilization meant that the killer knew the area and felt secure enough to bury the body without being detected.

Michael stood and glanced around the local area. Farms extended for miles into the distance. The terrain was mountainous, and the separation was several miles between buildings or trees. People minded their own business out here — that much Michael already knew. Only the landowner might be suspicious of someone who didn't belong on their land and check out the killer, if they were even seen. At night? It would be very dark out here, far from a major city. On a moonlit night, you could drive on the road for quite some time without your lights. If the killer was familiar enough with the terrain, he could drive out with his lights off, park near the building, and bury the body undetected.

That was Michael's working hypothesis.

Someone familiar with the area did this.

That could mean one of the landowners or his family members. Or it could mean one of the current set of suspects in the serial case tied to Kincaid. Eugene was known to spend time on the road between Paradise Hill and Seattle on local deliveries.

He could have done the killing and buried the body in the ground beneath the floor of the old shed.

It felt like Eugene to Michael, however, he knew it was way too soon to be speculating on who did the killing. There was a lot to do before he got to that point, but of course his mind went there.

He couldn't help his nature.

"Any idea of how long the body has been buried?"

Keller sat up and glanced up at Michael. "Same as usual at this point in the process. More than a year, and anywhere up to a dozen years. Can't say more until I do a soil analysis."

Michael nodded. "I'm an impatient sort."

She laughed at that. "Not me. Too busy to be impatient. Wish I had more time to fret about time passing, but not in this job at this time."

She went back to her work as the sun fully set and the floodlights provided the only light for the location besides a crescent moon off in the distance. Keller's forensic team was with her, as was the local Sheriff, checking out evidence and cataloging it on the off chance it was tied to the killer.

Once she was finished, and was done removing her overalls, she turned to Michael.

"You hungry? I don't want to drive back on an empty stomach. Besides, they have a really good barbecue at Henderson's in Riverbend. We could eat there on the way back."

Michael smiled. "A woman after my own heart," Michael said. "I'd love to join you."

While Keller finished up, he texted Tess and let her know he'd be late and was having dinner with Dr. Keller before he drove back to the cabin.

MICHAEL: *I'm going for BBQ with Dr. Keller. Figure I'll be home around midnight. Don't wait up if you're tired.*

TESS: *BBQ? Lucky you. I had leftover lasagna. I'll be awake, and looking forward to a debrief.*

MICHAEL: *Okay. Not much to go on yet as to ID of victim or killer. See you later.*

TESS: *Bye.*

He put his cell away and followed Keller out to the vehicles, which were parked a few hundred feet away from the shed.

It would be a long evening of driving before he got back home, but Michael was glad to be involved right at the ground level in this investigation. It made him feel less helpless. Maybe he wasn't on the CARD Team or FBI any longer, but he could still do something worthwhile until he started his PhD.

Working with Keller was enjoyable. He hoped that once his PhD was finished in a couple of years, he'd be able to alternate between teaching and doing research, working with police departments and the FBI around the country to track and stop serial killers.

CHAPTER SEVEN

Penny Morrison. That was the name they gave her.

It wasn't her real name, but since no one knew her mother's name, they gave her the name of the man whose name had been used to rent the car. There were no other names connected to her and you needed a name.

She didn't remember much of the time before she was abandoned.

Her strongest memory as a child was the floor beside the double bed where she slept, because that was where she was often sent when her mom had someone over for a visit. She was supposed to be quiet and keep her eyes closed until the friend left and Dennis came back, but sometimes it was hard because sometimes the friends weren't very nice to her mother. She'd become used to staying on the floor between the bed and the wall and had set up a little play area there, with her Rainbow Bright and My Little Pony toys under the bed, waiting for her.

She started to play there by choice, and it became a safe space for her. Her mommy and Dennis often sat at the sofa or slept on the other bed during the day, and so Penny played by herself by the wall in her imaginary world where there was no shouting or yelling or hitting or crying.

There were just pretty pink and purple and blue and yellow ponies and tiny dolls and miniature furniture.

She needed a safe space because the men who came to visit often made her mother cry. On the nights the other friends came, her mother made Penny sleep on the floor against the wall so they couldn't see her. Other times, her mother put her in the bathroom in the tub with a blanket and pillow. The tub was always cold and hard, but it was better than the floor.

Penny didn't like sleeping on the floor, because there were often bugs there and it was hard and cold, but she knew she had to be quiet. She couldn't complain or she'd get spanked.

The spankings were harsh, and she'd cry afterwards, but her mom would just tell her that she wouldn't get spanked if she was a good girl.

"Keep your mouth shut and then he won't have to spank you," her mother always said but no matter what she did, Penny could never seem to make Dennis happy.

The place they lived was a motel — that much Penny learned afterward, when she was put in foster care, when she was shunted from home to home and had to stay at one for a month while they waited for a new family to take her in. The room she remembered from before was dark and dingy by comparison to her foster homes. The room was often cold, and she was hungry much of the time. Her little spot on the floor beside the bed next to the wall felt like a punishment but Penny couldn't understand what she did wrong. She tried not to cry, but sometimes, when there were scary noises from her mom's friends, she couldn't help it.

She learned to cry into her pillow and keep quiet so that no one heard her.

Now as an adult, Penny still couldn't cry out loud. If she cried, her tears were silent. Her therapist told her that was her attempt to keep from getting punished. She needed to learn to let out her emotions, to feel her feelings or she'd never know happiness.

Happiness required letting go of emotions.

Penny couldn't do that. She understood that she had been abused as a young child, and that she wasn't 'bad'. She knew now that she tried to be good, but it was hard for a four-year old to know what good meant in such a chaotic family. Sometimes, her mom seemed angry and took it out on her for simply being there. Other times, Dennis spanked her to shut her up or make her behave. She'd even gone to the emergency room a couple of times when her wrist had been dislocated after Dennis pulled her too hard, when he put her in time-out in the bathroom. He said it was an accident, and that it happened when she fell, and he had to grab her hand to prevent her from falling off the stair-case beside their room at the motel.

But that wasn't how it happened.

Whatever the case, Penny's therapist said she had PTSD from the abuse, mistreatment and abandonment.

Anxiety, panic attacks, depression.

She had the trifecta.

She received Cognitive Behavioral Therapy for the panic attacks and anxiety. She took drugs for the depression. At eight, she had stopped going to school altogether and had been taken to the local emergency ward to see the on-call child psychiatrist. Diagnosed with panic disorder, she'd been put on one antidepressant or another, adjusting doses, taking other drugs to treat the side effects of the first drug, until she felt like a total zombie. Luckily, she was in a good foster home at the time. The mother was a former teacher and had some progressive ideas with how to treat a child like her.

Penny took online classes, and soon, safe in her bedroom in the Parker's house in one of the wealthier Seattle suburbs, she blossomed scholastically.

"You're very smart," Mrs. Parker had told her. "You have straight A's and could have straight A+'s if you keep at it."

That made Penny feel worthwhile for the first time in her life.

She was smart.

She may have had PTSD and she may have been home schooled because of panic attacks, but at least she was getting good grades.

Sadly, after a few years, Mrs. Parker developed cancer and had to stop taking foster children. After a tearful farewell, Penny had been shunted into another foster home, but the environment wasn't as enriched, and the parents didn't understand a child like her.

She continued doing online classes ahead of her age, but the family lacked the warmth of the Parkers. She stayed with them for only a year.

She finally found a family who was willing to accommodate her peculiar needs, both in terms of studying online and her various medications, and for the rest of her childhood until she reached fourteen, she stayed with them. When she turned fourteen, she was put in the group home with other kids like her, struggling with psychological problems, anxiety and depression. Most of them had families, and so she was the only true orphan.

She had no one to go home to on holidays. Instead, she'd spent time with the group home staff, eating turkey they cooked in the group home kitchen. It wasn't as nice as it had been with the Parkers, but at least she had her own room, with a desk and chair, a flat screen television, internet access. There was good food, she learned to cook, and the other residents often spent time together in the games room, playing pool or foosball or video games.

It could have been worse. She understood that.

Still, there was this place in the middle of her chest that always hurt just a bit. She would often wake up in the middle of the night and cry out, woken from a bad dream of her mother fading away, reaching out from the boat, but not being able to grasp her hand.

That was her recurring nightmare — that her mother hadn't wanted to leave her and was forced to by Dennis or the shadowy man on the boat who met them.

"Leave her," Dennis had said. That much she remembered. "She'll be fine until we get back."

"You'll be fine, sweetie," her mother had said, trying to console her.

But Penny hadn't been fine.

They never came back for her that cold March morning when she was only five and there was a hole in her heart where her mother and father should have been.

She was surviving, and now that she was taking classes at the University of Washington in Seattle, she'd moved into a dorm and had a single room to herself, and she was almost thriving. Her past, which she could barely even remember, was receding farther and farther into darkness.

Then, it all came crashing back.

One afternoon in October, she received a call from a number she didn't recognize. She stared at her cell and wondered who could be calling her from British Columbia, Canada.

She declined the call, figuring that it was probably a telemarketer wanting to sell her something. She'd received dozens of calls from some company asking for someone with a name she didn't recognize, and she'd stopped answering. She figured if it was important, they'd leave a message with a number to call and some kind of explanation. She had no credit cards, she wasn't in debt with anyone.

There was no one from Canada who would be calling, so it was a mystery.

In a moment, there was a ding indicating a message and so she checked her voicemail, her interest piqued.

After entering her password, she listened to the voicemail.

Hi, Penny Morrison? This is Detective McGregor from the Victoria police department here in British Columbia, Canada. I wanted to talk to you about a cold case I'm working. I wonder if you could give me a call and we can talk. I don't want to say much until you call me, but if you could call and speak with us about the case, which has a family connection to you, it would be a big help.

Of course, Penny's first thought was her mother and Dennis, who went missing fourteen years earlier.

Had police located either of them? Penny's heart rate increased. She'd always believed that her parents abandoned her years earlier when she was five, leaving her on a deserted stretch of beach near Old Town. When she was older, she researched her background, and learned that she'd been returned to the Seattle area when local police had been notified that she was likely from Seattle, since that was where the vehicle found near Old Town had been rented. Her identity was unknown because she didn't remember her name. The man who she knew as Dennis had rented the car found in the parking lot nearby with a stolen ID, but it had been rented in Seattle. The person whose names had been used to make the ID was homeless, living under a train bridge in the

Seattle area, and probably didn't even know his ID was missing.

Why had Dennis been using a stolen ID?

That was the real question.

For the past fourteen years, Penny had been shunted from foster home to foster home until she aged out of the system. For the past year, she had been living on campus and was attending the university to study criminology. Although her life had been hard, in and out of different homes, not all of which were even nice to her, she tried hard to do well in school. It was the one thing she could be proud of — her near perfect grades. The rest of her life had been crap, but her grades were stellar. Because of that, she got a scholarship to the University of Washington to study social science and especially criminology. The scholarship paid for tuition and books, but not much else so she worked part-time at a local coffee shop, pouring fancy coffee drinks for minimum wage.

On a whim, she'd paid for the Ancestry DNA kit and had sent off her sample of saliva to the genealogy company in the hope she might find relatives. She'd also registered with several agencies that help people search for their birth parents. She hadn't received her results yet and it had cost a considerable amount, especially for a young woman barely making ends meet, but she was hopeful the test would turn up some relatives.

Most of all, Penny longed for a family of her own. There had always been a hole in her chest where love and memories of a real family might have been. At least, that's the way she thought about the pain in her chest somewhere near where her heart was when she thought about her mother and father and what happened to her as a child.

She'd been put in foster care but had never been adopted. When the time came to apply for a social security number, she'd had to apply for a name change, and had added Morrison as her legal surname.

Morrison had been the name Dennis had used to rent the car. It stuck to her despite it not being her real name, or even his real name, but she kept it even though it really belonged to a homeless man in Seattle who denied ever having traveled to Old Town. When Penny saw a photo of the man, with disheveled hair in dirty dreadlocks and a beard down to his collarbone, dirty clothes and plastic bags for shoes, she knew that wasn't her real father.

Her real father had dark hair and eyes and was clean-shaven, according to a faded picture her mother had shown her. That much she remembered. He was rich and he died, her mother said.

Still, Morrison had stuck and was the only surname she knew growing up that was in any way attached to her.

The truth was, she didn't know her father's or mother's names or their fates.

She hoped that Detective McGregor from the Victoria Police Department might have some information.

CHAPTER EIGHT

Michael sat across from Dr. Keller at Henderson's in River-bend and watched her eat her ribs with gusto.

Considering she'd just been digging up the ribs from some poor unfortunate young girl or woman who had been murdered and buried in a shallow grave, it was pretty amusing. Michael figured experts had to be able to go from crime scene to dinner without a second thought or they'd never be able to work.

"It doesn't bother you to eat ribs after digging up two skeletons?"

Keller glanced up from her rib, a look of exasperation on her face. She laughed out loud.

"I'd never be able to eat if that was the case," she said and took another bite off the ribs, which were dripping in tangy BBQ sauce. "Back in high school, I used to dissect a fetal pig in anatomy class and then eat a ham sandwich, and never thought a thing about it. My dad said I was made to be a medical examiner. I have one of the strongest stomachs of anyone I've met over the years. You have to, if you want to be in my business."

SUSAN LUND

"I suppose so," Michael said with a smile.

He felt her gaze on him and looked up from his plate of coleslaw to find her examining him through half-lidded eyes.

"You had some problems after a case, if I recall correctly. Dealing with abducted and murdered children is a whole different kettle of fish than dealing with what I do on a regular basis. I know the people I'm going to see are dead or have been dead for a long time. With the CARD team, you're out looking to save a child's life. It has to be a lot harder to deal with when you don't succeed in rescuing one."

Michael nodded. "I had one really bad case that did me in. A young boy the same age as one of my own. I had to take a break, and then when I was injured and lost the use of my right arm, I wanted to get out of the FBI completely. It seemed like the universe was sending me a great big hint to that effect."

"You could have done supervisory work," she said and picked up her drink — a non-alcoholic soda.

"I didn't want to be in HR or a manager. I like investigative work, but just not on cases where my decisions might mean the difference between life and death. I could do cold cases, I suppose. I really enjoyed teaching one year when I did a few seminars for local police on the CARD Team and its work. That's why I decided to go back and get my PhD. I could do both."

"Sounds like a great plan," Keller said. "I'd like to see you continue on in law enforcement, but if you prefer teaching, that's good, too."

"I could still consult on cases with the FBI and police," Michael said. "But I'd also be able to spend most of my time teaching. Maybe even at the Academy."

"That would be the best of all worlds, wouldn't it? You could teach FBI Special Agents. What area are you most interested in?"

60

Michael considered. "Criminal profiling. Maybe how to track and find a serial killer. Trafficking."

"You like working for Nick at the DA's office?"

"I do," Michael said. "A lot. He's a great boss and the work is right up my alley. I get to go to crime scenes, keep track of where investigations are at, and at times, interview witnesses. What I don't have to do is chase bad guys or shoot them. Seeing as I'm still not a great shot with my left hand, that's a good thing."

"It is," Keller said. "I could never imagine being in law enforcement. Scared to death of guns. Don't own one and don't want to. I'm happy to leave that up to people in law enforcement."

For the next half hour as they finished their meal, Keller told Michael about her background and past, and how she'd been a child prodigy at music but had caught the forensic bug in high school and went to college two years early on a scholarship to become a medical doctor. She didn't like actually having to deal with people so instead of dealing with live bodies, she dealt with dead ones.

"In case you didn't notice, I have Asperger's. Don't really feel all that comfortable with the social world. Total geek and nerd."

Michael made a face. "I would never have pegged you as having problems with the social world. You've always been very easy to talk to and friendly."

"That's because we're dealing with my field, and I'm an expert and could talk your ear off about things I know. Get me in a party with people I don't know, and I absolutely crash and burn. Don't know what to say."

Michael shrugged. "Luckily, we're both crazy about forensic work, I guess."

"Exactly. If I had met you at a social event, you'd see me

standing in the corner terrified, at a loss for words. But get me started about my work and I could talk for days. My husband always said you couldn't shut me up."

"You're widowed?" Michael said, having read about her husband dying in a profile of her on the ME's website.

She nodded. "Yes. He died in a car accident five years ago. We didn't have children, so it's just me now. Me and work. That's all I do. It's my entire life and I don't expect anything will change any time soon, which suits me just fine."

Michael thought that was a shame. Dr. Keller seemed like such a nice woman. He supposed that now she was alone, she could focus completely on her work.

"You don't want to retire and travel the world?"

"Actually, I do," she said and pushed her plate away. "I was thinking of going on a cruise to the Galapagos Islands. Retrace Darwin's journeys."

Michael smiled. She really was a total geek and nerd.

He liked her. A lot. She was like a crazy aunt who always had the most interesting things to talk about.

They finished eating and after paying the bill, they walked out to the parking lot and their respective vehicles.

Michael stopped at Dr. Keller's car — a Volvo SUV. Electric, of course.

"Can I call you later this week to see what you think about how long the two bodies have been buried?"

"Sure can," she said and got into the driver's side. She closed the door and rolled down the window.

Michael smiled and watched as she drove off.

He liked watching her work and listening to her talk about what she was doing. He figured it was all part of learning as much as he could about forensic science. If he wanted to teach, and he did, he needed to learn everything possible. Dr. Keller was a leader in her field, and he could learn a lot from her.

He got inside his Jeep and sent Tess a message to let her know he was on his way back.

Then he drove off, feeling tired after a long day of work, but energized by his very enlightening talk with Dr. Keller.

CHAPTER NINE

Tess was sitting on the sofa when Michael arrived home after midnight.

"You're still up," he said when he entered the cabin.

"I am," she said and held up her notes. "Burning the midnight oil trying to figure this all out."

He hung his jacket up in the closet and shucked off his boots then came over to the sofa where she was sitting. He bent down to kiss her and then went to the refrigerator to grab a glass of water from the Brita.

"What's up? What's got you unable to sleep?" He plopped down on the sofa beside her, his glass in hand.

"Just reviewing the missing girls and women in the Pacific Northwest, starting with Oregon. I'm making a list of those who might be potential victims of Eugene and who might have been in the sex trafficking circuit. There's a lot. Eugene picked younger victims, but girls under eighteen are also potential sex trafficking victims, so I'm going back and looking at everyone between twelve to eighteen." She shook her head. "So many young women in that age range have gone missing from the area. I've got twenty-two from Oregon who are under eighteen and I'm only into the first one hundred missing persons out of over eleven hundred official cases. There could be over two hundred under eighteen in Oregon alone. Add in Washington State, and Idaho and there could be a thousand or more."

"Welcome to my former world with the FBI CARD team." Michael glanced over her shoulder. "It's depressing when you actually stop and think about it. We're supposedly so advanced when it comes to human rights and morality compared to say, Ancient Rome, but it seems like it's even easier to exploit children today. The internet and the isolation of individual families makes kids vulnerable in a way they weren't before."

Tess smiled and leaned over, to kiss Michael. "You already sound like a professor."

He laughed. "Hopefully a good one."

"Of course you'll be good. You'll be great," she said and smiled. "You have a passion for the subject matter and were almost killed when investigating it. That alone will make you a favorite of your students."

"Hope it's good for something," he said and raised his injured arm. "It's getting stronger and I'm getting better at the gun range, but it's not as flexible as it should be. Maybe one day."

"Do you really want to go back out into the field?"

"No, not at all," he said with a heavy sigh. "But I'd like to be able to defend myself or someone else. Like you, for instance. You keep getting yourself into these dangerous situations. I need to feel like I can defend you."

"I need to feel like I can defend myself. You can't always be there."

"I know," he said and leaned down to kiss her. "Ready for bed? I'm exhausted after my afternoon and evening of driving."

"You go ahead," Tess said and exhaled. "My mind is too preoccupied. I won't be able to sleep for a while."

"Okay, Lady Sleuth," he said and got up. "We should go out for breakfast in the morning. I feel like some good waffles and bacon."

"That sounds good. I'll be in later."

He bent down to kiss her once more and left her alone in the living room with her papers and laptop to sort through the missing girls of Oregon. She knew she should have gone to bed, but her mind was far too active for that.

When she did finally go to bed closer to one thirty in the morning, she felt exhausted, but maybe her mind would be so tired that she'd be able to fall asleep. For the past few weeks, sleep had been a long time in coming when she lay down in bed beside Michael. Nothing — not long walks in the fresh air, not listening to relaxation podcasts on iTunes, not even a cup of chamomile tea before bed, seemed to help. Part of it was her fear of the nightmares that came frequently when she did fall asleep.

They weren't images from the traumatic events that sent her to the hospital. They were different — dreams of her drowning, of being trapped in quicksand, of her being in dark rooms or deserted streets late at night with someone following her. She'd wake up, her heart racing, panic filling her and it would take a half an hour to calm down and be relaxed enough to close her eyes once more and try to sleep.

Michael had gone through a similar stretch of insomnia and nightmares after his own trauma, so he completely understood and supported her, but it had definitely put a damper on their romantic life.

Maybe one day, both of them would be free from the negative effects of their run in with Eugene.

. . .

The next morning, Michael was already up and had been for a run before Tess even opened her eyes. He came out of the bathroom, a towel wrapped around him, and went to the closet to get dressed. Tess turned over and watched him.

"You're an early riser," she said. "Why didn't you wake me?"

"You're awake," he replied and came over after pulling on his slacks to give her a kiss. "I didn't wake you because you need the sleep. Do you want oatmeal or bacon and eggs?"

"I thought we were going to go to The Stop for waffles?"

"Don't have the time. I got a call and have to go into work for an early meeting. The best I can do is whip something up myself."

"Okay," Tess said and made a mock pout. "In that case, how about oatmeal. And coffee. Strong. I need to get going on my article or Kate will look for someone else to write it."

"Never," Michael said, shaking his head. "She'd be crazy to take you off the story, considering your experiences, but you're supposed to take it easy, remember?"

"I remember." Tess shrugged, not feeling as positive as he was. She left the bed and went to the bathroom for her morning shower. By the time she was finished and dressed, Michael had oatmeal ready and handed her a cup of coffee fixed just the way she liked it.

"Thanks," Tess said, taking the cup and sitting at the kitchen island in front of her bowl of oatmeal. Michael sat beside her and together, they ate their food and drank coffee. Michael handed her half the morning paper, and she read the opinion pages while he read sports.

"How did your afternoon go in Riverbend and Bandera? I suppose it's too early to have IDs on the remains?"

"Yeah, that won't happen for a while," he said. "I'll revisit the missing persons records to find any matches, but the girls could be from anywhere."

"Do you think they're Eugene's? He started to confess to a number of girls, but then retracted his confession."

"One was buried under the floorboards of an old shed. That made me think of Eugene and little Melissa."

Tess nodded, remembering the day she arrived in Paradise Hill to bury her father. "Do you think Eugene wanted to be caught? He lit the cabin on fire purposely."

"Sometimes, killers do want to get caught. I never got that feeling from Eugene. I think he was bored and wanted to play with police. He got regular updates from Chief Joe and so probably loved to watch local police scramble around in the aftermath. He wanted to keep killing so he could get in the record books. That I am sure of."

Tess nodded. That's what she'd thought as well. He just got sloppy because she and Michael had returned to Paradise Hill, dredging up old memories and jealousies. Tess was certain that Eugene was envious of Michael, who was the all-American athlete in high school, who went to college and became an FBI Special Agent. Eugene on the other hand, had barely graduated high school, didn't make it to college, and had never done anything with his life outside of delivery services for his grandfather.

Michael must have been a real target of Eugene's hatred.

As for Tess, she had reminded Eugene of that night Lisa went missing when he was really after Tess. He'd wanted to kill Lisa but had been prevented by his father and John Hammond. He'd consoled himself with seducing and getting Kirsten pregnant, but what he really wanted was to kill Tess, as he'd most likely fantasized doing for some time before he ever made the move.

Tess shivered at the thought. She'd been so close to being picked off that night in Paradise Hill. The next time he tried something was at the hotel, when he'd attacked her. Michael saved her life by staying at the hotel and being alert for trouble. The third time was when Tess followed Eugene up to his mountain hideout, rescuing Elena from his clutches. Finally, he'd almost killed her at the cabin, but had stopped his assault to catch Lisa and Kira.

But way back in the beginning, if Eugene hadn't acted that night and taken Lisa, he might have succeeded in killing Tess. Instead, Lisa had spent a decade in the child sex trade and then trafficked as an older girl until she managed to escape and make a better life for herself.

After their brief visit in the hospital, Lisa had contacted Tess a couple of times via email and texts, promising to come and spend time with her, catch up on life, once Tess was recovered. Tess hoped Lisa meant it. There was a small part of her that thought Lisa just wanted to move on with her life and forget her past and everything connected with it. Time would tell. If Lisa did call and ask to come for a visit, Tess would be overjoyed to see her, but she'd let Lisa make that decision.

Tess couldn't begin to imagine what kind of life Lisa had led between that night in Paradise Hill and when they'd finally reunited. Lisa had to be incredibly strong to survive everything. Now, with Eugene dead and Lisa having a real job and new life, perhaps she could move on.

Maybe Tess would be in the way of that forward progress. It was something she seriously considered when she thought about reuniting with Lisa.

Would friendship with Tess be more harm than good? If so, Tess would back off gracefully.

She would never expect anything from Lisa.

It would all be up to Lisa whether they became friends once more.

CHAPTER TEN

Penny debated with herself for a few hours after she'd listened to the voicemail from Detective McGregor, but finally, she decided to see what he had to say. She dialed the number and bit her bottom lip, then chewed her thumbnail while she waited for the call to connect. When prompted by the Police message system, she entered the extension Detective McGregor had provided and soon, she was transferred to another line.

Finally, after four rings, a man answered the phone.

"Detective McGregor," he said. "How can I help you?"

"Oh, hi, Detective McGregor. It's Penny Morrison returning your call."

"Oh, yes." She could hear papers shuffling in the background. "Sorry, Ms. Morrison. I'm really sorry to be the one to bring you this news, but we matched your DNA to a set of unidentified female remains that has been in our database for a quite a while. Since 2012, actually. We recently hired an American lab to search DNA databases for matches to a number of our unidentified remains in cold cases, and came up with a match."

"Remains?" she asked, her stomach clenching at the prospect that her mother had been found dead.

"Yes, unfortunately. A woman's foot in a running shoe turned up in February 2012 on a stretch of coastline between Mystic Beach and Jordan River. It sat in our Medical Examiner's office ever since. We searched every DNA database we had access to at the time but were unable to identify it. Our department regularly revisits cold cases, and so the company we hired in the U.S. ran a new match last week and got a hit off of one of the databases. It looks like the deceased was a first degree relative of yours. We're pretty sure it's your mother."

Penny covered her mouth with a hand. She'd always hoped that her mother was alive somewhere but just unable to find her. In her fantasy, her mother was held hostage somewhere, prevented from finding Penny and that was why fourteen years had passed since she was abandoned on the beach.

That hope was now dashed.

"Oh," Penny said, her throat tight. "Oh, I didn't know for sure that she was dead. 2012? She died that long ago?"

"We don't know for sure when she died. It could have been in 2012. It could have been earlier. With these floating shoes, the range of time is wide. For some, until we identify the remains, we can't know."

Penny thought back, doing the mental calculations. "I was abandoned in 2005 when I was almost five. I never saw my mother again after that. I never knew who my father was."

"2005? It could have been any time after that. There have been a number of shoes washed up along the shores of the Salish Sea over the past two decades. Some of them are found in the same year. Others take years before they surface."

"Her foot was still in the shoe?" Penny said, horrified at the thought, her chest tightening. "Someone cut up her body and dumped it?" Tears sprung to her eyes despite the intervening years since she saw her mother.

"Just to be clear, we have no way of knowing how she came to be in the water. Often what happens with bodies that are in the water is that the joints disintegrate and separate, due to decomposition and," he said and paused. "Predation by sea creatures."

Penny closed her eyes at the image in her mind of her mother's body being consumed by sharks and eels.

"Running shoes of modern design are quite buoyant and when the foot separates from the ankle, the shoe floats on the currents," he continued. "The bones were protected by a thick nylon sock, and there was enough," he said and paused again, like he was trying to decide on the right words to use. "Enough material that we could pull a decent DNA sample. When we did, we had no match and so it's been a Jane Doe in our records. When you entered your DNA into the databases, we got a hit after I ran another search."

"I see," Penny said, her voice shaking. "I have no idea who she is or what her name is."

"I checked the other matches. It looks like there are a couple of cousins identified in the database. You could contact some of those people and try to figure out who your mother was. There are techniques to identify people through genealogy databases."

"Yes," Penny said. "Yes, of course. I haven't got my results back, so I'm surprised you have them already."

"It was the luck of timing of our request. Your DNA was in the database, but your notice hadn't been sent yet. You should be receiving it any day."

"I want to know who my mother was. I want to know what happened to her, too. I suppose you can't tell, based on a foot in a running shoe."

"No," he replied. "We have no way of knowing the cause of death. Many of the victims we have identified were suicides, who jumped off bridges or drowned when swimming, so it's entirely possible the same happened to her. We have no way of knowing for sure."

That hurt — the thought that her mother might have been so unhappy that she killed herself, jumping off some lonely bridge, probably in the darkness. She had a vivid memory of her mother — long dark hair, warm brown eyes, and a ready smile, despite all the hardship in her life. She had shown Penny love — as much as she could have given the circumstances of her life. After she'd learned more about the sex trade and human trafficking network, Penny had come to the conclusion that her mother was likely a young sex worker who got mixed up with some bad people and probably thought it was better that Penny was adopted by some family. Perhaps she and her father had decided to leave Penny on that stretch of coast in the hopes that someone would find her and adopt her.

That's what Penny hoped.

Now, she might have to change her constructed fantasy of her mother and father. Perhaps her mother was an addict — many young sex workers were substance abusers. She mostly likely was being controlled by a pimp, her life an endless cycle of sex with strangers to earn money and get her next hit. Maybe she had actually been murdered, her body dumped in the Salish Sea. Maybe she had taken her own life.

Penny took in a deep breath and tried to control her emotions. She felt close to tears and was surprised at how much the news affected her.

"How long do you think it will take to identify her?"

"I can't say," Detective McGregor replied. "Once you get the results, you can start contacting your matches and ask them for information about your mother. If you find anything out about close relatives, please call me. If you give me your email, I'll send you my contact info and a number you can call at any time, day or night, if you want to talk."

"Thanks," Penny said. "I will."

Detective McGregor ended the call and Penny sat staring out the window for a few moments, trying to take it all in.

Her mother was dead. That much Penny now knew for certain. How she died was unknown. Police couldn't tell from the foot. Whatever the case, Penny was never going to see her again. As for her father, maybe once they identified her mother, the pieces might fall into place. She might find out who her father really was.

At that point, Penny would be happy to meet an aunt or cousin.

For someone who'd been alone all her life after being abandoned, who was never adopted because she was so withdrawn, any connection, however tenuous, would be a gift.

The people working to find her a permanent family tried really hard to bring her out of her shell over the years. She'd gone into therapy and had seen dozens of psychiatrists and psychologists. She'd done talk therapy and play therapy and art therapy. None of it worked. She just couldn't connect to the strange people and their families, like she'd been holding out her heart from connecting until her real mother and father came to collect her. It was what kept her going, despite the sadness of her life.

Now, that hope was crushed.

There would never be a mother, and maybe never a father who loved her and waited to see her come home on vacations or for holiday dinners. No one would remember her birthday or call her to see how exams went. There were a few therapists who were nice and who she felt close to, but they were just once a week or two weeks for an hour. She had a few friends in school, but even Kassie, her lab partner in Chemistry, had gone somewhere else to study when she graduated.

A ready-made family wasn't just going to materialize one day out of the blue, complete with mother, father and siblings. She knew she'd better stop waiting and hoping for it.

If Penny wanted a family, she'd have to make one.

She spent the next few days researching missing women in Washington State. There were a number of databases, but if her mother was on one of them, Penny didn't find her. She'd examined photos of young women with dark hair, but none were her mother. Had no one reported her mother missing?

Had she just disappeared into thin air?

Her mother had to have family somewhere who cared about her. Penny was almost five when her mother and Dennis abandoned her. She remembered her mother saying she had been still a child herself when she gave birth, so she must have been under sixteen. Her mother must have been nineteen when Penny had been abandoned. Penny searched earlier years, thinking that perhaps her mother had run away from home when she was under sixteen, but there was no one who matched her mother's description or who resembled the image Penny carried around of her mother. A narrow face, with a pointed chin, dark eyes, dark hair parted in the middle. Freckles on her nose. That was her mother. Penny could see her face in her mind's eye.

There were girls who had dark hair and brown eyes who went missing years earlier, but it was nearly impossible to be sure whether one of them was Penny's mother.

There was no Charlene going back for a decade.

There was one woman, Julia, who went missing at eleven, with dark hair and eyes, but the girl's face was too round. It couldn't be Penny's mother. The name was wrong, and the face was too round...

Still, Penny did what she could to find out more about the young girl, who went missing five years before Penny was born.

It could be Penny's mother.

She went missing from Tacoma.

Penny printed off the image and tucked it into her file on potential matches.

The next article she pulled up was from Seattle's *Sentinel*, the local newspaper. It was about the missing and murdered girls and women from Washington State, and chronicled the writer's own experiences with a serial killer who was responsible for more than two dozen murders in the Pacific Northwest.

Eugene Kincaid.

He was dead, recently killed by one of his first victims.

That gave Penny a sense of satisfaction, seeing the killer dying at the hands of his first victim. Life wasn't fair — that's something Penny's therapist had driven home to her over the years. Bad things happened to good people. Children were abused. Parents died. Some parents did bad things.

All you could do was try to build up your strength and deal with the negative, never forgetting all the positive around you.

Penny tried to keep the positive in mind at all times, but some days it was harder than others. Reading about all the girls killed by Kincaid made her angry and sad.

A story by Tess McClintock detailed the killing of a big shot in the sex trafficking business in the Pacific Northwest. The man's name was Ericsson, and he had been involved in selling girls into the child sex trade for years. He had been killed by one of the girls kept prisoner at a wealthy pedophile's mansion near Bellingham, where she'd been locked in a room and raped repeatedly.

That made Penny shudder with revulsion.

At least the pedophile millionaire was now in custody and charged with multiple counts of abduction, rape and other sex crimes against children. Police were investigating the death of one of the girls who had been a captive at the mansion. She had been murdered and Ericsson was one of the suspects. Hopefully, police would charge Parkinson with murder in that case and he would be put away for the rest of his disgusting life.

Penny hoped so.

Her heart rate actually increased when she thought about him and his perverted friends, abducting young girls and keeping them as child sex slaves.

Had her mother been one of those unfortunate young women who got caught up in the sex trade?

CHAPTER ELEVEN

Michael went into work and met with Nick to update him on what he'd observed the previous day.

"How was your trip?"

"Good," Michael said. He placed the file on Nick's desk and sat across from him. "I always enjoy working with Dr. Keller."

"What did you find?"

"Two sets of remains, both skeletal, been there for a minimum of one year and possibly up to a decade. Dr. Keller has to run some tests to determine just how long and will know more in a few days."

"What's your view of the two sites? Any sense of whether they're connected or who might be responsible? How did police find two sites so close together? Do you think they're Kincaid's?"

Michael shrugged. "One set near Bandera was found when the landowner pulled down an old shed on the property and dug up the floor, finding the remains under the floorboards."

"That sounds like Kincaid," Nick said and Michael had to nod in agreement. He'd thought the same thing.

"The other was from a tip called in the same day," Michael

replied. "Clearly, someone wanted the second set of remains to be found — the ones near Riverbend — but didn't want to be identified. That much seems certain. Someone involved who wants the killer to be caught? Or the killer himself?"

Nick nodded and examined the photos Michael had taken of the locations and skeletal remains. "If they were Kincaid's victims, it was someone who knew it was him. Both young female victims?"

"Yes. Keller thought they were between twelve and sixteen years of age. Hard to tell exactly before eighteen when wisdom teeth come it but definitely under eighteen."

"Kincaid liked them younger," Nick said and closed the file on the desk. "These might be by someone who had an older age preference."

"My thoughts exactly. Kincaid preferred girls around ten to twelve, definitely before puberty. John Hammond and Daryl Kincaid used any age for their porn business, but mostly girls a bit older they picked up along the trucking route. Girls who were runaways or who were working the streets of the cities they delivered to. Fourteen to eighteen. From what I saw of their videos and print material, most of the girls were under eighteen. That was their business. *Not Even Legal.*"

"Yeah, the creeps will pay a premium for underage porn. Rape porn. Snuff." Nick shook his head. "What are your next steps?"

"I'll check out our missing persons cases for any girls from the area that match the age range, see if we have any DNA evidence from the families. Keller will run DNA analysis and we'll see if we can find any matches. The thing is, if they were being trafficked, they could be from anywhere. They could be unconnected to the local area."

"Okay," Nick said. "If it looks like it's connected at all to our cases in Bellingham or Seattle, I want you coordinating with the police and FBI on this. Keep me updated."

"Will do," Michael said and retrieved his file.

He left Nick just as Nick was answering a call and went back to his desk. He filed the photos back with the others he'd collected since working the case. He glanced at the map on the wall beside his desk and the two new pushpins he'd added to mark where the remains had been found. So many cases were linked in the state. So many runaways, who got lost or forgotten. Girls from families that were struggling to provide for them and who lacked the resources to look after them. Such girls were vulnerable to pimps who promised money in return for sex. Who praised them and offered them what passed for love and concern.

It was sad that these girls were targets of these men, but that was reality.

He spent the morning reading over the missing persons cases from the area, trying to decide which if any might be a match to the two sets of remains. There weren't any that were an obvious match, so he widened his search to the entire state. There were at least a dozen young women under eighteen but over twelve who were on their list who fit the age profile. He knew that there were probably dozens of young women who simply walked away from their families and weren't reported to police. These girls may have had intermittent contact with family, enough so that they wouldn't be missed if they didn't call. Family problems like alcoholism or substance abuse made it so that no one would be looking for them. They were simply written off as lost.

That made it almost impossible to identify them unless

there was something else — some piece of evidence or DNA profile to help narrow it down.

He sighed and rubbed his chin, wondering whether to close the files and turn to something else when Dr. Keller called. He picked up his cell and answered, hoping she had some info that could help narrow down the ages of the girls.

"Hello, Dr. Keller," he said when she identified herself. "What have you got for me? Some good news, I hope."

"Yes, I think so," she replied. "I ran some tests of the soil and my estimates, based on the soil composition, is that the post-mortem interval is less than five years for both sites."

"Okay," Michael replied, leaning back in his chair. "That's good to know. The last five years. Any better idea of the ages?"

"Definitely under eighteen and past puberty. Probably between thirteen and eighteen. Maybe younger than that. Thirteen to fourteen, based on the height estimates."

Michael considered that. Could be Kincaid's victims. Could also just be girls in the sex trafficking trade. "That gives me a better idea of what to look for," Michael said. "We should hold a news conference and let people know we're looking for young girls and women who went missing in the last five years who were in the age range. We might get a few more missing persons reports and that might help us identify the victims."

"That's your bailiwick," Keller said. "Let me know if you learn anything useful and I'll keep you updated with anything I find. I'll submit DNA profiles on each set of remains, but you know how backed up they are."

"Tell me about it," Michael said. "Thanks for calling."

"Anytime," Keller said and ended the call.

Michael exhaled, rubbing his chin thoughtfully. The victims weren't likely Eugene Kincaid's. Given the proximity to John Hammond and Daryl Kincaid's usual trucking routes, he suspected that maybe they might have been involved with the trafficking ring operating out of that area. Who else did John Hammond work with?

Since the events in Paradise Hill, Michael had done some digging into Hammond's background. He pulled up some files from the server on John Hammond and Garth Hammond's deaths. He'd spend the next hour or two going over everything again, getting caught back up with the materials found in their homes and at the service station. There was something there that might lead him to the unidentified remains.

He felt it in his bones.

CHAPTER TWELVE

PENNY CONSIDERED CALLING Tess McClintock after reading all her articles on missing and murdered women in the Pacific Northwest.

The description of some of the victims who had been identified sounded so much like her mother that Penny wondered if her mother wasn't involved in the sex trade in some way as a young girl. She'd read studies for her criminology class on women in prostitution, and found that most of them started in the sex trade when they were thirteen or fourteen, which was below the age of consent. Most of them came from disadvantaged homes and their poverty made them vulnerable. They may have come from broken homes, with one parent missing. There may have been drugs and alcohol and abuse involved in their homes, and the girl — or boy — left home to find some love and affection elsewhere. They may have been temporarily homeless and became involved with a pimp that way, after the pimp promised them a place to live.

Once in the pimp's clutches, they would be plied with drugs and alcohol, and then 'turned out' — used as prostitutes.

But they weren't technically prostitutes — no child can consent to sex, and so they are really victims of child trafficking and rape. They would usually become the pimp's girlfriend and the pimp would play up that angle, giving the girl the appearance of love and affection, but it was really just meant to abuse them, exploit them, and keep them under the pimp's control.

Penny shuddered to think of that happening to her mother, but she knew that her mother had to drop out of school in middle school, because she became pregnant. That meant she would have only been thirteen at most.

Pregnant at thirteen… Penny couldn't imagine it.

It happened. Penny knew girls from the group home she lived in after she turned fourteen who became pregnant, but they got abortions. Those who didn't, moved out and went to other homes for pregnant girls.

She even knew a few girls who exchanged sex for drugs or money, working for their boyfriends. Who, Penny now realized, were their pimps.

Dennis had been her mother's pimp, of that Penny was certain.

Back then, before they abandoned her, Penny knew Dennis wasn't her father. He didn't even try to be a father to her.

He was her mother's pimp.

That was the only thing that made sense. He didn't live with them all the time. He came and went. He brought money, and drugs, and food. Then he left her mother alone and the boyfriends came.

Her mother tried to explain it to her — that they were her boyfriends and Penny was to be completely quiet while they were there and stay in her special place while they played. If she made a sound, she would get slapped and so Penny learned soon enough to keep quiet.

Quiet as a mouse.

. . .

Penny read over Tess McClintock's latest article on a very rich man called Parkinson, who had been arrested for various sex crimes charges with minors. She also wrote about a man called Ericsson, who ran a sex trafficking business out of his homes in Bellingham and Seattle. Parkinson had kept various girls as sex slaves in his mansion up in Bellingham, and Ericsson had been killed when a young victim tried to escape. The girl's name was being withheld due to her age, but Penny knew she was young — maybe only thirteen or fourteen and had been held captive in the mansion. She had been raped and filmed for pornography.

It made Penny sick to her stomach to think of it.

She couldn't get enough news about Parkinson, and hoped they put him in jail for the rest of his life. The trial wasn't for months, as each side fought over legal issues, but his day in court would come. Penny even considered going to sit in the court and listen to the proceedings.

That would be interesting. For her class in criminology, Penny decided to write her paper on the issue of consent and how the age of consent had changed over the years. There were big name lawyers who argued that the age should be moved lower, to fourteen, and others who argued it should be increased to eighteen. There were even organizations that advocated for sex between adults and children.

Penny thought the whole lot of those people should be put in jail. Her mother's life had been miserable as a child in the sex trade. Sure, her body had been mature at twelve, but she was far too young to be working as a prostitute. It was only because girls like her mother were poor or came from abusive homes that they also became caught up in the sex trade.

Instead of calling McClintock, Penny debated with herself.

Did she really want to talk to someone about everything? Someone in the press?

She should really focus on her studies. That had always been her best bet in life.

Her foster mother had always said, 'Keep your eyes on the prize and you can't go wrong in life.'

The prize was a good job working in the field of criminal justice, either as a victim's advocate or maybe even keep going to earn her MA and PhD and teach at a university.

It was a big dream for a girl who didn't even know who her mother and father really were, but that 'prize' kept Penny going. Other young women and men she met who were attending college with her didn't really know what they wanted. They were going to school because it was expected of them, by their parents and their social class. For Penny, no one expected anything of her.

She expected it.

That had to be enough.

Penny's Ancestry DNA results arrived the next day and she spent the next few days trying to track down relatives that were matched to her. She was interested to learn that most of her relatives came from England, Ireland and Scotland, with some from Europe and Sweden. She never knew anything about her family or background and knowing that was where her people came from gave her some sense of identity.

Most of her ancestors came from the area around Oxford, and that made her think about a book she'd read in high school, *Jude the Obscure* by Thomas Hardy. Poor Jude had always wanted to study at Oxford University, but he never got the chance. He was a poor boy from a working-class family and despite the fact he could see the spires of Oxford University from where he worked as a stone mason, he never made it there. It made Penny sad to think of poor Jude, whose attempt to have a family ended so tragically.

At least Penny had made it out of her humble birth circumstances. Her therapist always said that Penny was one of the few lucky ones to escape the pull of her family's past. Going to college on a full scholarship was Penny's ticket into the middle class, and she was determined to work as hard as she could to make something of herself.

She wrote down a list of names of people to contact, who might have information leading to her mother's and her own real identity. All the people on her Ancestry page were distant cousins and apparently, neither her mother or her father had registered their DNA with the database, nor had any of their close relatives. But Penny might be able to contact the distant cousins and see if they knew of a female relative who became pregnant as a young girl of thirteen or fourteen and had a child. One who went missing perhaps, and wasn't seen after she was nineteen or twenty.

It wasn't much, but it was a start.

She sent a message to one of her matches, a second cousin, who had a pleasant face on the website. The woman was an avid genealogist and had an extensive family tree built up. But when Penny sent her a message, she got such a long list of potential family members, she didn't know where to start. The cousin, whose name was Gina Warren, said she didn't personally know of any young relatives who became pregnant while still in middle school, but that she should keep checking.

Gina sent her a nice text, that Penny copied and printed out.

GINA: *Be honest with everyone you contact. Tell them you're looking for your mother and father and that all you know is that your mother became pregnant while she was either thir-*

*teen or fourteen and may have given up her child for adoption
when the child, a daughter, was only four or five. She may have
gone missing after that, and may have committed suicide at
some point before 2012. They will either know of a cousin or
niece that fits the bill or they won't. That's your best bet. It will
be a long slog to get any results, but a lot of people have found
their parents this way. Keep at it! Let me know when you do find
out so I can fill in some more of my family tree. In the meantime,
welcome to the family!*

PENNY: *Thanks so much for your help and encouragement.
I have dreamed of finding my mother and father since I was
almost five years old. You have given me hope. I won't give up
until I find something about them, and once I do, I will definitely contact you. Even though we are only distant cousins, I
am glad to know something about our shared families.*

Penny now had a lot of names to track down, but at least
she had something to work with. Before, all she'd had was
Charlene and Dennis. That was it. Dennis used a fake name,
stolen from a homeless man living under a bridge, to rent
the car.

It was something.

The first three names she would check included several
members of the Stewart family, who owned a big shipping business. Curtis, Frank and Sean Stewart. Members of the Stewart
family side of Gina's family. Gina's aunt was a Stewart. She
hoped one of them would be willing to talk to her.

Maybe if she called Tess McClintock, she could help. The
crime reporter working for the *Sentinel* seemed really
committed to finding those responsible for trafficking in
underage girls and abducting and killing women and girls in the
region.

If anyone could, Tess would know how Penny could find
her real mother and father.

CHAPTER THIRTEEN

THE COTTAGE on Whidbey Island was built on thirty-three acres of prime waterfront land north and west of Greenbank, nestled in a small wood in a nicer part of the coast. Worth over two million dollars when he bought the land five years earlier, it was his home away from home.

Frank's refuge.

He rarely took anyone there, because it was really meant for him. It was where he did most of his most interesting work. Certainly, it was the work that made him the most money. He'd had several rooms specially built in the lower level, which was locked and private. There were hidden cameras in several spots in each room, recording the activities that took place inside. People asked where he made his money, and he used to always say it was through his connections. He knew rich people and he knew how to invest their money.

That was only partly true.

He did know a lot of rich people. People with more money than sense. He also knew how to invest their money, but that wasn't the secret to his success.

No, it was knowing which people were ripe for the picking. It was knowing which men wanted fresh meat.

He provided it, he filmed them sampling it, and then he showed them the videos, and they were more than willing to fork over millions of dollars for him to invest and of course, for his fees. Powerful rich men who lost sight of what was lawful and feared the consequences when they were discovered to prefer their girls on the younger side.

Once, he took his brother Curtis there and when Curtis asked why they couldn't use the lower level of the house, Frank used the excuse that it contained his business offices, and there was privileged information on his clients stored there. He couldn't allow anyone not in the corporation into the room to protect their privacy.

It was a good enough excuse.

Another time, his half-brother Sean, who shared a father with him but different mothers, joked that he had a dungeon down there and that was why he never took them out there and kept the lower level locked.

He couldn't have been more right. Except it wasn't a dungeon. More like a candy store.

Frank acted suitably insulted. "What the hell are you talking about — a dungeon?"

Sean laughed, but then shook his head. "I was just kidding."

"I hope so," Frank said. "I have to keep a spotless public profile. The last thing I need is my brother joking to anyone about a sex dungeon in the basement of my cottage. You don't understand what it's like having to keep up a corporate image."

"I would never do that." Sean rolled his eyes and went back to poring them both a stiff drink.

That shut Sean up. Frank was focused on the success of the legitimate family shipping business, which he'd inherited when his father died, and wouldn't do anything to risk tarnishing its very upstanding corporate profile. His investment business was very profitable, but it was separate from the family business and he aimed to keep it that way.

After their parents divorced, Frank Sr. married another woman, who gave birth to Sean. Sean wasn't Frank's favorite, but they were family and he had to keep up a good public profile. He'd given Sean a mid-level executive job, which the man had proceeded to screw up royally, but he was family and had to stay in the fold. He hired an assistant for Sean, which seemed to fix things. Sean was happy to let his assistant run the shop, and so it was all good.

How Sean came from the same father as he, Frank couldn't understand. At least Curtis was a competent company executive, if not extremely naïve about human nature.

Frank sat in his covered patio at the cottage, and re-read his email.

It was from a Penny Morrison, and the message sent a jolt of adrenaline through him.

PENNY: *Hi, you don't know me, but we may be related. I got your email from your brother Curtis. I'm searching for my birth parents and a DNA test shows that we're related although it's not clear how closely. I was hoping I could come by and sit down with you, go through your family and see if there's anyone who might be my birth mother. I'm meeting with Curtis tomorrow afternoon. Is there a time I could come by?*

Frank glanced out at the bay and felt his fists clench. What the *hell* was wrong with Curtis? Why was he meeting with the woman? She was obviously a grifter, looking to extort money from the family. The Stewarts were a powerful force on the West Coast, all the way from San Diego, California, to Seattle,

Washington. Every port along the coast had a branch of the company, providing shipping between the U.S. and Asia Pacific region.

Frank liked to sit on his patio and watch the ships traveling through Puget Sound. Across from his property was Port Townsend. It was relaxing after a long day of running the family business, which was doing even better than it ever had, given the increased trade. He came to the cottage to decompress.

That was ruined with the woman's text and news that Curtis — gullible Curtis, the happy-go-lucky simpleton of the Stewart family – was going to meet with her and give her claim some legitimacy.

The girl had a lot of nerve coming to him looking for relatives in his family. There were always people trying to get money from Frank. Young businessmen who wanted funding, old friends who had some cockamamie idea for a business collaboration. Women claiming their bastard offspring were his or Curtis's or Sean's.

Damn little bitch...

Frank decided to ignore her. He had enough on his plate, let alone some young grifter searching for long-lost family members.

He put it out of his mind. It wasn't the first time some person came along, alleging that they were family looking for connection — and cash.

She wouldn't be the last.

CHAPTER FOURTEEN

Tess's cell chimed around three in the afternoon, and the voice assistant said it was a call from an unknown number. She didn't answer, letting the call go to voice mail. Since her involvement in the Kincaid serial case, Tess had been contacted by news agencies from around the country and the world. Reporters asked for a few comments on the ongoing investigation and her role in the case, but so far, Tess had declined, wanting to save up her comments for her articles, keeping it exclusive to the *Sentinel*. Journalists weren't supposed to become the news story, and she didn't want to be one, so she usually ignored the requests.

Once notification of a new voicemail chimed, she took her cell in hand and checked her voicemail.

Hi, you don't know me, but I wanted to talk to you about your articles on missing and murdered girls and women in the Pacific Northwest for the Sentinel. I think my mother was one of the victims and thought you might want to talk about it. You can reach me if you're interested at...

The young woman left her phone number and so Tess called right back, feeling bad that she didn't answer right away.

"Hello," Tess said when the young woman answered. "This is Tess McClintock. I'm sorry I didn't answer, but I try to screen my phone calls as much as possible. I've been working hard to meet a deadline and am trying to keep pretty focused."

"Oh, I totally understand," the woman said. "I can call back later if it's better for you."

"No, no," Tess said quickly. "I can talk now. What's your name, if you don't mind me asking?"

"Penny," she replied. "Penny Morrison. That's not my real name. Actually, I have no idea what my real name is. It's just the name I took when I was first placed in foster care when I was four."

"Okay, Penny," Tess said, grabbing her notebook and pen. "Why do you think your mother might be a victim?"

There was a pause for a moment, and then Penny spoke. "I got a call from the Victoria Police Department last week. My DNA was matched to a foot that washed up on the shore near Mystic Beach seven years ago. They were able to match it to me through my Ancestry DNA profile."

That sparked Tess's interest. "The Victoria Police Department? Are you from British Columbia?"

"No," she replied. "I'm in Seattle, but, well, I was abandoned when I was four, near Redwood Bay boat launch west of Old Town, in Clallam County. My mother and the man I think was her pimp left me on the beach and were never seen again. The assumption is that we were visiting the area when they abandoned me. Then, a woman's foot washed up in 2012 near Mystic Beach on Vancouver Island. The only reason the Victoria Police found me was that I provided my DNA sample to several ancestry databases and the FindMe database, when I was trying to identify my birth mother and father."

"Ahh," Tess said, writing down the information on her notepad. "You didn't know their names?"

"No," Penny said. "I was almost five — we don't really know exactly because they still don't know much about my mother or even who my father was. I didn't even know my own first name and I called the people I was with Mommy and Dennis. We think her name was Charlene, but I have nothing else beyond that. I had no idea what my last name was. I honestly don't think the man with my mother was my real father. I called him Dennis, but I was shown a photo of a man who my mother claimed was my father. My memories of that time are really sketchy. There were a lot of different men coming and going to our motel room..."

Tess heard Penny sigh on the other end of the line.

"This is hard for you," Tess said softly. "I understand. Looking back, do you remember where you lived or any details that might identify the location? You said you live in Seattle now. Do you remember a place in particular?"

"No," Penny said. "The only reason I know we lived in Seattle is that the Sheriff's office in Port Angeles traced the rental car that Dennis rented to Seattle. He was from Seattle -- or his fake ID was from Seattle, so we all assumed I was, too. Port Angeles authorities sent me to Seattle when they couldn't find any biological relatives and I went into the foster system."

"What about the man who was your mother's pimp? What about his family?"

"They checked everyone in Seattle with that name, but no one claimed to know who I was or whether I was his child. The family of one man whose ID was used by my mother's boyfriend said his ID had been stolen."

"What do you know about this man?"

"He was in and out of a mental hospital, and had a record like shoplifting and was homeless. It wasn't him."

"Hmm," Tess said. "Doesn't sound like it was the man who was with your mother, especially if you remember your mom saying he wasn't your father. Do you remember a home where you lived before you were abandoned?"

"A motel room. Pretty dingy. Like I said, I suspect my mother was involved in the sex trade based on the number of men who visited our place. I really think Dennis was her pimp. I don't know... Maybe I was a burden to her continuing to work for him and so they got rid of me. But I don't understand why her foot would wash up on Mystic Beach on Vancouver Island unless she died there."

Tess heard a hitch in Penny's voice and knew it was still painful all those years later.

"For the foot to turn up so much later and in Canada seems pretty suspicious to me," Tess said, remembering what she'd read about the mysterious floating shoes with feet in them found throughout the Salish Sea over the past decade. "I read about the feet turning up in the Salish Sea. Most of those that were tracked to a missing person were likely the result of a suicide or accidental drowning. They turned up within a year or a few years at most, somewhere that the many currents and tides took them once the foot disarticulated from the rest of the body. So far, based on what I read, there are no cases of foul play among those who had been identified."

"I know but there are quite a few feet that remain unidentified. Who can say if they were murdered? No one can. I spoke with a relative who's building a big family tree using Ancestry DNA, hoping she could help me determine who my mother was," Penny continued. "But so far, she has nothing except distant cousins identified through me. No one I've spoken with has any knowledge of a missing woman named Charlene who would be my mother's age, but we just started digging. When I read your articles in the *Sentinel*, I thought you might have some ideas."

"Have you contacted anyone else in your Ancestry family tree?"

"Yes," Penny said, her voice sounding resigned. "But everyone is distant. Like third or fourth cousins. I'm still trying to extend the family tree, but there are so many possible connections and not everyone has submitted their DNA to the databases, so..."

"I understand," Tess said. "I can help you with that. I've done some work in this area and can probably give you some tips on how to trace missing family members. I might even want to add your mother into my cases."

"That would be great," Penny said. "I've been wondering for years who my mother is, or was, but so far, she's just this vague memory of a woman I have with nothing to even look at. The Detective I spoke with from the Victoria Police Department assumed that my mother's foot washed up on the beach far from where I was abandoned, and thinks she might have committed suicide. Most of the feet that wash up on the beach have been from people who went missing and most likely drowned or jumped off bridges. From what the Detective told me, my mother could have died any time after I was abandoned in 2005. It might have taken seven years for the foot to be removed from the leg and then was washed up onto the beach during the King Tide. The King Tides were especially high seven years ago."

"Yes, I've heard about the King Tides," Tess said, feeling bad for the woman. How hard it must be for her not to know who she really is except for some very distant relatives, none of whom can help her. "I'll do some thinking and call you back as soon as I have something, okay?"

"Thanks," Penny said, her voice sounding relieved. "I'll

send you the names of the Deputy and man who found me, so you can contact them if you want," she said. "I'll text you when we're done."

"Thanks. I'll contact both of them, and get their stories."

"I know you've written about girls and women who went missing over the past two decades in our area so you might be able to help."

"I'm glad you called. If you have any questions or think of anything else you remember from your past, don't hesitate to call me. I'll make sure to answer right away next time."

They said goodbye and Tess ended the call.

She leaned back in her chair and took a pushpin from her collection in the top drawer of her desk, then pressed it firmly over Mystic Beach, near Jordan River, B.C. More remains of a missing and unidentified young woman who may have been in the sex trade.

Her cell dinged and Tess checked the message from Penny. She provided the name of the Deputy from the Clallam County Sheriff's office in Port Angeles, Deputy Gallagher and the name of the man who found her — Derek Henderson.

Tess wondered how many girls there were who had been caught up in the sex trafficking ring in the Pacific Northwest. Kate would be very interested in this new story, so Tess took out her laptop and started outlining the possible storylines. The new online ancestry databases had turned out to be a boon for cold case investigators trying to close old cases of unidentified remains. There had been a very old cold case recently closed and the perpetrator arrested after police had been able to trace the victim to her killer and brought him to justice. He'd die an old man in prison, and to Tess, that was too good for him, but it was justice at least.

Working the missing cases and reading the details of the depraved killers of young girls had turned Tess from an anti-capital punishment advocate to one who was willing to make the exception — cases involving child murders. Anyone involved in the rape and murder of a child did not deserve to live in civilization. She knew it was wrong to feel that way, given her own religious morals, but it was hard not to want to see murderers like Eugene punished — to see them suffer like their victims had suffered. She totally understood the Old Testament view of an eye for an eye. Eugene had been killed quickly. He suffered for only a short while before he died, choking on his own blood. He probably didn't even know who killed him and while it was poetic justice that it was Lisa, he should have suffered more.

She tried to put aside her bloodthirstiness and focus, but it was hard not to want to see each and every person involved in the sex trafficking of children punished severely and every child serial killer executed.

Whatever she could do to end that industry and bring those killers to justice was worth it.

Maybe after she healed from her injuries and had her nightmares under control, she would seriously consider joining the FBI or even a local police force. Maybe she could study forensic science and work for police if she didn't get into the FBI.

She had time to figure it out, but she knew that in some way, she'd be fighting to stop men like Eugene.

One way or another.

CHAPTER FIFTEEN

PENNY SAT in the chair across from her therapist and took in a deep cleansing breath to calm herself.

"How are you doing?" Mrs. Katz asked, closing the file on her desk and leaning back. "How are you *really* doing? Don't put on a happy face if you're not happy."

Penny exhaled. "I'm doing okay," she said. "School is going well enough. I like my classes."

"Do you have enough money for everything? Are you eating well?"

"Well enough," Penny replied. She'd had some issues with anorexia for a time when she was younger but had been receiving therapy for several years and had it under control. "I make it a point to eat the right number of calories every day. And take vitamins, so I'm good. My weight is stable."

"Good," Mrs. Katz said. "Stress can exacerbate eating disorders. You need to balance things, so you don't get overwhelmed. What have you done about contacting your family?"

Penny told her about contacting a dozen people on her

potential family tree to interview them and see if any of them could shed light on her mother's identity. And her father.

"I'm meeting Mr. Curtis Stewart tomorrow," she said. "He's related to one of my cousins, so I hope he or one of his other family members might know my mother. I also contacted his half-brother, Sean and his other brother, Frank, but I haven't heard back from them."

"Good luck," Mrs. Katz said. "Don't get your hopes up too much. Go into it like a detective rather than someone who wants to find their mother and father. Evidence. Facts. Keep it at that level, like you're filling in blanks rather than finding your family. That way, you won't be disappointed. Sometimes, people don't want to be found and they have every right not to be."

"They should at least be given the chance," Penny said, unwilling to leave the issue alone. She wanted to know. Just *know* who her mother really was and who her father was. Why did they abandon her? She'd already decided they were probably down and out and couldn't afford to keep care of her, but what else? Why did her mother commit suicide, if she did? What happened to her father? Did he really die, or did he abandon her mother and her?

The only way to know was to keep pushing deeper into her Ancestry contacts, talking to each of them, going back in time to try to find some young woman who disappeared off the face of the earth with no reason. That might be her mother.

"They should be given a chance, but if your father says he doesn't want to meet, you have to respect that."

"I don't have to meet him," Penny said. "I just want to know who they were and why they left me. That's all."

"I understand. You have every right to try to find the truth. Just be prepared that it might be a truth you don't really want to know."

Penny nodded. "I spoke with the Detective in charge of the unidentified remains. He said that most of the feet that wash up on shore in those running shoes are suicides or accidental drownings. So, my mother probably jumped off a bridge somewhere and it took a year or more for her shoe to turn up on the coast. I realize that means she probably didn't have a very happy life. She probably abandoned me because of it. Maybe she killed herself soon after."

Mrs. Katz gave Penny a sad, sympathetic smile. "I'm sorry. It must hurt to think that."

"It hurts worse not to know. All my life, I've had this hole in my heart where family should be. I remember her face. I just wish I knew what happened to her and why she'd abandon me and kill herself."

They talked for a few more minutes about her plans for the coming week and then Penny stood up as the session was over.

"You can come in next week or in two weeks."

"Two weeks is good," Penny said.

"It's up to you. Call my office if you feel a need to see me sooner. I can squeeze you in next week during one of my emergency sessions."

"Okay," Penny said. "Thanks. I think I'm good."

Mrs. Katz smiled and walked Penny out of the office. "Take care of yourself," she said and squeezed Penny's arm. "Eat."

"I will."

Penny left the building and walked out into the rainy Seattle afternoon. When her cell phone chimed to indicate an incoming text, she checked it.

The text was from Curtis Stewart, a member of the famous Stewart family who had a shipping business on the West Coast. He was one of her potential cousins identified when she spoke with Gina. Gina went through everyone on her mother's and father's side of the family going back and forward, to help Penny identify as many potential relatives as possible.

Curtis Stewart was just one of many, but despite the fact he came from such a powerful family, he agreed to meet with her and chat.

CURTIS: *I'll be in town and in the downtown area this afternoon from 3:00 to 4:00 if you want to have a coffee. We can meet at The Dock Cafe, if you want.*

She checked the time. It was just after two in the afternoon. She could make it no problem.

PENNY: *Thanks. I'll be there. How will I know you?*
CURTIS: *I'll have a black umbrella and a grey overcoat.*
PENNY: *Okay. See you around 3:00.*

That was it. Penny glanced around and went to the other side of the street so she could catch a bus that would take her to the downtown area. If traffic wasn't too bad, she would probably make it by 3:00 no problem.

The bus was fast and so Penny arrived at the stop closest to The Dock Cafe just after three. She crossed the street and glanced inside the small cafe nestled in the middle of the block, surrounded by office buildings and next to and army surplus store. Across the street were some docks, so the cafe was aptly named but it really didn't have that great of a view of the water.

She went inside, curious to see who her potential relative was, and there, sitting at a table along a red brick wall, was a man in his late fifties with a black umbrella, wearing a grey overcoat. He glanced up when she walked into the cafe and smiled when he saw her.

She smiled back hesitantly and went to his table. He had warm brown eyes and dark hair with quite a shock of grey at the temples. He was tall, a bit heavy, but had a pleasant face.

"Mr. Stewart?"

"Call me Curt," he said and stood, extending his hand. "You must be Penny. We could be related, I hear."

"We could." She shook his hand.

"Go get yourself a coffee," he said, putting a ten-dollar bill on the tabletop. "And then come back and have a seat."

"Thanks, but I can get it," she said, not wanting to take his money.

She went to the counter and ordered a small latte and then went back to the table, sitting across from him. She took out her notebook and pen, and glanced up at him, smiling. "Do you mind if I take notes? I don't want to forget anything."

"As long as you don't quote me," he said with a laugh. "I have a notoriously bad memory for dates and things like that. You could talk to my brother, Frank, if you want actual hard data. I'm more of a story guy. He's the numbers guy in the family."

"I will," she said and opened to an empty page. "He's your brother?"

"Yes. Gosh, you look like my mom when she was young," he said and shook his head. "If I didn't know better, you could be a close relative."

"Really?" she said, her eyes widening. "How come? I mean, how come you think I look like your mom?"

"Same mouth and pointed chin. She had those lips -- bow shaped she used to say."

Penny smiled, already loving the idea that she was related to this man and his mother.

"Maybe I'm one of your cousins. Do you have any pictures of your mom I could see? Can we look at her brothers and sisters and see if they might have kids who might be my mother?"

"Sure," he said and pulled out his cell and paged through a

Facebook page until he came to a photo. "I only have Frank and a half-brother, Sean, but here's our mom. Maria Stewart, née Ross, if you want to know her maiden name. Look at that nose. See how it's turned up at the end? You even have her freckles. She hated them, but we always loved them."

Penny held the phone with a photo of the woman in her hand, wondering if it was a great aunt or cousin. How wonderful if so...

"She passed away?"

He nodded. "Yes. Two years ago from an aneurism. Our family was devastated. Her side of the family usually lives into their nineties, but it was a flaw in her blood vessel just waiting to burst, and that was her time. The good thing is that she didn't suffer. She just dropped to the floor in the kitchen, where she was baking cinnamon buns — her favorite. Her maid found her right away, but it was too late. She was already gone. How she loved to bake," he said and stared off into the distance, a wistful expression on his kind face. "We always told her she should have started her own shop and sold her baked goods, but she never wanted to work outside the home."

"I'm so sorry," Penny said, imagining the vivacious older woman lying dead on the floor of her kitchen, the sun streaming in the window, the smell of freshly baked cinnamon buns in the air... "You sound like your family is really close."

"Well, I'm close to my immediate family," Curtis said. "But not really close to my cousins. There was some family drama back in the early days of the company, and a split between my father and his brothers over ownership of the business."

"That's too bad."

Penny examined the photo. Mrs. Stewart sounded like the kind of grandma Penny always dreamed of having. If they were related, Penny would be sad that she never had the chance to meet the woman.

Maria Stewart, née Ross.

Penny now had another family line to investigate.

"Would you mind if I took a photo of this? I mean, even though we don't know for sure how close we might be? It's for my files."

"Sure," he said and shrugged. "I think she'd be tickled pink to find out she had another niece or cousin. She was really upset by the family division."

Penny took an image of the photo on the screen and then handed the phone back to Curtis.

"So, did you think about any young women in your family who might have had a child when she was young?"

He shook his head. "Not off the top of my head. I have two daughters, but neither of them ever had a child out of wedlock. I did some thinking before I agreed to meet with you and can't come up with anyone. My cousin Alice got married and had a grandson, who would be your age, I guess. No, I think everyone is accounted for. No missing girls."

"My mom might have gone missing about fourteen years ago or later — after she had a baby back in 2000. She abandoned me in 2005. Her foot washed up on a beach on the coast in 2012 so it was probably in the water for at least a year but could be much longer. Can you think of anyone who your family lost touch with? Someone who might be my mother? She was maybe nineteen when I was abandoned. I remember her saying she had to drop out of middle school when she had me and had been doing nothing for a couple of years, so if she left school when she was fourteen, that would make her about nineteen when I was abandoned."

Curtis shook his head. "Like I said, I don't know much about my cousins on my father's side because of the divide, but everyone is married and accounted for except for Dean," he said. "Frank's son, who's still single and old enough to have been around at that time your mother would have been in junior high school. He was known as a bit of a Romeo so maybe it was him. He isn't married and we don't know how many children he might have," he said with a laugh. "None legal, at least. Hey, he might even be your father." Then, his smile fell. "I'm sorry— that was thoughtless. I didn't mean to..."

She shook her head. "Don't worry about it. I know you didn't. I contacted both Frank and Sean, but I haven't heard back yet. Tell me about Dean. How old is he? I was born in 2000. How old would he have been then?"

He shrugged. "He would have been seventeen or eighteen when you were born if you were born in 2000. Joined up after 9/11, in 2002 when he turned nineteen. Been posted all over the U.S. and Europe, so he probably wasn't your father, now that I think of it, unless he got your mother pregnant before he left, and we didn't know about it. Since he got out of the service, he's been working for the family business, in and out of Seattle and Singapore."

"Tell me about your brother. Frank?"

"He's sixty-eight, a businessman who refuses to retire, working out of San Francisco, Portland and Seattle, managing the family business and also has his own investment company — Stewart Investments. He's got three stepdaughters from a new marriage to his third wife. He had Dean with his first wife, but she died accidentally, and he remarried twice. He lives up in Broadmoor."

Penny raised her eyebrows. Even she knew that was one of the wealthier neighborhoods in Seattle.

"He's doing really well for himself," Curtis said. "Sean has a son, Will. He would be about Dean's age, too, so there's another link you could check."

Curtis told her more about the Stewart family, and how they came to New York in the early 20th Century from

England, migrated to San Francisco and then Seattle, when the shipping business took off.

"Tell me more about your family," Penny asked.

"My father, Frank Sr., taught engineering at SFU. Made some money, started a company there then decided to move up to Seattle. Frank stayed in San Francisco to manage the office there, and then came up here after the death of his wife and brought Dean with him."

Penny nodded. It would be nice to be from such a well-to-do and educated family.

"Frank Jr. had two previous marriages?" she asked, writing everything down in her notebook.

"Yes," he said and frowned. "His first wife, Louise, died in a hiking accident. Terrible tragedy. They were climbing along the coast and she slipped and fell down a steep embankment. We were all really crushed when we found out. It was a rough few years, as you can imagine, with Frank a new widower and single father to Dean."

"I'm sorry to hear that. What a horrible tragedy." She tried to imagine how a husband would feel to see his wife dead at the bottom of a cliff. His son just a little kid...

"Yeah, Frank was really unlucky in love, but they say, three's a charm. He married his second wife Anita within a year, but she left him after three years and we haven't seen or heard from her since. I believe she was Dean's nanny, actually. Up and left him and little Dean, left town to live by the Gulf of Mexico or so we heard. Now, he's with his third wife, Lena. She had three girls from a previous marriage. Frank gladly took in the girls and has been a real great father to them."

"That's good," she said and gave him a smile, but immediately her mind thought that it was pretty convenient for him to find new wives so soon. Some men were happy to take over their new wife's children, but others weren't.

"Frank had no other children with his new wife, Lena?"

"Nope. Apparently, she got a tubal after her first three, so he had a ready-made family. He's a bit older than her, so." He shrugged.

Penny nodded and asked about Sean, and his son, who might have been the right age to have been with her mother, and they went through his cousins and their cousins.

"Sean's son, Will, lives in Tacoma, from what I remember. I don't know much about him. He wasn't really part of the family. Sean never really did feel part of the main group of Stewarts."

Penny sighed. None of the young women in the family who were around her mother's age went missing or were unaccounted for. The only ones who were no longer around were Frank's first and second wives. His second wife was older than Penny's mother would have been, so she was out.

She smiled sadly. "If you can think of anyone who might have known a young girl who went missing about fifteen years ago, let me know. Otherwise, it doesn't look like anyone fits my mother's profile."

"That's too bad," he said. "You sure do look like my mom. Do you mind if I take a photo of you? I could show it to Frank and Sean. Maybe they can fill in some blanks."

"Sure," she said and shrugged. He held up his cell and snapped a picture of her. The lighting was pretty decent in the café, so it turned out okay.

He examined the image and shook his head. "Strange. You look so much like her when she was young. You could be her daughter, but of course, she was past menopause when you were born. Did Frank or Sean agree to speak with you?"

She shook her head. "Not yet."

"I could talk to them and see if they have any ideas. Frank may be your best bet. Maybe there was a girl back in high school Dean got pregnant and didn't know about — or kept secret."

She nodded. "Thanks. I'd appreciate it. I'll make sure to ask Frank about Dean if I meet with him."

They finished talking and shook hands once more. "I really want to thank you for talking to me."

"You're very welcome. I hope you have some luck with Frank."

"Me, too. I'll call and see if he can meet with me, if you think he's a good source of family information."

"Yes, he's the one. He has a better memory than me. He might even know a few of Dean's girlfriends. Maybe one of them is your mother. He was pretty close to Dean when he was growing up."

"It would be nice to know," she replied as they walked out of the café and onto the street. "Thanks again for meeting with me."

"Don't mention it. If we are related, we'll welcome you officially into the family the next time there's a holiday."

"Great," she said and waved as he walked away.

She exhaled and glanced around. Across the road were the docks. She felt like walking there for a while, getting some fresh air now that the rain had stopped. She had a few new leads that could turn up something. That gave her hope. Maybe Frank would agree to meet with her. He sounded like the kind of man who had a lot of information about the family.

She tried not to be too optimistic, but the fact Curtis thought she looked so much like his mother was something to hold onto.

CHAPTER SIXTEEN

Tess entered the coffee shop, searching the patrons for Derek Henderson. She knew he was sixty-six and had retired from his job working as an economic analyst. He'd moved closer to Seattle after retiring, and so they met at a coffee shop that was half-way between his home and hers.

A grey-haired man wearing thick dark-rimmed glasses sat in a booth at the back of the coffee shop. It had to be him.

She went over and smiled at the man. "Mr. Henderson?"

He glanced up from his paper and smiled back. "That's right."

"Tess McClintock from the *Sentinel*," Tess said and extended her hand. "We spoke on the phone."

"Yes, of course. I didn't think you'd be so young. Please, sit down."

He pointed to the seat across from him and Tess sat, sliding in the booth so that she faced him. She removed her cell and pointed to the app to record the conversation.

"Are you okay with me recording our talk? It's for accuracy."

"No, of course," he said and waved his hand. "Please feel free. I understand."

"Thank you," she said and pressed record on the app. She placed the cell on the table between them and then cleared her throat. For the first few minutes, Tess recounted the story of how she had been contacted by Penny Morrison about her mother's foot being found on a deserted stretch of beach on the coast of Vancouver Island, Canada.

"Oh, that's terrible," Derek said, frowning. "Poor girl. How is she handling that?"

"As well as can be expected. She really wants to find her real family, so I agreed to help her and will be writing about her case."

"Understood. How can I help you?"

"I understand you were the one who found Penny on the beach when she was four years old. Tell me about that morning. What you can remember? Tell me everything you can remember just as you saw it and how you felt. I want to be able to tell the story of that morning in my article. Every detail you can think of. The weather, the scenery. The girl, of course. How you felt. That kind of thing."

"Okay. It's been a while," he said and shrugged. "But I'll never forget it. It was one of those experiences that is written into your memory. My wife and I lived in Old Town, just east of Port Angeles. We had a nice little house that overlooked the Salish Sea. That morning, I went for a walk along the beach after breakfast, about an hour after sunrise. I do some carving and make walking sticks for fun, and so I look for interesting branches and wood that can be used for crafts."

"That's interesting," Tess said. "Do you have an Etsy store?"

"As a matter of fact, I do," he said and took out his own cell, swiping across the screen to reveal his photos. He showed her one of a walking stick polished to a high shine. "I found this one on that very beach. It made me think of my favorite movie and book series — The Lord of the Rings. I liked to imagine I held Gandalf's Staff. You can see that the top of the stick is similar to its twisted crown. The only thing missing is the large crystal in the center."

Tess looked at the image more closely. It showed a younger, darker-haired Derek with the staff in hand. "It's very nice."

"I had that with me when I found her. This is a picture taken that day."

He showed her another photo of him wearing a black rain slicker and rain hat, the staff in his hand. He was right -- it did look a bit like Gandalf's staff.

"You walked a lot on that beach?"

"I walked every day and still walk now that I'm retired. I come from a long line of men who die soon after retirement. Unlike them, I intend to keep as fit as possible to avoid the family curse. I figure that a vigorous walk each morning along the beach should do the trick, but now I walk along the beach near Edmonds."

He showed her another image -- of the small bay where Penny was found, the beach littered with rocks and logs. To the north was the Salish Sea between Vancouver Island, Canada and Washington State. Tess had already checked Google Maps for the location. To the south was an evergreen forest.

"What did you see?" she said, trying to get him back on track. "Tell me what the scene was like where you found her."

He took in a deep breath and narrowed his eyes like he was remembering. "I was walking along the beach, looking for interesting sticks and I saw a small dark mound poking up from the huge rocks and logs that lined the beach. At first, I thought it was some kind of animal in between the rocks. I stopped for a moment and watched, but it didn't move. Whatever it was, it looked like it had fur. I took my walking stick firmly in hand

and approached it, trying to decide whether it was a harbor seal. When the mound turned, I realized it was a small child. A girl. "*God,*" he said, his voice filled with emotion even then, fourteen years later. "It shocked the hell out of me. I searched around for her parent or caregiver. I thought, surely the child isn't alone on the beach that early in the morning. There was a brown sedan parked in the lot a few spaces down from my car, but I didn't see anyone inside and there wasn't anyone else on the beach."

"What did Penny do when she saw you?"

"She seemed really calm despite being all alone. I said hello when I got to her side," he said. "I didn't want to scare her. I thought at the time that she was only three, because she was really small, but I later found out she was almost five and seriously underweight, poor child. She'd been practically starved. She was wearing a dark toque over brown hair, which was wet from the rain. She wore a thin grey jacket with fur around the neck but with no hood and had on pink polka dot leggings and white running shoes. She was holding a stuffed doll of some kind and looked really patient. I asked her where her mom and dad were, but she didn't respond. Finally, she pointed to the water. I looked out, but there was nothing to see except the sea. You couldn't see Vancouver Island because of the clouds."

"What happened next?"

"I asked her if her parents went out on a boat, and she nodded, but still wouldn't speak. All she did was watch the water, holding on to the stuffed doll. I asked her how long ago her parents left, but she just shrugged. 'Did your parents go out there just now? Or a while ago?' I asked. But she didn't respond. Maybe she'd been taught not to talk to strangers."

Tess smiled. "Probably. What happened next?"

"She finally said it was dark when her parents left. I couldn't believe it — poor child," he said and looked at Tess pointedly. "She'd been there for several hours if that was the case because the sun had risen at least two hours before I got to her. I asked her what her name was, but she shook her head, like she decided to be quiet again. She seemed intent on watching the water in case her parents came back. I checked up and down the coast, but I couldn't see any sign of a boat. I asked if the brown car was her parent's and pointed back to the parking lot. She shook her head, but I figured that had to be wrong. How else would she have gotten there? So I asked her if she came to the beach in that car. Sometimes, kids are too literal. You know — you have to ask them the right question. She nodded her head, so I knew that they'd at least come in the car. I figured it was possible that the mother and father had come to the beach with a boat and went for a ride, but the car had no trailer so they must have met someone on a boat. Why leave her when it was still dark? Why not take her with them? Whatever the case, leaving her behind alone was reckless and downright dangerous. It was negligent, no matter if they returned to get her. My wife and I," he said and shook his head, an expression of horror on his face. "We would *never* have even considered leaving our five-year old daughter alone on the beach while we took a boat ride. Never."

"What did you think?"

He took in a deep breath. "I thought that something bad happened and that's why the girl was still alone. The parents left their child alone for some reason that I couldn't fathom. I mean, who does that? Drug dealers out to pick up a shipment? I figured that they abandoned her there on purpose. Why else leave her behind?"

He searched Tess's face like he was hoping she could explain it. She couldn't except that there were monsters in the world. Sometimes, the monsters had children.

"It must have been really upsetting for you," she said, seeing the obvious concern on his face, the anger in his eyes. "What did you decide to do after that?"

"What else could I do? I had to wait for the parents. I was angry that anyone would even consider leaving their child alone like that. But first, I called the Clallam County Sheriff's office, which I knew was responsible for the area. I told them I was on a stretch of the beach west of Old Town with a small boat launch. I said that I found a young girl on the beach alone who said her parents left her and took a boat ride. They asked me to ask her name, so I tried. I said, 'Sweetheart, what's your name?' but she just shook her head. The dispatcher said that deputies from the Sheriff's Office were on their way and that I should stay with the girl until they arrived. They'd likely want to question me before I could leave, and I told her I was happy to cooperate in any way I could. I just couldn't imagine anyone leaving a child alone on a beach at that hour while they took a boat ride. Of course, I suspected that there was foul play involved."

"What happened next?"

"I asked the dispatcher if I should bring her to the office, but she told me to just wait for the deputies, just to be on the safe side in case her parents came back. She said I could wait in my vehicle because it was pretty cold and rainy that morning. I told the girl to come with me and wait in my car where it was warm and dry, but the girl shook her head and hunkered down on her spot. She wouldn't go with me. I hesitated to force her," he said. "I was afraid to even touch her, if you understand my meaning."

"I understand," Tess replied. "Please continue."

Derek took in a deep breath. "The dispatcher asked if I had a blanket or umbrella in my vehicle that I could use to keep her dry and warm until officers arrive if she wouldn't go willingly with me to my car. Frankly, I was glad I wouldn't be expected to just pick the girl up and take her into my car, even though that was the right thing to do. You never know today whether someone would misunderstand if they found me with her."

Tess nodded. Of course, the right thing to do would be to pick up the poor child and take her into the car, keep her warm, but she could understand how a man in his forties might look alone in a car on a deserted beach with a child who wasn't his own.

"Continue with your story," she said and smiled. "What happened next?"

"I ended the call with the dispatcher and went to my vehicle. I had an old wool blanket on the back seat for my miniature Poodle-Bichon cross, who died a few months earlier from old age. I took the blanket and an umbrella and went back to the girl. I wrapped the blanket around her and opened up the umbrella, placing it over her shoulder so it blocked out the drizzle. At least it kept the rain off her face and out of her eyes. Then, we waited for the deputies, watching the sky and the sea. She seemed so patient, like she had been left alone before and was used to waiting. I felt so bad for the poor thing."

"How long did it take for the sheriff's deputies to arrive?"

"About ten minutes," Derek replied. "They arrived in a black SUV from the Clallam County Sheriff's Office in Port Angeles. They drove up into the parking lot and two deputies came down to where we were. Deputy Foster and Gallagher. That was their names."

"Continue," Tess said, smiling to encourage him.

"They introduced themselves and then we spoke about what I'd found, what I was doing there. That kind of thing. I told Foster that I came here to walk the beach every morning and found the girl and spoke with her, but I hadn't seen any sign of her parents. I was pretty sure they simply abandoned her there. No one had shown up to claim her, so I figured they just left her there or something bad happened when they went out on the boat. An accident, perhaps. Deputy Gallagher knelt down to her. She was really good with the girl, calming. Finally, the girl said she didn't know her name. Her mother called her Baby Girl and that she was supposed to be waiting there for her mother to come back. When Gallagher asked how old she was, she held up four fingers. She didn't want to leave the place where she was sitting, but finally, Gallagher convinced her, and they went to their patrol vehicle and sat inside. Foster took my statement, and then the evidence team's vehicle drove up. The techs spoke with Deputy Foster and then one went to the brown Honda and began his examination while the other put on protective clothing and began a canvas of the area for evidence."

"Did you stay and watch?"

Derek nodded. "I felt a bit ghoulish for staying, but I was concerned for the girl and curious about how the Sheriff's department would process the scene. I'm a big fan of those forensic shows on TV." He smiled guiltily. "The forensic team took prints and photographed the car and beach where Penny had been sitting. The evidence techs placed yellow markers on specific spots, marking footprints, and other items -- a cigarette butt, a juice bottle, and some other things I couldn't quite make out. Then, Foster went to the vehicle and spoke with his partner for a few moments and then came back to my car. He told me I was free to go, but I should provide them with a foot-print before I left, so they could rule out mine from the others. I went over to the techs and apologized for walking all over their potential crime scene, but they waved me off, telling me they'd be able to rule out my footprints after they had a cast. So, once I gave them a print, I went back to my car."

"That was it? You left at that point?"

"No. Foster came over and thanked me once more. I told him there was no need to thank me. It was my duty as a citizen.

I asked him if he had any idea what happened and whether the girl said anything to Deputy Gallagher, but he said no. He told me that if I thought of anything, I should call him or Deputy Gallagher or the Sheriff's office in Port Angeles and someone would be glad to speak to me. Foster handed me a business card with his name and the info about the Sheriff's office. I asked whether I could call in and find out what happened to the girl because it would be hard for me to sit and wonder. He said sure and thanked me once more. Most of all, I felt really bad for her. She had such sad eyes. Think about a child being abandoned on the beach amidst the rocks and logs." Derek shook his head, his voice catching. "I just can't imagine the kind of monsters who would do that to a child. I'd led a very privileged life and never experienced anything like what I expected she'd been through. How would she deal with it over the coming days, months and years? While my own daughter was fully grown, I remembered her at that age and couldn't fathom the circumstances that would lead to abandoning a five-year-old on a beach on a drizzly late winter morning. How on earth could parents do that to their child?" He looked at Tess, his eyes haunted.

She smiled softly, understanding completely how he felt. She'd lived with guilt all those years after Lisa Tate went missing and was presumed dead.

"You'll be happy to know she's doing really well, going to college."

"Believe me, I am very happy. It makes me feel relieved to know she's well. But it must be upsetting for her now that she knows her mother died."

"She told me she always felt sad that her mother abandoned her, but she always figured it was because she couldn't take care of her anymore. She thought that her mother hoped someone would adopt her and give her a better life. We think she may have been in the sex trade, maybe a victim of sex traf-ficking. There were many men who visited their motel room, strange men, and there were drugs. So, it's possible that her mother truly couldn't look after her any longer. But they could have left her in the motel, if that was the case. Leaving her on the beach? It sounds like something happened that kept them from coming back to pick her up."

"Foul play?"

Tess nodded. "The majority of cases of these feet washing up on the shores around the area are the result of suicides, but it's possible something bad happened to Penny's mother and that's why she was left on the beach. It's pretty hard to find out this many years later. Plus, Penny still doesn't know her real name. She has some names of second cousins from Ancestry DNA results, but no one more closely related to her."

"I hope she finds her family and that they're welcoming to her. After what she's been through, she deserves some happiness."

"I couldn't agree more," Tess replied and turned off the recorder. "Thanks for meeting with me and telling your story. I'll keep you updated on anything we learn during the investigation."

She stood and so did Derek. She extended her hand, and they shook once more.

"Thanks. I'd appreciate it. Please tell Penny that I'm so very happy she's doing well now."

"I will." Tess smiled at Derek and left the restaurant, a clearer picture of that day Penny was found on a beach bordering the Salish Sea.

CHAPTER SEVENTEEN

Frank sat in his Cadillac and listened on his cell while his stupid brother bleated on about the girl.

"She looks so much like Mother," Curt said, sounding all emotional. "We have to be related in some way, but the only eligible guys close to her mother's age are Dean and Will. I wonder if Dean didn't screw around before he left Seattle and got some young girl pregnant. It could be his daughter or Will's."

"You already said that. Three times, and each time, you were wrong. Dean is not the father, *period*. I don't know about Will, but I can tell you, it wasn't Dean."

"How can you be so sure? You don't know all the girls he was with before he joined up."

"He's *not* the father."

"You're not excited at the idea she might be one of our cousins? Maybe even your granddaughter?"

"That's bullshit. If Dean had gotten some girl pregnant, he would have taken care of it. *We* would have taken care of it. I have cousins I don't even know about, and I'm fine if it stays that way."

"Party pooper," Curt said with a laugh. "You should meet her. You'd be shocked. Like Mom before she got married."

"Did she try to grift you for money?"

"What? No. Of course not. She merely wants information on who she might be related to. She was raised in the foster care system her entire life, and was never adopted, so you have to understand how much it would mean to her to find her actual family."

"We have enough actual family members," Frank said, unable to keep the disgust out of his voice. "Family members we know are legitimate. We don't need some young grifter with a fake claim coming along to family dinners, hoping to get some pity money."

"Why would you even think that?" Curt said. He sounded mad.

"I think that because I know human nature, Curt. Something you apparently have no clue about. People who have nothing are always angling to get something from those of us with means. I'd think you'd realize that, so you should just let the girl go. Forget about her. She's nothing to us."

"How the hell do you know? She has DNA evidence that she's related to us."

"*Distantly* related," Frank said and shook his head. What the hell was Curt thinking? Didn't he realize that the only reason the girl was interested was for money? She probably wanted to get some kind of compensation or child support.

He just knew it. There was no other reason. She was searching for her father. She probably wanted a sugar daddy. Well, Curtis might be stupid enough to take the bait, but he was not going to comply.

"I'm not going to meet with her, and I'm not going to be inviting her to any family dinners, so get that out of your head."

"I will," Curt said defiantly. "The more the merrier. You really should lighten up, Frank. She never asked for anything. I even offered to pay for her coffee, but she refused. She's *not* a grifter.

"That's the perfect thing for a grifter to do — refuse to let you pay so that it looks like they're not interested in money. Then, once they've weaseled their way into your life, they spring it on you. The pitch. That's when they stick their hand out for a handout."

"Jesus, it must really suck to be you," Curt said. "Suspicious of some poor girl who lived her entire life in foster care with no mother or father? Christ. Get a life..."

Curt hung up.

It wasn't the first time Curt had done that — gotten angry at Frank over something and ended the call without saying goodbye and on bad terms. Curt would get over it the next time a holiday rolled around, and he wanted to have a family dinner.

Frank checked his watch. It was late and he had to get back to the house to take the girls to swim practice. He'd drop them off and then swing by the motel, where he had a new girl waiting. It would pass the time until he had to get the girls and take them home to his wife. He'd told her that he'd been working late on a big project — but she was at her once-a-week book club that night and so Frank had to take the girls to practice. It was okay. They were too focused on the practice to notice him sneaking out after the first fifteen minutes to go to see his new girl.

Last week, his daughter Shelly asked where he'd gone, and Frank had to say he did a teleconference in his car using Skype. That had shut the girl up.

He arrived home at just after six and went inside. The

three girls were sitting at the island in the kitchen, all dressed and ready to go. Frank wasn't hungry. He was never hungry when he knew he was going to meet a new girl at the motel. He ate afterwards, not liking how a full stomach interfered with his ability to enjoy their sessions.

"You kids ready?"

"You're not going to eat?" Lena asked, frowning. She was all dressed up and ready to go to her stupid book club, even had makeup on. Most of the time, she stayed home and surfed the internet but once a week, she went to meet with other middle-aged women to read the latest murder mystery.

He had to laugh at that. He leaned over and kissed Lena on the cheek, knowing that she'd just applied lipstick and wouldn't want to smear it. "Have a good time, dear. What are you reading?"

Her eyes widened. "We're reading a series of murder mysteries set in Sweden. Really good."

"Great," he said. "Maybe you should write your own murder mystery."

"Oh, Frank," she said and waved him off like he was crazy. "I wouldn't know where to start. What do I know about real murderers?"

"Murderers look like everyone else," he said and raised his eyebrows. "Who knows? Maybe even someone you know. One of your family members. I've always been suspicious of Alan..."

She laughed, for her older brother Alan was a priest and had always been the one everyone turned to for comfort during a crisis. "You're so silly. Alan couldn't hurt a flea."

"You know what they say about Catholic priests..." He watched her react. Her family's Catholicism had always been a sore point between them, but he'd never really pushed his atheism on her.

"Don't say that," she said and frowned. "He would never hurt a child. Never."

"I hope not," Frank said. "Considering he's taken our girls out camping before. Hey, did your Uncle Alan ever molest any of you?"

The girls had equally horrified expressions on their faces. "Dad! How could you even say that?" Frank's youngest girl Kaylee said. "He's never touched me."

"Me, either," Jana said, the eldest, her expression equally horrified.

"All right, all right, I was just kidding. Of course, Uncle Alan never abused you. But if he did, you should tell us."

"He didn't, okay?" Jana was really upset. Frank reminded himself not to joke with the girls too much. They were too sensitive.

The girls grabbed their gear and they all piled into the SUV. Lena waved to them as they drove off and Frank was excited at the prospect of spending an hour with his latest girl.

As he drove to the pool, he thought about the girl. He'd found her while searching through prospects provided to him by his talent scout Martin. Martin had a line on girls who didn't have much in the way of a home life and who were willing to exchange their bodies for cash to spend on drugs or whatever. Girls who, a thousand years earlier, would have been populating legal brothels.

He didn't feel bad paying them in exchange for sex.

They were just following capitalism's dictates — exchange what you have of value for money. It was a straight transaction. Only the social prohibition against sex between adults and minors got in the way but he rejected it. Those girls he used knew what they were getting into. They were clearly old enough to consent. Hell, some of them looked more than eighteen years old, with makeup and the right clothes, but they weren't. That made all the difference.

When he arrived at the pool, he dropped the girls off and told them he was going to go get a coffee and that he had to make a phone call about work.

"It's night," Shelly said. "You make your employees still work?"

"This is someone from Japan. It's tomorrow morning there. My business is international."

Shelly nodded, apparently satisfied.

"I'll be back in about an hour. Have a good practice."

"Okay," Shelly said. He watched as the girls carried their gear inside.

He drove off, his excitement growing at the prospect of a session with the girl. He'd sent her a text earlier in the day, telling her he wanted her freshly showered and naked, waiting for him in the motel room. He knew she'd comply. She was a little vixen, eager to do anything he asked in exchange for her fix.

Money and meth.

She was a willing partner in their little sessions, so eager to get her drugs she'd do anything.

I'm on my way. Be ready.

He put his cell down and took the highway to the motel on the edge of the city. He had about twenty minutes to spend with her if he got there quickly. Then, he'd grab a bite to eat and return to the pool where he had to spend at least half an hour watching the practice.

He had to keep up appearances -- Frank, the doting father. The loving husband. The upstanding community member. The successful businessman.

It was only in the motel room that he was able to let his carefully constructed façade drop to reveal the real Frank.

The one who loved blow and young nubile girls and kinky sex.

That Frank no one outside of a few very select fellow travelers in the trafficking world knew.

He aimed to keep it that way.

CHAPTER EIGHTEEN

The following Saturday, Tess walked the beach west of Old Town near the Dungeness Wildlife Preserve and wondered how it all went down.

Michael was in the car, which was parked in the small lot a few feet away from the path leading down the cliff face to the beach. He got a call from Nick, but he would join Tess once the call was over.

The beach itself was below a cliff, sheltered by trees on all sides and was hidden from the road, so whatever happened there wouldn't be visible to anyone driving by. Dozens of old logs laid in a jumble up near the cliffs. Tess could see the tide line from the seaweed that rotted on the sand. It was currently low tide and so the water was far out from the beach, revealing rippled sand and small tidal pools of seawater. She walked over to the logs and stepped among them, wondering exactly where Penny had been sitting in wait for her parents to return. Tess sat down on one log and glanced out to the Salish Sea beyond the bay. In the distance, she could make out the coast of Vancouver Island.

She felt an immense sadness for Penny.

Poor child – to sit alone in the darkness, waiting for her mother to return. Penny had texted Tess the name of her therapist and had authorized her to call and talk about Penny's childhood for her article. What Mrs. Katz told Tess painted a picture of a troubled young girl, anxious, withdrawn.

When she was finally fostered by a woman who was able to break through Penny's protective barrier, Penny had blossomed. She did well-enough in school to assure teachers that she could learn, but then Penny's foster mother died, leaving Penny alone once more.

After that, Penny lived in two more foster homes and finally, a group home with other troubled youth who had anxiety or depression for various reasons. Fellow survivors of mental and emotional problems, they kept mostly to themselves, finding it hard to warm up to anyone.

Her only focus had been to get good enough grades that she could get a tuition scholarship to the University of Washington, where she wanted to study Sociology and Psychology, perhaps to try to understand what happened to her and her mother, whom she was certain had been sex trafficked as a young teen. It would explain all the strange men coming and going to their motel room.

Tess stood and walked along some logs that had washed up on the beach and thought how scared must Penny have been on that early morning. She'd have been sitting by the ocean in darkness while her mother and her mother's boyfriend went out on a boat. Waiting for hours until a stranger found her and her life as an abandoned orphan began...

Michael arrived and stood beside Tess, shading his eyes from the bright sunlight as the sun broke through the clouds.

"This is where they found her?"

"Yes," Tess said. "Around here, in these logs or ones like

them. She was hiding between two big logs, waiting for her mother to come back for her. I guess she didn't want to talk to Derek Henderson, the man who found her, but she finally spoke with a Sheriff's Deputy, a woman, who was able to get her to talk."

Michael scanned the coastline. "They could have gone anywhere. To Port Angeles, or to Vancouver Island, for all we know."

Tess nodded and sighed heavily. "I want to help her find her family and figure out what happened to her mother. Do you think you could talk to someone in the Bureau about how to find out who she really is? I've done what I can to develop a history of her life after she was found, but she was too young to even know where she was living, what her name was. All she knew was her mother's first name. That's it."

"I'll make a few phone calls and see who I can talk to about the case," Michael replied. "At least I can provide you with background from law enforcement's point of view."

Tess smiled. "Thanks. Penny found some relatives through Ancestry, but she only has third cousins so far. No one who is a close family member. Now she knows her mother died, probably by suicide years ago, but she doesn't know anything else. I feel like I want to help her as much as I can."

"I completely understand," Michael said, his arm around her shoulder. "Like I say, I'll do what I can to see if anyone her mother's age was reported missing from Seattle around the time Penny was found. I doubt I can turn up anything more than you can when using online resources. Sometimes, there are people with no one else in their lives, so no one even notices they're missing."

"That makes me so sad," Tess said with a sigh, resting her head on Michael's shoulder. "It feels something like Rachel's past. No one reported her missing either. I can't imagine not having a parent who cared about my safety."

They sat on the log for a while, talking about the case and what would have happened in the days after the Sheriff's department took custody of her. They had a date that Penny was found. They had her mother's first name, and the fake name used by the man who rented the car they had driven from Seattle to the small bay. It wasn't much to go on, but it was a start.

"This really matters to you," Michael said, reaching out to take Tess's hand.

Tess smiled sadly. "It does. She came to me after reading my stories about missing girls and women in the Pacific North-west. It makes me feel like my work matters. Sometimes, I feel so sad that I'm covering the kind of stories I do – girls and women who were trafficked, who were abused and murdered. If I can help Penny find her family, and maybe find out what happened to her mother, it would feel really great."

Michael nodded. "That's how I felt when I worked for the CARD team. Finding missing kids." He shook his head. "Sometimes we were successful. Too often, we weren't. I like working for Nick. I don't have to worry any longer about finding a child before they're murdered or trafficked. Now, I'm only helping prosecutors get killers and traffickers and put them away. It's far less stressful."

Tess smiled to herself, thinking of the last case they both worked on.

Eugene Kincaid.

It wasn't much less stressful, all things considered. But like her, Michael had the crime-solving bug and could never be happy unless either of them were doing something constructive to solve crimes.

Tess spent her time writing articles and researching cold

cases. It gave her the sense that she was doing something useful. Calling attention to the magnitude of the sex trafficking problem in the Pacific Northwest wasn't the same as actually catching the criminals and putting them in jail, but it was better than nothing.

Maybe one day when she had fully recovered from the ordeal of Eugene Kincaid, she would consider becoming more involved in police work, but for now, she was focused on finishing her series on missing and murdered women and girls.

"Let's blow this popsicle stand," Michael said and stood, extending his hand to Tess. "That is, if you want to make it back before supper."

"Could we stay here tonight? Maybe go to the motel where Penny might have stayed?"

Michael frowned. "You really want to stay there? There are nicer hotels in the area…"

"No, we can stay somewhere else, but I want to go and look around the motel if it's still there and see where Penny stayed. For my research."

"Of course," Michael said and consulted his smartphone. "We can stay at the Best Western nearby. If you want, I can make a reservation now."

"Yes," Tess replied, glancing out at the Salish Sea. "I'd like to stay overnight."

"I'm seeing the boys tomorrow for lunch," Michael said. "I can drive to Tacoma tomorrow after I drop you off at the apartment. I'll be sad to leave the cabin, but we can go back on the weekend if we want."

"Sounds good," Tess said, remembering that Michael had visitation rights for the day because it was his son's birthday. He only had them for a few hours in the afternoon before supper, when they would be home for the birthday party, but at least Michael would spend time with them during the day. He'd take them out for lunch and then to a local amusement park to go on a few rides.

It wasn't much, but it was a start.

Tess glanced around, imagining Penny as a small girl, only five, skinny, malnourished, her hair a mess, sitting on the beach with her doll, waiting for her mother to return. The thought of it made Tess's throat constrict.

"I feel so bad for Penny," she said, her voice filled with emotion. She took in a deep breath. "The coast is so beautiful, but I can never look at it again without thinking of Penny all alone, probably crying her eyes out."

Michael put his arm around her shoulder and squeezed. "Hey," he said and pulled her into his arms. "She's doing well. She's a success story. People pulled together and did what they could to help her and she's fine."

Tess buried her face in his shoulder and squeezed her eyes shut. It was making her far too emotional for her own good.

"Let's go. I've seen enough that I can write about this place."

They walked up the path to the small parking lot and got in Michael's Jeep, then drove off in search of the tiny run-down motel where Penny and her mother and the boyfriend might have stayed. When they found the motel, Tess felt so bad for little Penny, to have stayed in such a run-down place. The low single-story building was worn and dirty, but there were still people staying in the rooms. She could only imagine the kind of motel Penny lived in back in Seattle, if that was indeed where she and her mother lived. Penny had said she spent a lot of time between the wall and the bed while her mother entertained her man friends, keeping quiet so that she wouldn't interrupt their business.

Given how young Penny's mother was, Charlene was a probable victim of sex trafficking. She'd most likely been pulled into the trade when she was twelve or thirteen and had been used and abused, got pregnant, had Penny, and then was forced to sell herself to stay alive — like so many other vulnerable young girls Tess had read about over the years. That, more than anything, motivated Tess now. She never tired of working on her articles for the *Sentinel*, hoping to cast a harsh light on the dark underbelly of modern society.

Maybe one day, she'd write a book about it, but for now, finding out as much as she could about Penny and Charlene was more than enough to make her feel she was doing something important, and valuable.

Beside her, Michael held up his phone. "We have a room at the Best Western for tonight. Do you feel like Chinese? There's a restaurant with pretty good Yelp reviews nearby."

"Sounds perfect."

They turned and left the motel parking and drove to the Best Western, where they would stay for the night.

Penny was doing well, all things considered.

There weren't many things to celebrate when you studied the sex trafficking trade, but Penny's story was one.

That was something.

CHAPTER NINETEEN

Frank remembered an old saying that was appropriate to the moment: Keep your friends close and your enemies closer — unless you can get rid of your enemies altogether, that is.

That's what he thought when he realized that the girl was not going away.

Penny.

She was insistent, curious about him and his potential relationship to her mother. The damned DNA results said that they were related, but luckily, he and his closest family members had never done the tests. He didn't trust them. He knew that business and government were salivating after the DNA data and facial recognition software so it could track and monitor every citizen's activities — all the better to sell you things, or watch your political activities, of course.

He had refused any attempt to do DNA analysis of his genome and had prohibited his wife and his kids from pursuing it, telling them that he knew personally that the genealogy companies were colluding with government to create a Big

SUSAN LUND

Brother state that knew your every move, thought and genetic weakness.

That had paid off. While the girl had made a distant connection to his family, there was nothing to prove that she was more closely related.

He aimed to keep it that way.

Still, it was possible that someone really capable could get a sample of his DNA by stealth — humans shed their DNA like dogs shed their hair, if the truth was told. He'd personally talked to a friend who worked for one of the biotech companies in San Francisco who said that your hair, your skin cells, even your sweat at the gym, could be collected by someone intent on getting your DNA and used to profile you.

Cops did it all the time...

He stopped going to the gym when he learned that. He started to be much more careful about what he did and where. It wasn't possible to stop all body hair from being shed, but he did his best, shaving his head and sporting a Kojak look from back in the day when that show was popular. Lena didn't particularly like the shaved-head look, but he figured it was the safest.

He had an amazing security system installed in the house, with cameras in every damned room, so he could watch what everyone was doing at all times. Not that there were a lot of visitors to the house, since he liked to keep a close watch over the girls, but if anyone broke in and tried to get his DNA, they'd be seen on the cameras, which fed directly to an app on his smartphone.

So, the girl was a problem.

He hadn't worked so hard for all those years to let it all fall apart now because of her snooping around in his family tree, looking for her father...

"Where are you?"

He glanced up and saw that Lena was watching him, her voice dragging him back from his reverie and into reality.

"Oh, sorry. Just thinking about work." He gave her a smile that he didn't really feel and forked his food, no longer hungry.

The two of them were eating dinner at a high-end restaurant in the neighborhood after he'd finished a particularly good meeting with some investors who were helping him fund his latest project. He really had to focus, and not raise suspicion in Lena. That was the last thing he needed. He'd crafted such a perfect life with her in the years since he left San Francisco.

He wasn't going to let that perfect life crumble because of one persistent and stupid girl.

"Did that girl contact you?" she asked, raising her eyebrows.

"What girl?" He frowned, not realizing that the girl had called Lena. How the hell did she get Lena's number? It was unlisted...

"You know. The girl. Penny something. I don't remember her last name. She called the house and left a message, so I called her back. She seems to think you are related and she's trying to find out what happened to her mother and if you knew her father. Haven't you spoken with her?"

"As if I'm going to talk to a complete stranger who's probably hoping to grift us for money. You shouldn't talk to her either, if you know what's good for us."

Lena frowned. "She's trying to find her father. Maybe it's you?" She gave him a smile that was far too amused for his liking.

"It's not me, so don't even say that. I kept it sheathed back the day when I was sowing my wild oats, thanks. I didn't get anyone pregnant, least of all her mother."

He stabbed his filet a bit harder than he meant to and the fork scraped on the china plate, grating his nerves even more.

"Did you know her mother?"

"Of course not," he said, trying to calm himself. "I meant some random girl off the street. What is she — a homeless kid hoping to extort us for money? She was in foster care all her life from what she said. As if I knew *her* mother..." He shook his head in disgust. "If she calls again, you tell her to take her grift somewhere else. I don't have time for any foolishness."

"She seemed really nice on the phone," Lena said. "Maybe it's one of your disreputable cousins who got a girl pregnant back in the day. Or Dean. You have to admit your family is pretty licentious..."

"Not Dean and whatever my family did, I'm not like them," he said, shoving a piece of meat into his mouth and chewing hard. "I've spent my entire life trying to build this corporation and empire. You have to be kidding me if you think I would ever have associated with this girl's mother. Besides, I was busy creating the business. I didn't have time for screwing around with street waifs."

Lena frowned and it was then he knew he'd said the wrong thing.

"How do you know her mother was a street waif?"

He shrugged, trying to downplay it. "The mother abandoned her, right? For drugs or something? Isn't that what she said? Like I'd be involved with someone like that."

"Still, you could help her. Tell her about some of your less-savory relatives who might have been involved in drugs and crime back when she was born. Your half-brother is a good candidate, if that's the case. Sean was wild before he got married. Maybe he might know who her mother and father were. Maybe Will?"

"I'm not helping her, Lena, so get that out of your mind. As far as I'm concerned, this matter is over. I don't want to talk about her and her little drama of finding her parents. If we encourage her, the next thing you know, she'll be wanting to come for Easter Sunday dinner or something crazy."

Lena laughed at that. She picked up her napkin and wiped her mouth. "Would that be so bad? What if she's a niece or cousin?"

"I don't need any other relatives, sweetheart," he said, hoping to damp down Lena's interest in a new family member. "We have enough already, okay? Besides, we need to look after our own children. I don't want this girl to make us feel like we owe her anything."

"Why would you think she'd do that? She's just looking for family. Everyone wants family."

He didn't say anything in response, figuring that being quiet was the better option. Lena would move on to a new topic soon, but if he resisted her, she'd keep pushing. He'd learned that after a decade married to her.

"I think she sounds like a sweet girl," Lena said, unwilling to give up the topic. "Poor thing, not knowing who her mother is, or her father. Growing up in foster care and in youth homes. She didn't even know her own name. We should check into your family and see who her mother might be. You never know."

"Someone else can deal with her," he said. "Speaking of family, did you hear that Tim was trying out for spring training this year? I guess he was scouted. I suspect that boy is going to go places."

"You think?" Lena said, her eyes widening. "That would be so awesome."

Good. Distract her from the girl by talking about Lena's nephew.

Lena then launched into a discussion of her brother's wife and their home in Tacoma, and that was the last he heard about the girl looking for her mother and father and who might be related to them.

Thank God...

He checked his cell on the way out of the restaurant a half hour later, and there was a text from the girl.

PENNY: I was hoping I could come by and sit down with you, go through your family and see if there's anyone who might be my mother. I met with your brother Curtis and he feels that there might be a connection and that you know the family better than him. Is there a time I could come by?

He frowned.

Maybe he'd have to humor her. Frank was what people called an "upstanding citizen" and he intended to keep it that way. He wouldn't let some girl claim that he was her father. That would destroy his carefully constructed façade as a God-fearing man.

He responded to her text.

FRANK: Sure. You can meet me for lunch at the wharf. I like this little place that does fresh fish and chips. Gordon's Seafood. Meet me there at 1:00.

The girl replied.

PENNY: Thanks so much. See you then.

He didn't want to have to deal with her, but he needed to know what she knew. He needed to know who she talked to.

"Who are you texting?" Lena asked as they reached the SUV.

"That girl, Penny," he said. "I'm meeting her for lunch tomorrow to talk about family. Does that make you happy?"

"Oh, good," she said and squeezed his arm, smiling. "You're such a good-hearted man. I'm sure she'll appreciate it. Maybe one of the black sheep in the family got her mother pregnant. If so, think how happy she'll be to find us. She'll have a real family for the first time. Won't that be great?"

"Wonderful," he said with just the right amount of emotion, despite the distaste he felt inside. If he could, he'd like to knock the girl off and get her out of his hair, but he'd have to find a way to deal with her that didn't raise any suspicions. He figured she was an orphan with no known family. She'd lived in a group home. There was no one looking out for her.

Seriously — she'd be very easy to pick off if it came to that.

He hoped it wouldn't come to that, but if she was going to raise a bunch of very uncomfortable truths about his past, it would.

CHAPTER TWENTY

PENNY HAD a hard time sleeping the night before she was scheduled to meet with Frank.

The older brother of Curtis Stewart, Frank was a very wealthy businessman, who ran a shipping empire and his own investment business.

Curtis had given her a few names to track down but assured her that Frank was much better with those kinds of details. He might remember all of Dean's ex-girlfriends from before he joined the service, or maybe could talk to him about it on her behalf. Curtis thought that she looked so much like their mother that maybe she was one of Dean's bastards.

Dean might have met her mother when he was in high school and they'd had sex, she'd become pregnant and then he'd left to join the military. It was a story that she dreamed might be the case.

Her father — a handsome young warrior who fought in Iraq and Afghanistan after 9/11, now a successful businessman working for one of the biggest shipping companies in America.

He'd be about thirty-six. A few years older than her mother would have been if she were still alive.

She could imagine it in her mind's eye -- the two of them meeting when Dean was in high school and her mother was in middle school, maybe at a game. They saw each other several times and had sex — he was her first of course. Then, she dropped out of school and he left for boot camp in 2002 and that was it.

Her mother was pregnant with his child.

She probably didn't want to tell him because it would be frowned on by his much-wealthier family. Instead, she'd gone ahead and had the baby.

Then, her mother's life fell apart. She'd dropped out of middle school, becoming a sex trade worker to make ends meet. She'd met her boyfriend — who probably turned out to be her pimp — and had grown too depressed to care for Penny any longer. She'd left Penny, gone on a boat with her pimp, and that was it. She probably thought that someone would find Penny and give her a proper family life.

Of course, that didn't happen. No one seemed to want her -- the abandoned girl with emotional problems. Attachment disorder, it was called.

One terrible day, depressed and without hope, her mother jumped off a bridge somewhere along the Salish Sea and died alone. Some years later, her running shoe with her foot still inside, washed up on the shores of British Columbia.

It was a tragic story and made Penny sad to think that her mother had been so depressed that she wanted to kill herself. For several years, Penny had been angry at her mother for abandoning her, and that anger was like an acid in her chest burning a hole that lingered to that day. Then, her therapist convinced her that forgiveness was better, so she could move on and make a good life for herself. Wallowing in self-pity never accomplished anything.

Penny tried to forgive her mother, but it was hard.

Now, she had a real reason to forgive her. She most likely thought she was giving Penny a better life by abandoning her, knowing that Social Services would take her and look for a new family. Maybe she'd been planning to kill herself all along and abandoning Penny was done to protect her. Penny knew that, sometimes, women who were depressed killed their children before they committed suicide.

Whatever the case, Penny hoped that meeting with Frank might clear up some of the mystery in her life.

She'd looked up Dean's Facebook page and he was a handsome man in his late thirties with brown hair and golden-brown eyes. She tried to find some resemblance to him, and there was a hint of the same mouth and nose, just like Curtis said.

It warmed her heart to find someone she was related to at long last. Even if she wasn't Dean's daughter, they were maybe cousins in some way. That would have to be enough, but maybe, just maybe, Frank would know someone who she could talk to in order to find her mother and learn finally who she was.

When she woke up the next morning, Penny showered and chose her best causal clothes for the lunch meeting. If Frank was her grandfather or great uncle, or even a distant cousin, she wanted to make a good impression. Then, she sat at her desk and went over her Ancestry DNA results once more, adding in Frank, Curtis and Dean to her makeshift family tree on a pasteboard tacked up to the wall in her tiny room in the dorm. She drew a line from her mother to Dean with a question mark.

Was Dean her father?

Could Frank finally tell her who her mother really was?

Would Dean consent to do a paternity test?

She'd contacted Dean but hadn't heard back. There was nothing to be done but wait.

Waiting was hard. She'd been waiting all her life. It was time that something went her way.

She arrived at the fish and chips restaurant just before noon and waited outside, sitting on one of the patio chairs and waiting for Frank to arrive. The sun had actually peeked out through the clouds, signaling a change in the weather. She'd read the forecast and saw that they were in for a few days of sunshine, which was a pleasant break from the usually rainy fall weather. Maybe they were in for a warm winter.

At quarter after one, she checked her cell for any text from Frank, telling her he'd be late but there was nothing. At one twenty-five, she sent Frank a text.

PENNY: *Hey, I'm at the restaurant. Are you here?*

There was no answer. She went inside and glanced around once more but there was no one waiting. He hadn't shown up.

Dejected, she sent him another text.

PENNY: *I'm leaving. I have a class to prepare for but if you want to meet another time, let me know. We could Skype if you can't meet in person. It's just that Curtis said you had the best memory for the past and might know of one of Dean's girlfriends who might be my mother.*

There was still no answer, so she exhaled in resignation and left the patio, taking a walk along the street bordering the port.

She made her way back to her dorm room on campus and plopped down on the bed, finally allowing herself to cry. Why hadn't he at least responded to her, to let her know he couldn't make it? He probably didn't want to have to face her and deal with the fallout of having a bastard granddaughter, if Dean really was her father.

At around three o'clock in the afternoon, she got a text from him while she was sitting in class.

FRANK: *Sorry I missed you earlier. Had an emergency at work and wasn't able to reply to your texts until now. I spoke with Dean and he says there's no one in his past who might be your mother. He knows every girl he dated back in high school and none of them ever became pregnant or ran away from home so he can't be your father. Sorry. I hope you find your family.*

She read his text over several times and tried to hold back tears. She'd been so foolish to think that Dean had been her father.

PENNY: *Thanks anyway. Can you send me a list of your cousins and uncles and aunts anyway, on both sides of your family? Even if we aren't immediate relatives, someone more distant might be able to help.*

She tried to focus on class while she waited for his reply, but it wasn't easy. Her mind kept wandering to the photos of Dean that she'd seen.

Even Penny had to admit that they looked like they could be father and daughter. Besides, maybe Dean didn't want to tell anyone about the girl he got pregnant or the girl he had sex with who he lost track of. Maybe, just maybe, if she contacted Dean directly, he might be more willing to talk.

If Frank wouldn't help her, she'd talk to Curtis again and see if he was willing to give her Dean's contact information.

Finally, around six that night, after she was finished with her classes and was back in her dorm room, she got a text from Frank.

FRANK: *I'm sorry. I really don't think I or any of my family can be of any more help. Please don't contact us again. Best of luck.*

Penny sighed and lay back on her narrow bed.

She wanted to cry, because she'd become so enamored with the prospect of being Dean's daughter.

Instead of wallowing, like she could have very easily done, she sat up in her bed and sent Curtis a message.

PENNY: *Hi, Mr. Stewart. I talked with your brother Frank, but he doesn't think he can help me. Would you be willing to contact Dean on my behalf and see if he would be willing to talk to me? I emailed him to see if he's willing, but it would help if you could contact him yourself. Whatever he prefers if he's willing.*

She quickly added:

PENNY: *Also, could you please please please ask your family members to think of any young girl who would have been around fourteen or fifteen when she had a baby and maybe nineteen or twenty when she disappeared. Or any story of a family member or even acquaintance who had to give up her daughter to the foster care system and then disappeared in the last two decades?*

Then, she spent the rest of the night focused on her studies. Maybe the Stewart family itself was a dead end in her quest to find her mother and father, but at least she had some new names to add to her family tree and a few more leads to follow.

Surprisingly, she got a text back before nine that night.

CURT: *Sorry Frank was so uncooperative. I guess he's worried you're going to hit up Dean for support payments if you find out he's your father or something! Anyway, I did send a text to Dean, who's in Singapore right now on business but he's coming back to Seattle in a week or so. We'll see what he says. He'll let you know if he wants to talk. I gave him your cell number so he may text you if so. Take care.*

She texted right back, her heart rate increasing from excitement.

PENNY: *Thank you so much! Even if he doesn't agree, I*

really appreciate the help you were willing to give. Thanks a million.

Then, Penny waited.

Due to the time difference, she didn't expect to hear anything until the next day at the earliest. As she fell asleep that night, she held out a small smidgen of hope that Dean might agree to talk to her and that — hope against hope — he was her real father.

CHAPTER TWENTY-ONE

FRANK THOUGHT that was the end of it.

He'd driven to the restaurant and watched the girl from across the street. Just seeing her and how much she resembled others in his family, made him realize that he couldn't meet with her. No way. He didn't want any links between them.

So instead of meeting with her as planned, he'd told the girl to take a hike, so to speak, and as far as he was concerned, she was nothing but a bad memory. For a few days, that belief held firm and he went to work and spent time at home with his family, completely happy in the belief that it was a tempest in a teapot. Nothing more.

Of course, that idiot Curtis, who didn't know when to leave well enough alone, blew that plan out of the water. The man had no sense of propriety.

Did he really think Dean wanted to learn whether this little bitch was either of their illegitimate spawn?

He didn't and he was sure his bachelor son Dean didn't want it either. Dean had a good thing going on. He was a dashing young former soldier, handsome and accomplished, an exec in the Stewart Corporation, and the last thing he wanted was some little bastard cramping his style.

Frank was absolutely certain of it.

Still, he might foolishly decide to do the 'right thing' and get a paternity test and if that happened, they would be in big trouble.

Right away, he could see it — everyone would start looking into Frank's and Dean's pasts. That would do nothing but open up a huge can of worms — earthworms — and expose them to even more danger than just being the father of a bastard daughter.

The police would call him in for questions.

He couldn't let that happen.

He sent Dean a message.

DAD: Hey, buddy. There's this girl who's been pestering all of us for info on family members because she's trying to find her mother and father — she was abandoned when she was a child. Curt has already spoken with her but she's persistent. If she contacts you, do not, I repeat DO NOT humor her. She's probably trying to find someone to scam. I've read about these kids who show up on your doorstep pretending to be a relative so they can scam you out of money. Ignore her, okay? Her name is Penny.

He sent the text and then expected to wait until the next day to hear back from Dean, but he replied soon after.

DEAN: Hey dad. I already texted with her and told her that I'd be out of town for a while so I couldn't meet her any time soon. I didn't get her mother or anyone pregnant to my knowledge, but I told her I'd look through my friends and see if any one of them knew of any girl of the right age who had a kid and just up and disappeared. She seemed nice, but a bit of a sad case, if

you ask me. Abandoned at four years old — that's quite a story.
Her mother's foot washed up on the coast of Vancouver Island
and now she wants to find her parents. Can't blame her. Can't
really help her either but I said I'd ask around.

At least Dean didn't think he might be the father. That was
a relief. Still, he might do something stupid, chivalrous, and so
Frank knew he had to warn him.

DAD: As long as you don't do anything else, that should be
fine. No paternity test, okay? I know you're not the father, but
I've warned you about getting your DNA profile done. These
businesses are in coordination with the government and they are
building this huge DNA database about all of us. Keep your
DNA private. Who needs the government snooping around our
family tree?

DEAN: Don't worry. I've avoided bastards so far in life. I
aim to keep it that way until I meet Ms. Right.

DAD: Good. Take care. See you when you're back in
the USA.

DEAN: You too, Dad. Love you.

DAD: Love you back.

Frank put down his cell and rubbed his forehead, glad that
Dean wasn't interested in helping the girl out besides asking a
few friends about missing girls they might know about. That
put his mind at ease.

Hopefully, without his cooperation and without Dean's,
that might be the last they heard of Penny and her dreams of
finding her real father and mother.

Of course, it wasn't.

A few days later, he got a call from Curt.

"Hey," Curt said, his voice sounding distracted. "I got

another call from Penny. She asked me if I ever put in a DNA test and so I thought you should know that I finally sent off the Ancestry DNA test I had sitting in a drawer for months. Maybe it will help her find a closer relative."

"What?" Frank's heart sped up at the news. "Why would you do that?"

"Well, I figured if I did a test, it would show how closely she's related to us. Or not. But she looks so much like Mom, I figured she has to be a close relative. Mom had two sisters and a brother, and one of their grandkids just might have been the father."

"Jesus Christ, Curt. What were you thinking? If she is related to us, do you think we want to know? What if it's Dean's kid? If he wanted to know, he'd have offered to do a paternity test!"

"You think she might be Dean's? He said he didn't get anyone pregnant that he knew of, but I figured that maybe she'd have a few more names to add to her tree if I did mine."

"Can you get the test cancelled?"

"Why would I?" Curt asked, sounding suspicious. "If she's a second cousin or even closer, I want to know. If she's a relative, the more the merrier."

"Christ," Frank said, rubbing his eyes. "I gotta go."

He ended the call without hearing Curt's reply.

He had to think fast.

Once the DNA test came back, it would surely identify Curt as a very close relative. He didn't need that. He had to handle the girl and shut all this down — *now*.

But how?

Now that she'd made contact with Curt and Dean, and had texted him, and left a message on his phone, they were all linked to her. He did *not* want her being associated with the family in any way.

Was it possible to cancel an Ancestry DNA test?

He went to his laptop and did a quick google search to see if there were any directions on how to cancel a test after it had been sent. Luckily, it was possible. He'd have to figure out what information Curt sent them in order to do so. He knew that Curt wouldn't agree to the cancellation, being the kind of man who always seemed to want to help out damsels in distress, so Frank would have to figure out how to do it himself.

He called the number on the website and asked them what info he needed to cancel. Then, he realized he'd have to go over to Curt's and find some way to access his Ancestry mail, so he could provide the kit number. But even if he did that, Curt would find out that it was cancelled, and then the game would be up.

Damned Curt and his gullibility... He'd really fucked things up.

"What's the matter, dear?" Lena asked when she came into his home office. "Your face is red."

He shook his head. The last thing he needed was Lena prying into his private business. "Nothing, dear. Just some crap at the office."

"That's too bad," she replied. "You really should take some time off."

"I can't," he said. Then, he had a brainstorm.

"Actually, I think I might have to go on a business trip for a week," he said. "Figure things out in Portland. Do you mind? I know you have your sister coming."

She shook her head. "Of course I'll miss you, but it's no problem. If you have to go, you have to go, right?"

She bent down and kissed the top of his head then gave him a big smile. He knew she wouldn't mind at all. It would give the two sisters time to do whatever they pleased. They could shop and gossip and get their manicures and pedicures and spa treatments to their heart's desire.

Good.

He needed cover for what he was going to do to get rid of his Penny problem...

CHAPTER TWENTY-TWO

PENNY SAT STARING at the image on her cell.

Maria.

She had a pleasant face, with kind eyes. Penny thought it would be nice to be related to her and her family — especially Curtis, who was so helpful.

While she waited to speak to Frank, Penny received the much-anticipated text from Dean.

DEAN: *I understand you're looking for your birth mother and family and think you might be related to my family. My Uncle Curtis contacted me about it. Please tell me about yourself.*

Penny's heart picked up speed when she read his text. It seemed pleasant enough.

She sent him a response right away, and had phrased it as nicely as she could so he didn't take offense or have a reason to deny her request.

PENNY: *Hi, Mr. Stewart. Thanks so much for texting me. As your Uncle Curtis may have said, my name is Penny Morrison. That's not my birth name, but I have no idea what it was.*

My mother, Charlene, became pregnant with me almost twenty years ago and dropped out of school. She lived in the Seattle area at the time, but we are not sure exactly where. I was born and lived with her for four and a half years, and then she abandoned me, and I was left an orphan. She died sometime after that and her remains, a shoe in a sneaker, turned up on the coast of British Columbia.

Penny broke the text up into several sections.

PENNY: *Now, I'm trying to find my birth parents. I was connected through several DNA databases to some second cousins, and they gave me a list of potential relatives. I did some checking with them, and your family was listed as a distant relation to them. I was hoping we could speak, and you could think back to your high school days and see if you might have known my mother, or if not, if you remember any young woman getting pregnant and dropping out of school. It would have been about 2000. I live in Seattle currently and met with your Uncle Curtis, who said that I look a lot like your grandmother, so we both hope there is some family connection between us.*

Then she waited to see what he said in response.

She saw the little dots and realized he was responding, and bit her lip in anticipation.

Finally, the text came through.

DEAN: *I remember a girl named Charlene from my high school years, but we were never intimate, so I know for certain that I'm not your father. In fact, I don't think she even went to my high school, but was friends with some of the girls on the cheerleading team. I'll go back to my yearbook and see if I can come up with some names you could contact for more information about her. As to how we would be related, maybe one of my other cousins was involved with her? Curtis would know the family tree better than me, but we were all from Seattle and Tacoma area, although I was born in San Francisco, when my father was working out of that office. We moved back when I was ten and lived in the same general neighborhood with my cousins so it might have been one of them. That's all I can think. I'll get back to you with some names. Hope that helps, but I know for sure if your mother is the Charlene I knew, I'm not your father.*

Penny was ecstatic.

PENNY: *Thanks so much! What do you remember about her? What did she look like? Can you send me a pic from the yearbook of the girls who were her friends? What yearbook is it? Is there one in any library that I could get hold of? What high school was it? What neighborhood? I'm so glad you contacted me. Thanks a million!*

DEAN: *Like I said, I don't think she went to our high school, which was a private school, but I played varsity football and our cheerleading team went along with us. I remember my girlfriend at the time, Dana Martin, had a friend named Charlene from another school. Maybe she was on the cheerleading team and that's how she knew her. That's it. As far as I know, Dana still lives in Seattle and she may know more about Charlene that I knew from back then.*

PENNY: *Oh, it would be so wonderful if it turns out to be her. Do you think one of your cousins might have been the father — my father? What are their names?*

DEAN: *Curtis is the one who is the keeper of that kind of information in our family, since my grandmother died. Talk to him some more.*

PENNY: *I will. And thank you so much for this lead.*

DEAN: *No problem. I'll send you whatever I find out. Good luck with your search.*

PENNY: *Thanks again. Take care.*

Penny sat with her cell in her hand, re-reading the texts over and over again, hoping against hope that maybe, she'd finally found someone who knew her mother back when she was in school.

In a moment, she received another text from Dean.

DEAN: The Yearbook is called The Echo, just in case you want to check it out, but like I said, the Charlene who hung out with Dana wasn't a student at Seattle Prep. She was from one of the other schools, if I remember her correctly. Maybe Garfield? You could check that one out.

PENNY: I will. Thanks again. You've been such a huge help. I don't know how to thank you!

DEAN: Glad to help. Let me know what you find out and I'll contact Dana and see if she remembers anything.

PENNY: Thanks!

Immediately, Penny searched for a Dana Martin, but if she married and took her husband's surname, she might be hard to find. Her first searchers turned up several possible Dana Martins, only one of which was in Seattle. She was a lawyer who worked for a big firm. There was a link to her Facebook page, and a LinkedIn entry. Penny spent the next hour collecting up whatever information she could about Dana, and even registered for the eYearbook site that hosted hundreds of yearbooks from high schools around the country.

She sent a message to the Dana Martin through the law firm website. She could have been Dean's girlfriend, and might remember Charlene.

PENNY: Hello, you don't know me, but I got your name from Dean Stewart, who said he knew you back in high school at Seattle Prep. I'm looking for my birth mother's identity and all I know is that her name was Charlene, and she would have given birth to a child when she was fourteen, back around 2000. Dean said he remembered a friend of yours named Charlene back in the day, so I hoped I could call you and talk about it if you do happen to remember her from high school. Thanks for your help if so!

Then, she spent an hour trying to find the yearbook for Garfield High School, just in case, as Dean said, there was a Charlene from there. There were several copies, but no Charlene. It was a unique enough name that if she found one, it was most probably her mother, but sadly, there were no matches.

Until she spoke to Dana Martin, she wouldn't know for sure if this was a dead end, but Penny was certain that the Charlene Dean spoke of had to be her mother. Curtis might have some names of their uncles and those uncles might have had some sons who might have been her mother's boyfriend...

By mid-afternoon, Penny was feeling a bit down after coming up empty with no girls named Charlene in the Seattle Prep *Echo* or at Garfield High School. There were a number of high schools in the Broadmoor area, and so began her long afternoon and night of searching yearbooks for any potential Charlene.

An hour after a bleak dinner of toast and tea, her cell dinged, and sure enough, there was an email from Dana Martin, Esq., who was a lawyer working with the firm Penny found when searching.

DANA: Hi, Penny. Thanks for contacting me. I do remember Charlene from when I was in high school. She was a friend of my best friend Brenda and wasn't yet in high school. Unfortunately, Brenda died of breast cancer recently, so she won't be able to help you, but they were friends because they lived in the same neighborhood. I think their moms were friends. Brenda got a scholarship to attend Seattle Prep so that's how she was there. I think Charlene was in Middle School. Maybe O'Grady in Miller Park area? She had a pretty hard life if I recall correctly. Charlene's father died when she was six, and her mom had a hard time afterwards. Char-

lene was an only child. I don't remember her getting pregnant, but she stopped hanging around with us at the end of the school year so that might have been why. I lost track of her after that. I don't think she ever attended Seattle Prep. It was a private school, so her family wouldn't be able to afford tuition. That's about all I can think off the top of my head. Good luck with your search.

Penny re-read the text and then responded.

PENNY: *Thanks so much for getting back to me. This helps a lot. I really think the girl you knew as Charlene was my mother. So, the last time you saw or spoke to her was at the end of the school year in 2000? Or 1999?*

DANA: *It would have been 1999 I think. June 1999 probably. I really can't think of anything else. Brenda would have been your best bet for more information on her. I remember sitting with her during games. Hope that helps! Let me know if you find your mom.*

PENNY: *You've been such a big help, so thank you so much. What was Brenda's last name? I might be able to talk to her family to locate my mom.*

DANA: *Her last name was Pender, but she got married and was Wallace. Her mom was Janice Pender.*

PENNY: *Thanks. I'll let you know if I confirm that the Charlene you knew was my mom. She died sometime after I was abandoned, so after 2005. We have no idea how she died, but her foot in a sneaker washed up on the shore of Vancouver Island in Canada in 2012, and I only learned it was my mother's remains when I did a DNA profile and the cold case investigators made a match.*

DANA: *Wow, sorry to hear that. I heard about those feet washing up on the shores around here. I hope everything works out for you. Take care.*

PENNY: *You as well.*

Penny sighed heavily and then opened up her web browser

and did a search for middle schools in Seattle. She didn't have much to go on other than the name of an old friend's mother, but if Dana's friend lived in the Miller Park area, that was a good place to start if their mothers were friends.

It was a good lead.

Penny was certain.

CHAPTER TWENTY-THREE

PENNY HAD a list of names and places, and intended to contact every person and visit every place. She would leave no stone unturned in her search for her mother's identity — *her* identity.

She'd contacted Brenda's family, and after talking to Brenda's very nice husband to confirm Brenda's mother's name, she called Mrs. Pender out of the blue, certain the older woman would either not remember or wouldn't cooperate.

She was wrong.

Mrs. Pender was only too happy to help Penny, and began to reminisce about her own high school days, and the extremely good luck Brenda had to attend Seattle Prep on a scholarship.

"You have to realize at the time, we were dirt poor," Mrs. Pender said. "Brenda's father was disabled after a bad accident on a construction site and on disability pension, and I worked two jobs, but Brenda's grades were so high, she was able to get a scholarship to Seattle Prep. We did everything we could to keep her there and she graduated and went on to college to study business."

Penny listened intently, glad to finally meet someone who might have known her mother.

"Tell me about Charlene, Brenda's friend. She lived in your neighborhood?"

"Oh, yes, Charlene. Her mom and I were friends. Charlene's family was really struggling, and then her father died when she was about six and Darlene was all alone with Charlene. She didn't remarry right away, and lived off a survivor's pension, on top of working part-time cleaning office buildings on the evening and night shift. Charlene was one of those latch-key kids. We felt sorry for her, and she slept at our place a lot when Darlene worked nights and Charlene was afraid to stay alone. Charlene and Brenda were best friends until Brenda went to high school and Charlene was still in middle school. They lost touch that year, although Charlene did still come by now and then, but Brenda and Dana became friends and things just came to an end, I guess. I heard Charlene ran away from home and was living with some new friends she'd made, but that was it. After that, we didn't hear from Charlene and I assumed she must have gone on to high school in the neighborhood. Darlene and I lost touch as well, after she eventually remarried. I can give you her name and number if you like."

"That would be fantastic. What's her last name?"

"It was Schafer. Darlene Schafer, but she remarried, and I think his name was Tim Wood. I believe they moved to Tacoma for work, but I don't know where they are now. We lost contact after that."

"So Charlene was a Schafer?"

"Yes, I believe her father was George Schafer. But he died when she was six."

Penny wrote that all down and sighed. "Thanks so much, Mrs. Pender. You have been such a big help. Do you have any photos of Charlene or Darlene Schafer?"

"As a matter of fact, I just might have. Darlene and I spent a lot of time together, cookouts and Sunday dinners. Brenda had some photos and we kept them in an old album. If you want, you can have them if you think Darlene and Charlene Schafer might be your relatives."

"I do," Penny said. "Charlene is the right age for my mother and has some of the same traits as her. From a working-class background," she said.

Mrs. Pender interrupted with a wry chuckle. "You mean impoverished."

"Yes, impoverished is a nicer way to put it. Charlene also seemed to have run away when she was about thirteen or so, which is similar to the story my mother told me about her past. She always told me that she became pregnant with me and had to drop out and never finished school. I've checked all the schools in Broadmoor for any Charlene, but the name wasn't very common."

"We lived in Miller Park. Charlene would have gone to Meany Middle School where Brenda went. You could check their school yearbook, but I do have some old photo albums you could check out if you want some photos. I'm here all day, so you can drop by anytime you like."

"Thanks," Penny said. "Can I come by tomorrow? Morning or afternoon — you choose. I have the day off."

"Mornings are best for me. I get tired in the afternoon, usually."

"Can I bring you anything? Coffee? Donuts?"

"That sounds nice. We can look at photo albums and talk."

"I'll see you around nine," Penny said, happy that she might have finally found her mother. "Is that a good time?"

"Perfect. I like my coffee with lots of cream and sugar. There's a Dunkin Donuts right around the corner from here and it's been a long time since I had any."

"I'll pick some up on the way. See you then."

"Goodbye, Penny. I hope Charlene is your mother."

"I'm sure she is, so thank you. This means so much to me."

"Well, you're very welcome."

With that, Penny ended the call and sat staring off into space for a moment, wondering what photos Mrs. Pender might have of Penny's mother Charlene and her grandmother Darlene.

Charlene *Schafer*.

Penny might just be a Schafer.

If this turned out to be real, she had a breakthrough.

This might be her family.

The next morning, Penny was up early and after a shower and quick breakfast, she got on the bus and took it out to Miller Park where Mrs. Pender lived. It wasn't the nicest area of Seattle, but it wasn't too bad either. There were a mix of houses, some old and some newer infills along with a number of older and newer apartment blocks. The streets were tree-lined and pleasant enough. There were worse neighborhoods in Seattle, so it wasn't all bad. Still, there were a number of very small houses that looked like they'd been built during the war — tiny bungalows on very narrow plots of land.

Mrs. Pender lived a few blocks away from Edmond S. Meany Middle School, and Penny walked by on her way to Mrs. Pender's apartment block on East John Street.

She had two Dunkin Donuts coffees in a takeout tray and a bag of donuts in hand when she pressed the buzzer next to Mrs. Pender's apartment and waited to be let inside. The door buzzed and Penny entered, then took the stairs up to the second-floor apartment, noting the piles of flyers and old newspapers in the entry and the loud sounds coming from under the doors to a few apartments. The walls were dingy, and the carpets worn.

She knocked at the door marked 2 1 2 and waited, listening to the sound of the door locks unlocking. Finally, the door opened and there was Mrs. Pender in all her glory, hunched over a walker, her grey hair disheveled, a floral robe over her pajamas and slippers on her feet.

"There you are," Mrs. Pender said and smiled. She covered her heart and shook her head. "My God, do you look like Charlene...Come on in. Penny. Penny Schafer, maybe?"

"I think so, although my real name isn't really Penny. The social workers gave that to me," Penny said, her heart skipping a beat that Mrs. Pender thought she looked like the Charlene they knew. Penny placed the tray of coffees on the kitchen table while Mrs. Pender pushed her walker over.

"Have a seat at the table. It's best for my back when I'm eating or drinking. I got bad scoliosis, but it wasn't bad enough for an operation when I was diagnosed as a kid, but it's gotten worse the longer I live."

Penny took a seat on a chair, covered with a plastic floral fake-leather, and opened the bag of donuts, placing them on the plate Mrs. Pender placed in front of her.

"I got a couple of different kinds. You pick your favorite. I like the chocolate dip."

Mrs. Pender plopped down on the chair beside Penny, and in her hand was the photo album that she was so excited to see.

"Here you go, dear. I'll find the picture of Charlene, but you can look through as much as you like."

She opened the photo album and paged through it, then came to rest on a photo of four girls standing together at a football field, three of them dressed in cheerleading outfits and one girl, smaller than the rest, standing beside the three. All of them had big smiles on their faces.

The girl standing alone could have been Penny when she was that age.

Charlene Schafer.

Brown hair, dark eyes.

Mrs. Pender took one of the chocolate dip donuts and the cup of coffee and began eating, while Penny stared at the photo, too excited to eat.

"That's her," Penny said, a flood of memories making her throat choke up with emotion. "That's my mother. I remember the hair and smile. She was a small woman, fine boned."

"Like you," Mrs. Pender said. "I thought of Charlene when I saw you at the door. You could be twins for goodness' sake."

Penny smiled at that, glad that she looked like her mother. It was something she could hold onto.

They paged through the photo album and Mrs. Pender talked about the photos with Charlene in them. One was of Charlene and Brenda at the playground, sitting on swings.

"We took that on Brenda's birthday when we had a picnic in the park. That was a very nice day, and the girls had a good time. It was soon after my husband had his accident and was on disability, so we didn't have a lot of money, but we had a nice birthday for Brenda."

Penny smiled, thinking that Mrs. Pender was a very nice woman, to treat Charlene like another daughter, despite all their own family's hardships. "I'm so sorry about your daughter's passing." She smiled.

"Thank you. It's been hard, surviving your own child."

A moment passed, and then Penny pressed on. "Do you know of any boys that my mother was friendly with? Someone who could have been my father? She would have become pregnant in her last year of middle school."

Mrs. Pender shook her head. "She was always hanging out with the older girls from Seattle Prep. She went to games with

Brenda and the other girls. They sat on the bleachers and watched the games. I never saw her with a boy, but that doesn't mean she was never with one, obviously." Mrs. Pender made a face of sorrow. "I wish I could help you more, but that's it. I don't know what the girls did when they weren't at the house."

Penny nodded in understanding. Of course she wouldn't know. Penny's mom became pregnant in some way, and it likely wasn't at school. More likely at a party or while at her boyfriend's house.

"Did you know Dean Stewart?"

"Dean?" Mrs. Pender said, her eyebrows raised. "Oh, yes I did. I thought he and Brenda might get together at one point. They went to Seattle Prep together. The Stewarts from Broadmoor are famous around here. Everyone knew Dean Stewart. He was the star quarterback and he signed up to go to Afghanistan soon after 9/11. All the girls were in love with him, and I think he had his eye on Brenda, but it never developed into anything." She turned to Penny. "You don't think he's your father, do you? I don't remember seeing him with Charlene if that's what you're thinking."

"I don't know for sure," Penny said quickly, feeling silly. "We're related, I think, but maybe only distantly. I'm just wondering if he was ever hanging out with Charlene. I met with Dean's uncle Curtis Stewart, because we're related but we're not sure how closely. He did say I looked a lot like his mother. So, I wondered..."

She raised her eyebrows. "That's a very wealthy family to be related to," Mrs. Pender said. "I thought that maybe Dean and Brenda might get together but as soon as he finished high school, he joined up and went to war." She sighed wistfully. "He's still not married, from what I can tell. That's quite the family. They're very rich, run a big shipping business out of Seattle, but they have offices in Los Angeles, San Francisco, and Portland. They've seen a lot of tragedy. Mr. Stewart Sr., Dean's grandfather, was a scion in Seattle. He divorced and remarried several times and was a notorious womanizer. Frank Jr. and Curtis are from one wife who Frank Sr. met and married in California. Sean, their half-brother is from another wife who lived in Seattle. Frank Jr. came to Seattle after Dean's mother died. Frank Jr. remarried but they split just a few years later. Finally on his third wife, and she's a lot younger than him and has these girls from a previous marriage."

"You know a lot about them," Penny said when Mrs. Pender stopped to take a drink of coffee.

"I do," she said. "The Stewarts were pretty famous in Seattle. Their stories make the gossip pages."

They talked a while longer about Brenda and her illness and death, and finally, Penny felt as if she'd gotten all the answers she needed and said goodbye.

"Can I take photos of Charlene?" she asked and held out her cell.

"Of course. I'd give these to you, but I want to keep them for my own memories."

"No, that's fine. I can take photos of them with this."

She laid the photos down and took several images of them. Then, she turned and smiled at Mrs. Pender.

"Thanks so much for taking the time to speak with me."

Mrs. Pender nodded. "Let me know if you find out who your father is. I'd be shocked if it's Dean Stewart, but you never know. Stranger things have happened. Maybe he and your mother were sweet on each other and none of us knew."

"I have no idea if he is, but I'm sure we're related in some way. I'll let you know what I find out."

"That would be great," Mrs. Pender said and waved at Penny.

Penny closed the door behind her and left the apartment, glad that she'd reached out to Mrs. Pender.

She was pretty sure the Charlene who was friends with Brenda Pender was her mother.

Whether or not Dean was her father was another matter, she at least had pretty good idea that Charlene was her mother based on what Mrs. Pender said.

Penny felt a growing sense of excitement in her gut at the prospect that maybe, just maybe, she was finally on the right track.

CHAPTER TWENTY-FOUR

PENNY SPENT the next few days reading everything she could about Darlene Wood, née Schafer, Edmond S. Meany Middle School, Seattle Prep, and the Stewarts of Broadmoor fame.

There was a Meany Middle School yearbook and so she went to the website and was able to find a copy of the yearbook from 1999/2000 and 2000/2001. She spent an hour paging through the two copies, searching for her mother and there, on the page for the 8th Grade students, was her mother.

Charlene Schafer.

Light brown hair, brown eyes, and a small frame — just like Penny.

It was her, although a bit younger looking than Penny remembered. But it was definitely her.

Tears came to Penny's eyes and she immediately searched for Darlene Wood. There were dozens of people by the name of *Wood* listed in Tacoma but there was a T. Wood and a Timothy Wood, either of which could be the right one. She called Timothy and left a message on their voicemail system.

"Hi, you don't know me, but we may be related. My name is Penny and I lived in foster care all my life after my mother was unable to care for me when she was nineteen. I'm currently looking for my family and I think that her name was Charlene Schafer, whose mother was Darlene Schafer. Darlene married a Tim Wood and moved to Tacoma. If this is the Darlene Wood whose daughter was Charlene, I think Charlene might be my mother and I'm trying to track down any family members. Please call me so we can talk if so."

Penny left her cell number and then ended the call, leaving much the same message at the other T. Wood.

That done, she started searching for anyone connected to the Schafers in Seattle. There were over one hundred in the Seattle White Pages, and there was no way she could figure out who she might be related to easily. At least the white pages listed ages, names, addresses and previous locations for some of them, but it was an overwhelming task to sort through who might be related to Penny's mother and who might not. She settled on the Schafers in the neighborhood where Charlene was supposed to have grown up. There were a few Schafers in Miller Park.

She'd start there.

She listed their names in alphabetical order and would just start calling, hoping against hope that one of them might be a relative.

"Hi, my name is Penny and I'm searching for my birth mother and her family. Her name was Charlene Schafer and..."

She left the same message on a dozen of the Schafers who lived in the general area around Miller Park, in the hopes that even if Darlene never called, someone else may have been a relative and known what happened with Charlene. She didn't expect anyone to call. Even Penny had to admit that a stranger calling out of the blue with a story about maybe being related would likely not get many responses, but that was the only thing she could think of doing.

Penny turned back to her cell and searched through the photos while she took a break and made some coffee. She'd taken a picture of Dean's photo in the yearbook, and one of him from his Facebook page.

Was Dean her father?

He was a handsome young man when he joined up and went to Afghanistan. She looked at the picture of him from Seattle Prep — handsome as a younger man, too, with dark hair and eyes, a strong jaw and an easy smile. If Dean was her father, she'd inherited her mother's coloring and not his.

It was looking more and more likely that Dean was her father, even though he denied it. The Ancestry link to the Stewarts, the fact that Charlene knew one of Dean's girlfriends...

Probably what happened was that Dean had the sweets for Charlene, and they got together, but then when she got pregnant, she didn't want him to know and just stopped hanging out with the girls. Dean had said they never got together, but maybe he didn't want to admit it...

If so, how sad for Charlene, to have to face pregnancy alone?

Did she spend that year pregnant, dropping out of middle school when it became more obvious?

Penny hoped that Darlene would call and tell her what really happened.

With the photos printed off and the list of names, Penny kept busy for the rest of the day, leaving messages and ticking off a list of things to do in her search for her birth mother and father. She wouldn't give up hope, and used every spare moment when she wasn't studying for her classes to search.

. . .

A few days went by before Penny had any luck.

When she got out of class on Tuesday, she saw a message on her cell, which she'd turned off during the lecture.

It was from Darlene Wood.

"Hi, Penny. This is Darlene Wood. I'm Charlene's mother. I guess I'm your grandmother. Charlene ran away when she was fourteen, and lived with a friend's family — Teresa Williams, I think was her name. Charlene and I clashed a lot because I had little money and not much of a job and she didn't like the man I met and intended to marry. She just wouldn't listen to me or obey our house rules. I offered Charlene the chance to move with us to Tacoma, but she decided to stay in Seattle with Teresa's family. I tried to keep track of her at first, but Charlene didn't seem interested and we lost touch. I'd given up hope trying to find her. If you know where she is, please let me know. I'd like to re-establish contact after all these years if she's willing."

That made Penny feel terrible.

Of course, Charlene was dead, her foot in a sneaker washing up on the coast of the Salish Sea the only evidence that she had died. Penny would have to call Darlene — her own grandmother — back and let her know that Charlene was dead.

She hesitated, not wanting to upset the woman. Perhaps they could meet, and she could break it to her gently...

Then, Penny wondered if she wasn't getting the poor woman upset over nothing. Maybe that Charlene wasn't her mother after all...

Filled with a certainty that Charlene was in fact her mother, Penny called Darlene and chewed her bottom lip nervously as she waited for the older woman to answer.

When Darlene did, Penny took in a deep breath and began.

"Hi, Mrs. Wood," she said. "This is Penny. I left the message on your voicemail."

"Oh, yes, Penny! I'm so glad you called back. To be honest, I've long dreamed that one day, Charlene and I would reconnect, but she never has. Have you had any luck finding her?"

Penny cringed internally and made a face, glad that she wasn't actually with Mrs. Wood when she told her about Charlene's death.

"No, well, I mean, yes, but..." she said, stuttering, not really sure how she could phrase the information. "If Charlene was my mother, if your daughter Charlene was my mother, that is..."

"Yes?" Mrs. Wood said, her voice hopeful.

"To be honest, Mrs. Wood," Penny began.

"Call me Darlene," Mrs. Wood insisted. "Or grandma, if you prefer. Mrs. Wood just sounds like I'm the Principal or something."

Penny could hear the smile and excitement in the older woman's voice and closed her eyes, a weight of sadness in her heart that she'd have to tell her — Darlene — maybe Penny's grandmother — that Charlene was dead.

"Could I come by and talk to you in person? I have some photos and would love to see any you have."

"Oh, of course," Mrs. Wood — Darlene — said. "Please feel free to come by. Tim's busy in the shop, so it'll be you and me. I'll make some coffee and we can have some cake. I made some nice carrot cake with cream cheese frosting. It's my favorite and it's fresh so if you like, come on by around three."

"That sounds delicious," Penny said. "I'll drop by around three and see you then."

"Yes, see you then, Penny."

Penny ended the call. She didn't relish telling Mrs. Wood that her only daughter was dead, most likely a suicide. She likely jumped off some nearby bridge, her body decomposing at the bottom of Puget Sound. Then, when her foot disarticulated from her leg and floated to the surface, it found its way into the currents of the Salish Sea, coming to rest on Mystic Beach, Vancouver Island, Canada.

But if she was going to tell that story, it should really be in person.

She arrived at the small house just before three in the afternoon, having taken public transit all the way from her dorm to Tacoma. It had taken almost two hours, but Penny figured it was worth it to see where her possible grandmother lived and pay a visit.

The house was nice enough. A craftsman built in the fifties by the looks of it, the house was on a decent sized lot and had a nice lawn, with rose bushes and planters filled with flowering plants. Mrs. Wood — Darlene — was waiting at the door when Penny walked up the sidewalk and she was a delicate older woman, wearing a floral dress and sweater, her white hair pulled back into a ponytail. Her face was narrow and had a pointy chin — just like Penny — and light brown eyes.

She could be Penny's grandmother. That was clear.

"Penny?" Mrs. Wood said and opened the door.

"Yes, hello Mrs. Wood," Penny replied. "It's me."

"Come in, come in," Mrs. Wood said. "And please, call me Darlene. If we're related, you can call me Grandma if you like. That would be nice."

She held the door and Penny entered, taking off her shoes and following Mrs. Wood — Darlene — into the small living room at the front of the house, which overlooked the lawn and street.

The house was tidy and nicely decorated, so whatever Mr.

Wood did for a living, they had enough money to furnish their house nicely. In fact, despite the house being older, it was the nicest house Penny had been in. It was the kind of house she dreamed about having grown up in and could imagine walking to the local school, playing in the playground outside the school, and taking trips to the local 7-11 to buy Slurpees while growing up.

The house smelled wonderful — cake and coffee.

"Have a seat," Darlene said. "I'll bring the cake and coffee. Do you take cream and sugar?"

"Yes, please," Penny said and sat on the sofa in front of a glass-topped coffee table.

When Darlene arrived back, she had a tray filled with cups and plates with slices of carrot cake. It looked and smelled delicious.

They fixed their cups of coffee and Darlene handed Penny a piece of cake.

She tried it, and only for a moment did she stop to wonder if it wasn't poisoned, but then shook her head mentally. Why would the woman want to harm her? She was just a nice older woman who lost touch with her only daughter and was hoping to learn about her fate.

They ate and talked about the neighborhood and where Mr. Wood was, and how Darlene was sad that she never had any more children, but that Mr. Wood had a vasectomy after an earlier marriage and three children.

Penny smiled. Darlene was a talker, and filled the empty spaces with conversation about her life.

Finally, Darlene put down her cup and her face grew serious.

"So I expect you haven't found her," Darlene said. "Charlene, I mean. Your mother."

"I'm not completely certain it's your Charlene, although I think so, based on what I've read and heard from people who knew her. A week ago, I was contacted by a police officer working cold cases in Victoria, British Columbia Canada."

Darlene's expression turned serious and she took in a deep breath.

"Oh, dear," she said, her tone much less cheerful. "Cold cases you say?"

Penny nodded. "They found a foot in a running shoe in 2012 and it sat in their morgue, as evidence, until this year. They ran a DNA search and matched it to my profile. The DNA in the foot was determined to be my biological mother."

"Oh, my," Darlene said, a hand to her mouth, her brow knit. She shook her head and didn't look at Penny. "I was afraid of something like this."

Penny nodded. "The only thing I knew about my mother was that her name was Charlene. I was told that my father died when I was young and that my mother had to drop out of school to look after me. I never knew my father's name. We lived with a number of different men, and the last one was Dennis. One day, they took me to a small boat launch near Old Town in Clallam County, and left me on the beach. They took a boat and left. I was found a few hours later by a man walking on the beach. From that day on, I was in foster care."

"Oh, dear, I'm so sorry..." She shook her head. "That's such a sad story."

"Do you think she might be your Charlene? Would you do a DNA test to check?"

"I, I really..." she said and glanced away. "My Charlene dead? I always wondered, but the Williams's... Teresa's family... I always thought that she just stayed with them, finished high school, got married... Honestly, the last time I saw Charlene, she told me she wasn't ever coming home again. She didn't like Tim, you see..."

She wrung her hands and stared out the window, tears running down her face. She pulled a tissue out of her pocket and wiped her eyes, shaking her head the entire time.

"I'm so sorry," Penny said, feeling bad for the woman. "Maybe before you get too upset, you could submit your DNA to the police in Canada and they could see if it's a match. If it isn't, she's not your daughter."

Darlene shook her head. "No," she said. "I'm pretty sure it's my Charlene." She wiped her eyes and took in a deep breath, like she was preparing herself. "I didn't say anything to you earlier, but back in the day, I got a note from Mrs. Williams that Charlene had gone to stay at Sisters of Mercy, this charity home for unmarried mothers, to give birth. I learned she'd become pregnant, and well, Tim didn't want to bring the child into our house, or I would have offered for her to come and stay with me. We fought over it. He felt that Charlene was just going to take advantage of us and that she had to give the child up for adoption and go back to school, but Charlene didn't want to. You have to understand, I was all alone, I'd lost my job and was on welfare and then Tim came along, and he was doing so well, and we had a home in Tacoma..."

"I understand," Penny said and reached out to take her grandmother's hand. "It must have been really hard for you. I can't imagine. Did you know the name she gave me?"

"No, I never checked. I'm so sorry," she said and squeezed Penny's hand. "I hope you and I can be family. Other than Tim's side of the family, I have no one. It would be nice."

Penny smiled. "It would be."

She'd found her family. Her mother had been the Charlene from Miller Park, who got pregnant and ran away from home, giving birth in a Catholic charity home. She'd probably been trafficked as a young girl, and had died after committing suicide, jumping from a bridge in Puget Sound, her foot washing up on the beaches of Vancouver Island. It was a sad story, but at least she found her people. At least, half her people.

Now she had to find out the identity of her father...

CHAPTER TWENTY-FIVE

THE FIRST THING Penny did after meeting with Darlene was contact the Sisters of Mercy home for young girls, to see if they had a record of her mother's stay there. Sure enough, one of the administrators checked the records and there was a birth certificate, registering her birth, mother name Charlene Schafer, father unknown.

The name given to her at birth? Melanie.

Melanie Celeste Schafer. Born February 2, 2000.

She said the name, but it didn't feel right. She was Penny and had always been since that day on the beach when the man named Derek found her.

She couldn't imagine changing her first name, but she would gladly call herself Penny Schafer from then on. She'd googled how to change her name and had begun the process, but it would require a fee and having a notary public to complete the process.

Part of Penny was angry with Darlene for not caring enough to keep track of her own daughter. She tried to be generous, and understand that Darlene had a hard life, raising a troubled kid with no support, being a single mother, and on welfare. She met her new husband and was probably grateful when Charlene left, feeling like her life would finally be good.

Maybe if Darlene had kept in touch with Charlene, she would have had a family instead of living in foster care all her life.

Out of the blue and to her complete surprise, Penny got a text from Dean saying he was in town and could meet.

DEAN: *Hey, Penny. I know I said I was going to be out of town for a while, but I'm in town today and tomorrow for a quick business trip, so if you'd like to meet and talk, I'm staying at a hotel between Tacoma and Seattle. How about meeting me down by the wharf? There's a great coffee shop I used to go to with a nice view of the water. Blends. I've gone through a few more school yearbooks and some old scrapbooks I have from school and might have a few leads for you to follow.*

PENNY: *That sounds wonderful. The names you gave me really helped. I had some luck with the name you gave me, your old girlfriend, and the yearbooks. I tracked down a woman I think is my grandmother. Her name is Darlene Wood, but it was Schafer. So my mother's name was Charlene Schafer. She went to Meany Middle School, instead of Garfield like you suggested.*

DEAN: *That's great news. So you're still looking for your father? I wonder if it wasn't one of my great uncle's grandkids — my grandmother's brother Steven. We lost touch but that's an avenue you could explore. One of Steven's grandkids might be the right age to be your father and they were here when your mother might have become pregnant.*

PENNY: *Oh, that would be great if you have info on them. I have no idea who my father might be, but given that Curtis thought I looked like your grandmother, we wondered if maybe I was related to someone on your family's side.*

DEAN: *Yeah, the resemblance to my grandmother suggests*

one of her relatives might be your father. Her nephews were Greg and Pete, if I recall correctly. They have sons who would be about the right age. Her maiden name was Ross. My dad is still worried you're going to hit me up for child support or something, even though I told him I never touched your mother, but he's suspicious, I guess...

PENNY: *It's not like that at all. I just want to know. I want family. All my life, I've been alone.*

DEAN: *I can't imagine it. Anyway, see you tomorrow at 8:00 at Blends.*

PENNY: *Thanks again, Dean.*

DEAN: *Don't mention it.*

Penny smiled to herself, unable to damp down the happiness that she might get some more info that would help find her father. She wondered what Dean found. It might really help the search.

He wanted to meet and seemed really positive about them being family. Dean seemed really nice, like he was friendly and helpful, and she was glad he was in town and called about meeting. It was so great that he thought about her and wanted to help out more.

They were a nice family and even if she learned that Dean wasn't her father, she was still related to Curtis and Dean. Although they were only second or third cousins, it was something.

She might finally have a real family of people and she might be able to build new relationships. In her mind's eye, she imagined Christmas Dinner with all of them, sitting around a big dining room table, the decorations festive, a huge turkey surrounded by all the trimmings. Presents under a tree.

She didn't care about getting presents, but would love it if she had some cousins who she could buy presents for.

All her life, she'd yearned for a family. A real family.

Marnie had done her best to be a foster mother to Penny, but as nice and caring as she was, she wasn't blood.

There was something about the idea of people being her blood relatives that made a difference.

She arrived at the wharf and checked out the room. Sure enough, there was Dean, sitting beside the window. She thought he was such a handsome man. He had dark hair and brown eyes, he had that nose and chin, so he did have some resemblance to her.

"Hi, Dean?" she said and extended her hand. "I recognize you from a picture your uncle showed me. I'm Penny."

"Yes, please, sit down." He stood and pulled out a chair for her and she felt her cheeks redden. No one treated her like that, and she felt awkward. Still, it was nice.

Once they were seated, he shook his head. "My uncle was right. You sure do look like a relative. Like my grandmother. Wow..."

She smiled, blushing even harder. How she wished he was her father...

"Thanks," she said. "Curtis showed me a picture of her on his phone. She was very pretty."

"She was. So, here's what I wanted to show you. These are a few of the guys I hung out with at school. And here are a few of my cousins, just in case one of them was your father. I don't know where they all are, and I don't really want to be the one to contact them. I'll leave that to you."

"Thanks," she said and glanced down at a file he had opened on the table. Inside, there were pictures from a school yearbook and faces and names circled. He picked up one of the pictures of a soccer team standing near a soccer goal net. "This is my soccer team from high school. My father was an assistant coach, and my best friends played on the team with me."

She took the photocopy and examined the faces of the guys he had circled. The print quality wasn't very good, but the names would help.

"Great," she said. "I can at least start tracing the names to see if any of them remember my mother or who she might have been dating at the time."

"That's what I thought. I hope it helps. No one ever told me about getting a girlfriend pregnant, but that's not surprising. We're Catholics, so we shouldn't have been fooling around and if we did, we should have been using protection, so no one would probably brag about it. Like I say, I don't remember any of my friends talking about being with your mom, but some of the guys might remember something useful."

"What about your other cousins?"

He made a face and handed her another photocopy. "Here they are. You know, we weren't really a very close family," he said and shook his head. "We didn't hang out, so it's not like your mom would have met any of them when they were with me. But you look so much like my grandmother." He smiled.

"I won't tell them that you gave me their names. I'll just say I found them through research."

"I don't care," he said. "If one of them is your father, I think it's better that we all know. The more the merrier."

He smiled.

Penny smiled back, feeling like finally, she was on the right track.

She and Dean did look alike, with the same nose and chin, same coloring. He could be her cousin for sure.

They talked a bit longer and he spoke of the family fractures that resulted when the patriarch of the family, Frank Sr., divorced his wife and remarried. It had led to hard feelings on both sides.

"We're over it now, but at the time, there was a real rift between the two sides of the family. Sean and my father were almost enemies. My dad is still a bit negative towards my uncle but they're mostly over it. If you come to any family gatherings, you might pick up on the tension. I try to ignore it, but it's still there."

"I hope I can come to one of them one day," Penny said wistfully. "Maybe when I know for sure who my father is, I'll be a welcomed. Right now, it's all a big question. Just because I look like your grandmother, doesn't mean anything."

"Well, I hope you find him, and we can all be one big happy family."

He stood and they shook hands again. He pulled her close for a hug, and it warmed her heart that he was so willing to help.

When they were on the street, she said goodbye and waved, then walked away to the bus stop where she'd wait for her bus back to the dorm. There were tears in her eyes, but they were tears of happiness instead of sadness.

On the bus home, she got a text from Tess McClintock.

TESS: Hey, Penny. Just checking in to see how things are going and if you want to drop by the Sentinel and discuss your search for your family.

Penny smiled to herself. She would actually love to go to the newsroom and meet with Tess. She'd never been inside a newsroom and so it would give her the opportunity to see what went on.

PENNY: I'd love to. When do you want me?"

TESS: *I'll be going in again tomorrow. If you want to meet just after lunch, I have some time.*

PENNY: *Sounds good. I did actually meet with a woman who I think is my grandmother - Darlene Schafer. I also met with another potential family member. His name is Dean Stewart, and his father is Frank. They're apparently a wealthy family in Seattle. He knew my mother and thinks that maybe one of his cousins could be my father because I look so much like his grandmother. I'm hopeful one of them might have some info on my mother or at least might have known her. Keeping my fingers crossed.*

TESS: *That's great. See you tomorrow.*
PENNY: *See you.*

CHAPTER TWENTY-SIX

TESS SAT in the newsroom and pondered Penny's story. After their call, she read over what she'd written and after editing, decided to extend it.

Tess felt that Penny's mother was a classic case of sex trafficking. She was underage, she became pregnant, she ran away from home — or couch surfed because of family issues — and she disappeared after living in cheap motels for several years with her daughter and several anonymous fathers and "boyfriends." Penny spoke of how several men would come to the motel room and spend time with her mother, during which time Penny would hide on the floor beside the bed or in the bathroom in the tub.

Poor girl.

Tess always felt she suffered because of the breakdown of her parent's marriage, and moving to Seattle away from her father, but to have never known your father... To have been abandoned after being neglected and dragged around from motel room to motel room all her young life must have left permanent scars.

It was amazing that Penny was doing so well.

Penny's mother Charlene hadn't been reported missing, so she would never have been on any police or FBI list of missing persons.

She had just been forgotten.

In fact, if her foot hadn't washed up on the shores on Vancouver Island, she would have just vanished, and no one would ever have known of her fate. Her story was still only half-written, and Tess was determined to write a series of stories on her case.

She was one example of how child trafficking had such a tragic end and at the same time, showed how resilient humans were. Despite her harrowing childhood — the early days, the foster care, the lack of parents and family — Penny had survived and was thriving.

Tess would do whatever it took to help Penny in her quest to find family, and would tell her story so that other young girls out there might feel hope about their futures.

When she got home that night, there was a message from Michael that he'd be home late and not to wait on supper.

MICHAEL: *I'm going to the range to get some practice in and then I'm going for some burgers with Dr. Keller. She's going to update me on some of the cases that we're both investigating. I should be home after nine. Hope you had a good day. XO*

Tess smiled to herself and responded.

TESS: *Enjoy yourself. I feel like Dr. Keller gets to see more of you than I do. — Just kidding.*

MICHAEL: *It's the only time we could meet. She has some data back on those two girls who we dug up. Then, she's on her way to a conference so it was the only time we could meet.*

TESS: *You don't have to explain. I understand completely. See you at nine.*

MICHAEL: *See you.*

Then, she spent the rest of the evening in her pajamas, going over her notes from her meeting with Kate, and drinking chai tea while she waited for Michael to come home.

The first item on her agenda was to research the Stewart - Ross family, since Penny sent Tess a text indicating that she was likely related to both and perhaps was especially related to Maria Stewart, who she was supposed to look very much like.

There were many records on the Stewart family, and she was able to find a few that mentioned Maria in particular. Maria was the daughter of a banker, Warren Ross, who did business with Frank Stewart, Sr., the head of the Stewart Shipping corporation. Frank Sr. started the company in California in the 1950s. It was successful and he amassed a small fortune. His son, Frank Jr., took over the family business when his father had a stroke and was incapacitated. Frank Jr. married a young woman, the daughter of a business partner, a pretty blonde who had a son with him, and then who died tragically during a hiking trip along the California coast.

If Penny was related to that family, she'd be joining a very wealthy family and depending on how they accepted her — or didn't — she could have a future.

Tess spent the morning preparing for Penny's visit to the newsroom.

She hoped to help the young woman figure out what happened to her mother and who her biological family was.

Penny had given Tess some leads, and so Tess had been doing the legwork, creating a family tree of sorts so that they might eventually find where Penny fit in.

At least now they had one side of the family — the Schafer family from Miller Park area.

She had names going back three generations in the Schafer family, and she started to build a tree for the Stewart family, which had some third and fourth cousins who were related to Penny.

The two families were related but how? The only DNA matches were for distant cousins.

When Penny arrived at the elevator to the newsroom, Tess greeted her.

"Hey, Penny. Come on in."

"Wow," Penny said, glancing around the newsroom, which was currently packed as staff tried to meet deadlines. "This looks just like I imagined it."

"It's not normally this busy, but we have the weekend edition to finish, so they're all in to finish work on it."

Tess ushered Penny over to the small room which was now her office. She had set up a whiteboard with all the names of the various family members on it and files were strewn across the old wooden desk that had been targeted for disposal, but Tess claimed it. It reminded her of something one would find in an office from the 1920s.

Tess closed the door and pointed to the whiteboard. "What do you think?"

Penny leaned closer and examined the names.

"This is great," Penny said and turned to Tess, a smile on her face. "I had no idea how to do this. This really helps."

Penny sat down at the table and removed a notebook from her backpack and began copying down the family tree.

"I know my name," she said and smiled at Tess. "Melanie Celeste Schafer. I was born on February 2, 2000. My mother was Charlene Schafer and I met my grandmother, Darlene."

"Oh, that's so good! So we know your mother's side of the family. Now, we have to find your father."

"Yes, and I think it's someone in the Stuart family. Maybe one of the cousins."

"The Stewarts are a pretty wealthy family," Tess said, and took out her laptop, googling the Stewarts. "The Stewarts have been a pretty solid part of the city and state for more than half a century, at least. The Stewarts came to the West to California, Oregon and Seattle. The one branch of the Stewart family got into shipping, and made a fortune in trade with Asia. The other branch in California got into tech, and is located in San Francisco's Silicon Valley. The patriarch of the family, Frank Stewart, had two sons with one wife. "

Penny scribbled down what Tess was telling her.

"The real question is, how are the Schafers and Stewarts related? From what I can see, the Schafers don't have any immediate connections that I can find. Frank Sr. had Frank Jr., who is an executive in the shipping corporation and has his own investment firm. And Curtis, who is also an executive with the corporation."

"Yeah, Frank Jr. didn't want to have anything to do with me. I asked to meet with him, but he stood me up. I met with his younger brother, Curtis, who was willing and helped me quite a lot. Curtis seemed really nice. He's going to do a DNA test to see how we are related."

Tess googled Frank Stewart Jr. and read off the information she found at several websites.

"So Frank Jr. lost his first wife accidentally, according to this website that did a profile of him."

"Yes, Curtis told me. It's a tragedy. Dean, their son, is really nice. He was happy to help me and provided information on the family so I could find other contacts. Curtis thought Dean might have been my father, or at least, that Frank was worried I thought Dean might be my father," Penny said with a wry grin. "But Dean said that while he knew who Charlene was, he never was intimate with her."

"Do you believe him?" Tess said with a frown. "He was around the right age. He admitted that he knew your mother."

Penny shrugged. "I do believe him. He's more than willing to do a DNA test to prove it and said that he would when he was back in town, so I trust him. He's been on the road traveling for the family business. He started working for the Stewart Corporation after he got out of the service and is in sales."

Tess had googled Dean Stewart, had checked LinkedIn and other business-related websites, and had a small dossier on him and his father, Frank Jr.

Frank Jr. was a prominent member of Seattle's business community, and had a successful investment business that he started himself, with some money from his father. He'd spent some time in California, in LA and San Francisco, before moving to Seattle after the death of his first wife. Frank Sr. divorced Frank Jr.'s mother and remarried. They had a son, Sean Stewart, who then had a son and a daughter who were both the right age to have been contemporaries of Charlene.

"We could look at Sean Stewart. His son, Will, was your mother's age and went to the private school with Dean. He might have known her through Dean's friends."

"I've contacted Sean, but never heard back. I'll ask Dean if he has the contact info for Will."

"Apparently, the half-brothers aren't on friendly terms," Tess said, reading off a gossip page online. "I guess Frank felt that Sean shouldn't have inherited any of the family money, and there was some kind of falling out between Frank Sr. and Frank Jr., sometime when Dean was in high school."

They spent the remainder of the afternoon going over every

possible name that Penny had, doing searches of each name for information.

Penny showed Tess the photo of Curtis's mother, and Tess had to agree that she did look like the older woman when she was young.

Penny thanked Tess and said she had to go. She had a class from seven to nine, and then had to get up early to go to her part-time job at a coffee shop as a barista for the early shift until after lunch, when she had another class.

"Thanks so much for your help," she said and shook Tess's hand. "I really do think my mom was involved in the sex trade, based on what you told me."

"I'll keep looking," Tess said. "You let me know if you get any more DNA matches and we can keep building this family tree. You'll eventually find your father."

"Do you think so?"

Tess nodded. "I do. As long as you keep trying, you should find him eventually."

Penny smiled and Tess felt a tug at her heart. How sad for the young woman to have never known what happened to her mother and who her real father was.

When it was time for Tess to leave to meet Michael, she glanced once more at the family tree and saw all the empty spaces leading from her mother to the spot where her father should have been — and his father and mother, and any uncles and aunts, cousins, grandparents.

So many unanswered questions about her life. Who was her father? Did he know he had a daughter somewhere? Did he know the mother of his child was dead, possibly from suicide after a very sad life as a sex-trafficked young girl?

She took a picture of the family tree with her cell, sent the attachment to her email, and then printed it off so she could show Michael. Then, she left the newsroom, popping in to say goodbye to Kate on her way out.

"Any progress on the Penny story?" Kate asked, waving Tess inside her corner office.

"She identified her mother and knows that side of the family, but her father's side is still a big unknown. It was probably someone her mother met while she was still in middle school — maybe a high school student or maybe someone who met her and trafficked her. She most definitely had a pimp."

"She did?"

"Yes, Penny said that there was a guy, Dennis, who used to stay with them at night, but would leave during the day, and then other men would come and have sex with her mother."

"Poor child," Kate said, shaking her head. "To have that as a childhood and then to be abandoned."

"It's the dark underbelly of our society. It makes me so mad, that no matter how disgusting it is, I feel like I have to expose it, so people know and stop looking away. They feel like it's not their problem, but poverty and abuse and drugs all make it far more likely, and poor girls and boys are the ones to pay the price. Actually, Penny was probably lucky that her mother did abandon her, even though it was hard on her emotionally. At least she wasn't abused sexually or physically afterwards."

Kate shook her head and sighed heavily. "I'm glad I have you writing this story. I couldn't do it myself. Too depressing."

"I can't look away," Tess said. "Not after what happened to Lisa and all the other girls."

"You're a crusader for sex trafficked girls and women," Kate said and smiled. "I'm glad I have you on staff."

"I'm glad you actually pay me to do this."

"It's important work you're doing," Kate said and shuffled her files, indicating it was time to say goodbye.

"I'm happy to do it, and thanks for giving this work to me.

Now, I'll leave you. You going to burn the midnight oil again tonight?"

"Most likely," Kate said with a laugh. "Don't worry about me. I'm as addicted to this life as you are. Now go. Have dinner with that handsome man of yours."

"See you tomorrow," Tess said and left the room, closing the door to Kate's office behind her. Kate really was a workaholic.

She was also the kind of boss Tess was glad to have. She trusted Tess to do the work and left her alone. All she expected was an update whenever she had a new development.

Tess left the building and drove off, shutting off her work mind and thinking of Michael, waiting for her at the restaurant.

He'd be as interested as Kate in what update she had on Penny's case and might have something new of his own to report.

CHAPTER TWENTY-SEVEN

MICHAEL SAT at the bar and waited for Tess to arrive. He checked his cell and saw that she had just left the newsroom and was on her way. By his calculation, it would take about fifteen minutes for her to get to the restaurant. He had time to make a few calls.

The first call he made was to the Task Force to check up on any leads on the two sets of remains found near Riverbend and Bandera. His contact on the Task Force was Special Agent Ramirez, who specialized in cold cases. They'd only spoken once, and Michael wasn't sure how cooperative he would be. He seemed like a decent guy, but until you worked with someone, you never knew what they were like as a colleague.

Ramirez answered the phone on the third ring.

"Hey, Michael. I was wondering when you'd call."

"This is me calling, hoping you have some kind of update on those two sets of remains."

"We've been doing some legwork on the former owners of the property near Bandera. The previous owner, Mr. Ken McLeod, was a construction manager, overseeing several projects in town. He had no record, so he seems pretty clean. He said the shed was rarely used and had been on the property when the family bought it a decade earlier. The last time he was inside was at least five years before they sold it. It could have been someone who worked on the property who saw it as a good place to dump a body. Or the killer happened to see it and realized it was pretty remote and decided to dump the body there. Records show that both Daryl Kincaid and John Hammond drove along that route and might have seen it from the highway. I don't see McLeod as a suspect, frankly."

"Doesn't sound like it. What about the other remains?"

"Nothing on those yet. Dr. Keller excavated the dump site and found a few items that may have been connected to the victim. A ring, earrings, a pendant. We're going to post some information about the items and ask the public if they know of anyone who may have owned them. We might get a hit off that."

"Let me know if you get anything. It would be good to close a few more cold cases connected to either Kincaid or Hammond."

"Will do," Ramirez said. "Any time you need an update, please feel free to call me. Same goes on your part."

"Absolutely," Michael replied. He ended the call and exhaled, glad that Ramirez seemed like a cooperative guy.

He checked his watch just as Tess was walking into the restaurant. She smiled when she saw him sitting at the bar and came over, leaning up to give him a kiss.

She sat beside him and glanced at his drink. "Scotch? You must have had quite the day."

"It was a good day," Michael said.

The bartender came over and placed a cardboard coaster on the bar in front of her. "What can I get for you?"

Tess glanced around the rack of bottles behind the bar

against the mirrored wall. "I feel like something refreshing. How about a Bloody Mary?"

The bartender nodded and began making her the drink.

"So," Tess said, smiling when she turned to face Michael. "How was your day?"

"Good. What's new with the Penny case?"

"Oh, right. I want you to take a look at something." Tess removed a file from her satchel and opened it to show a family tree. "This is what we have so far."

Michael took the piece of paper and examined the tree, noting all the empty spots and names that were listed at the side as distant cousins and then relatives whose exact connection were not known.

A name stood out right away.

Stewart.

"*The* Frank Stewart?" he asked.

"Yes, Frank Stewart," Tess replied, leaning closer, her interest piqued that he mentioned the man. "Why do you ask?"

"The Stewart family is very well-known in the Seattle area. Wealthy, into shipping, and then investments. How is Frank related to Penny?"

"We think maybe one of Frank's cousins might be related. There's no DNA profile for Frank or his close relatives, so we don't really know for sure, but we know that Penny is related to them, at least distantly."

"It would be interesting if Penny was related to the Stewart family. Quite a scandal. Maybe one of the Stewart boys got Charlene pregnant? What about the young men who were her mother's age?"

"Dean Stewart, Frank's son, is going to submit his DNA. He was really helpful."

"Dean," Michael said and frowned. "Frank Jr. is his father, right?"

"Yes," she asked. "He lost his mother when he was just a boy, so I expect he feels sympathy for her."

"His mother died?"

"Yes, in California when Dean was just a young boy." Tess pulled out her cell and did a quick Google search. An obit for her from an archived site and a news story talking about the tragedy. Tess read it for Michael. "The article is titled 'Anniversary Tragedy at Pfeiffer Burns State Park.' It shows the place in the trail where she fell down an embankment and struck her head on the rocks below, dying immediately. Apparently, Frank was injured as well and had to be airlifted to a hospital where he treated for minor injuries."

"Hmm," Michael said, his senses pricking up with interest. "That sounds suspicious. Wife dies but husband miraculously suffers only minor injuries."

"Yeah, my thought exactly." She smiled. "I wasn't going to say anything because I'm at the point now where if a woman dies, I immediately suspect the husband."

Michael nodded. "Whenever a spouse dies, especially a wife, the husband is always the prime suspect."

"She was pretty young. Only twenty-three. He was thirty-nine at the time. So she was," Tess said, mentally doing the math. "She was only eighteen when she married him and had Dean. Wow."

She glanced at Michael and he could tell from the look on her face that she was now also intrigued.

"He liked them young," Michael said, his voice low. "He was thirty-three when he married an eighteen-year-old?"

"Correction. When he thirty-two when he impregnated a seventeen-year-old."

"How soon after was Dean born?"

Tess did the calculations in her head. "Less than nine months."

"So, she was likely pregnant before she married Frank Jr. What was her maiden name?"

Tess looked at the website. "Her maiden name was Connelly."

"Connelly. That's another famous name in Seattle. I think they're in the transportation business, too. She must have been the daughter of one of the Connelly brothers. So, Frank Jr, of the Stewart family, shipping magnates, got the daughter of another rich family pregnant and married her when she was eighteen, probably to make Dean legit. No scandals. She died six years later accidentally when out hiking with her husband. Where was Dean?"

"He was back in San Francisco with family, who were visiting from Seattle. Her parents stayed with Dean while Frank and Louise went on a weekend getaway for their sixth wedding anniversary."

Tess raised her eyebrows.

"My spidey senses are tingling," Michael said.

"Mine, too. Can you call the detectives who had the case back then and inquire?"

"I'll do my best."

They both picked up their drinks and took a long sip.

The next day, Michael sat at his desk at the DA's Offices and read over the news report after Tess texted him a link. He'd printed off the article and was on the phone, waiting to speak with someone in the Monterey County Sheriff's Department. When his call was answered, he introduced himself and asked to speak with someone who could help him with an old case from back in 1990.

"'90? Jeff Cole was Sheriff back then," the receptionist said. "He must be eighty now. He still lives in Monterey County.

You could also talk to Dan Palmer. He's Chief Deputy Sheriff. I can see if he can talk to you."

"Thanks," Michael said and waited on the phone, reading over an obit for Louise Stewart née Connelly.

The Chief Deputy Sheriff came on the line. After introductions and small talk, Michael got to the point.

"I'm investigating a cold case up here and wanted some more information on a case back in 1990. It's the death of a resident of San Francisco, Louise Stewart, while hiking in Pfeiffer Burns State Park."

"Oh, yeah, I remember that case. Sheriff Cole was coroner back then and attended the scene. Pronounced Mrs. Stewart dead and concluded that it was an accident. Her husband fell trying to prevent her fall and almost died himself."

"I thought he had minor injuries," Michael said.

"Well, yes. They were minor in comparison, but he fell as well and had to be airlifted to Monterey. They were celebrating their wedding anniversary and were on a hike near Big Sur. There was no reason for the Sheriff to rule anything but accidental, if I recall correctly."

"What did her family think?"

"They were unhappy with the ruling, but honestly, there was nothing in either her husband's past or hers to suggest it was anything other than a tragic accident. She was pregnant, too, so it was a double tragedy."

"She was pregnant?"

"Yes, just, I guess."

They spoke for a few moments, and then Michael said goodbye, thanking the Chief for his help.

He turned back to the family tree that Tess had provided and stared at it.

Until Dean put in his DNA and got results, there was nothing that directly linked the two except for distant cousins, but he had a feeling that there were more connections than currently existed.

That accidental fall?

Michael didn't believe it. He couldn't say why. Based on the case and evidence, there was no immediate reason to suspect that it was anything other than an accident, but something did not sit right with him.

Not right at all...

CHAPTER TWENTY-EIGHT

Penny spent the next few days tracking down the names that Dean had given her, happy to have some place to start. She began with her potential cousins, rather than the boys who had been on Dean's soccer team. In all honesty, she hoped one of Dean's cousins was her father instead of some random friends. She really wanted to be related to him and his family. Even though there were divisions among the brothers, they seemed like a really great family to belong to.

It might be wishful thinking, but Curtis and Dean both thought she looked like Curtis's mother. Maria Stewart. Dean's grandmother.

None of them were on Ancestry, so she couldn't track them that way. Instead, she would send them a Facebook message in the hopes that they would agree to talk with her. Without knowing their phone numbers or addresses, she had to guess. She sent out feelers, hoping that a few of them were actually potential relatives and that they might be willing to speak with her.

Hi, your cousin Dean Stewart gave me your name as a

potential family member. I'm looking for people who might have known my mother, Charlene Schafer, who lived in Miller Park back in 1999-2005. If you remember her, please contact me at PMorrison@hotmail.com. Thanks in advance!

Someone must remember her mother from school. Maybe even know what happened to her in detail, rather than the vague description she had from her grandmother, Darlene.

She sighed and after sending another message to one of the Stewarts in the phone book, she grabbed her bag and went on campus to her afternoon class. She walked along the streets leading to the building where he class was located, her hood pulled up to shelter her face from the drizzle, and smiled to herself that things were looking up in her quest to find her father.

It was while she was crossing the street that she first noticed an older man in the corner of her eye. He seemed to be watching her as she walked down the sidewalk, his head turning to watch as she crossed the street. She glanced at him and he looked away, then she shrugged it off, thinking it was just an old man people watching.

After class, she went to her favorite café and stood in line for her latte. After giving her order, she turned and glanced out the window. To her complete surprise, the old man was standing directly across the street, watching the café.

Was he looking at her?

She turned when the barista called her name and went to the counter to receive her drink and then she went to the front door, glancing across the street as she did.

The old man was gone.

Good. He was probably just a pedestrian people watching. She did that more than enough. On a nice day, she would often sit on a bench along the waterfront, watching people as they walked by, ran, skated, or rollerbladed along the walkway. She couldn't blame a man for doing it as well. Penny had always felt like she was an observer rather than a participant in the world.

Maybe the old man felt the same way.

Later, she went to the library, doing research for her Abnormal Psych paper. The library was busy as usual, and she grabbed her books and set herself up in one of the study carrels along one side of the quietest floor. Then, she immersed herself in the articles, reading them and taking notes. She figured if she put in a couple of hours, she could justify spending more time that night on her genealogy quest.

When she was finished, she checked her cell for the time. She'd been there longer than she anticipated — it was now almost nine thirty at night and the library would be closing soon, so she gathered up her books and papers and stuffed them into her book bag. Then, she made her way out of the library to the bus stop. There were a few other late-night library denizens waiting with her and she felt a sense of satisfaction that she hadn't felt in a long while.

Things were coming together for her. Life was good. She was on a full scholarship studying sociology, she was living in a dorm, she was learning more every day about her family.

She was close to finding her father — she could almost feel it in her bones.

Penny sat on the bus, watching outside the window as the streets of Seattle passed on her way back to the dorm. Before she got that call about her mother's foot, she had pretty much given up hope of finding any of her relatives. She had hoped that her Ancestry DNA would find relatives she could contact, but she never imagined she'd find her grandmother and dozens of distant cousins. And now, she knew her real name.

She felt like she had real roots for the first time in her life.

. . .

When she arrived at her stop, she grabbed her book bag and left the bus, stepping out into the cool misty Seattle air. She breathed in it, glad the rain had stopped.

The dorm was only a half-block walk from her stop, through a brightly lit parking lot. She passed by an old Volkswagen van and saw that the side door was open. It gave her a start, and she tensed when someone stepped out from the side of the van.

It was the old man.

"Oh, you scared me," she said, holding her hand over her chest.

"Not enough," the man said, and she saw him bring his arm up, a stick of some kind in his hand. He was fast and brought it down on her head.

Then, there was only darkness.

When she woke up, she was lying on the wet pavement and her head hurt terribly. She immediately tried to sit up, but a man was leaning over her. It wasn't the old man. It was a young man with fair hair and a well-trimmed beard.

"Hey, are you okay? You should stay lying down. You've got a pretty bad cut on your head." She reached up and felt a piece of cloth on her head. It was soaking wet — with her blood.

"What happened?" she asked and glanced around. Then she remembered. The old man hit her on the head. "Where's the old man?"

"I saw him from the bushes where I was smoking and chased him away from you. He was trying to drag you into his van, but I stopped him. He got in the van and drove off. I called 9-1-1, so someone should be here right away."

"Thank you," she said, holding her hand to her head. "What's your name?"

"I'm Joe. Joe Campbell. I live in the dorm."

"Penny Schafer," she said, using her mother's name.

"Hi, Penny. You're going to be fine." He smiled.

He had kind eyes.

A distant siren sounded, and soon it grew louder, and they saw flashing lights. Penny sat up, holding the piece of cloth against her head. Finally, the ambulance stopped and an EMT got out and came over to her while the other EMT opened the rear doors of the vehicle.

While the EMT checked her over, a police car drove up. The police officer spoke with Joe while the EMT shone a light on her head and then the two EMTs helped her up and onto the gurney. They loaded her into the back of the ambulance, and she said goodbye to Joe, who came over.

"I'm going to give my report to the police. Call me and let me know how you are," Joe said with a smile. "We can have coffee."

"I will."

She waved at him and watched as the EMT closed the back doors to the ambulance.

She'd never ridden in an ambulance before.

After they arrived at the hospital emergency bay and she was registered, a doctor examined her to check to make sure she didn't have a concussion, and she was sent for a CT scan just to be sure. She was glad she had good health insurance through her scholarship. When she was back in the tiny room in the emergency room, she spoke with a nice police officer from the Seattle PD, who took her statement about the attack.

"You say you saw the man earlier in the day?"

Officer Richmond was taking notes on a small leather-bound notepad, his face serious as he listened to her speak.

"I saw him twice. Once after lunch and then once again later in the day. I figured he was just people watching. I mean he looked really old. Maybe in his seventies or eighties. I didn't think he would be dangerous."

Officer Richmond shook his head. "It's strange. It's not very often that we get a senior as a suspect in an attack like this. Are you sure he was that old?"

"He had thin grey hair and lots of wrinkles. He looked really old."

Richmond shrugged. "Our witness, Mr. Campbell, said the same thing. He figured the man was in his seventies or older. Very spry for that age, all things considered. He ran to the van and drove off before Mr. Campbell could stop him."

"I saw him two times. He was definitely following me. He was outside the café when I went to get my daily coffee, and he was waiting outside my dorm tonight after I got home from the library. There's no way he lives at the dorm, so he had to be following me."

"Is there anyone you know of who might want to hurt you? Anyone of his age?"

Penny shook her head. "I've been researching my family. I was abandoned as a child and never knew who my parents were. I've recently discovered some connections through DNA matches and have been speaking to my relatives. Maybe one of them is upset?"

Richmond said nothing, but wrote the information down on his pad.

"Anyone in the dorm you can think of that might have an older relative who would want to hurt you?"

"No," Penny said. "I'm a very quiet person. I don't have a boyfriend. I don't have many friends. I lived in foster care all my life and went to a special school for kids with emotional problems. I know a few people from there, but really, I'm a loner."

"It's possible it's just someone who saw you and fixated on

you. It happens. But someone that old... It's not very common. Criminal behavior declines with age. Once someone is in their sixties or seventies, it's almost non-existent. Very strange."

Richmond folded up his notepad and tucked it into his uniform pocket. Then, he removed a business card from a pocket of his jacket and gave her a smile. "If you think of anything at all, please call me. Anything at all. We'll be checking whatever security feed we can find to see if we can see a license plate. I'll keep you updated if we find anything."

"Thanks. I will."

He left her and after the ER doctor came back in and checked her over once more, she was discharged from the emergency room.

"You should call someone and have them pick you up," the doctor said. "I don't want you traveling home on public transit."

"I can take an Uber," Penny said, not wanting to call anyone. Besides, there really was no one to call.

"Okay, if you're sure."

He gave her instructions with how to deal with the cut and bandage, and then she went to the hospital emergency room exit and waited for the Uber that would take her home.

CHAPTER TWENTY-NINE

Michael did a search for Louise's parents, who were living on Fidalgo Island. Mr. John Connelly was retired from his position on the board of the family-owned business, and they lived in a very expensive ten-bedroom, ten-bathroom mansion that overlooked Burrows Bay. He'd called the previous day to see if he could come out and speak to them about their daughter's death and see if they had the same misgivings about the Coroner's conclusions that the death was accidental.

He took his car and drove north, to the road leading to the island and arrived just after lunch. John Connelly met him at the front door of the house, wearing a thick grey cable sweater and faded jeans. Grey hair slicked back, and thick dark-rimmed reading glasses, he looked every inch the retired business tycoon that he was.

Connelly ushered him in, apologizing for the activity in the entrance, where several painters were working, putting on a fresh coat of paint.

"Please go into the study," he said and pointed to a door leading to a room with wall-to-wall bookshelves. "My wife,

Tana, is getting us some coffee. I have to speak with the workers for a moment."

Michael walked along the wall of books while Connelly spoke to one of the workers. There were books on business and finance, history and art. There were true crime books and crime fiction books on the shelves. A portrait of a much younger Connelly was perched over the fireplace, standing behind his desk in a very expensive looking business suit.

He looked like a business magnate and he was impressive.

Mrs. Connelly came into the study with a maid behind her carrying a tray with cups and saucers, plus a coffee pot.

"Hello, Investigator Carter," she said and extended her hand. "Please have a seat. Have a cup of coffee. My husband John will join us in a moment. He's just dealing with the painters."

She smiled and sat on the sofa across from his armchair.

"Thanks for inviting me. You have a very lovely home."

"It's old and in need of a lot of work, but we wouldn't trade it for anything."

Michael fixed his cup while she made small talk about the house being repainted. Finally, John joined them and plopped himself down on the sofa beside his wife.

"I'm so happy you called us," John said. "We've been wanting to speak with someone about what happened for a long time, but everyone wrote our concerns off as distraught parents, and dismissed us when we tried to reopen her case."

"You didn't think it was an accident?"

"We were never happy about the coroner's determination that it was an accidental fall," Mrs. Connelly said, frowning.

"Why?"

"We liked him at first," John said, running his hand over his head. "Frank Jr. He was destined to take over the company and we thought it would be a good match, even if she was too young to be involved with him. We thought that he really loved her. Or at least, he claimed he did. I guess he really loved the idea of not being charged with statutory rape."

"I never liked him," Tana said firmly. "Frank was always so fake, like he was acting. He'd always make a point of saying that he was merely being a good husband, a good father, a good son, a good CEO. Like everything was a performance. I never liked him, but John thought he was a good businessman and would be a good match for Louise, so I shut my mouth. I wish I'd told her to put the baby up for adoption and maybe none of this would have happened."

That shocked Michael. Usually, a grandmother was pleased as punch to have a grandchild and wouldn't wish their daughter had given them away instead.

"I know that sounds pretty harsh," she added, when he was at a loss for words. "You have to realize that I didn't like Frank from the start. I didn't want Louise to marry him, because her life had just started. She was secretly seeing him without our knowledge and became pregnant before she was even eighteen so technically we could have charged him with statutory rape, but John was friends with Frank Sr. The two of them put their heads together and decided that they should marry. If I had only put my foot down..."

"I'm very sorry for your loss," Michael said, keeping his voice soothing. "It must be hard to know that you had another grandchild on the way and lost it along with Louise."

"We loved Dean," Mrs. Connelly said. "We would have loved the new child as well. But that was that."

"Then he married again, and his new wife took over and we barely saw Dean," John said disapprovingly. "Frank was so busy with the business, and always traveling, Dean hardly saw him. When his new wife up and left him, we thought we'd see more of Dean since she couldn't control things anymore, but no such luck."

"His new wife was unhappy with the marriage? What was she like? You said she was controlling?"

"Well, that was Frank's excuse. She was in charge of the house while he was away, and Frank said we had to negotiate with her if we wanted to see Dean. He said that he couldn't tell her what to do when he was away, and she had responsibility for running the house and caring for Dean. We had to negotiate with her. She wasn't cooperative, to say the least. Then, she left, and we thought Frank would be happy if we took more of an active role in Dean's life, but no." She shrugged. "It was just more of the same."

"Where did she go when she left? His second wife?"

"Lord only knows," John said.

"He probably killed her," Tana said, her eyes narrowed. "He killed our girl. He probably killed her, too."

Michael glanced from John to Tana.

"Now, we don't know that," John said quickly. "They were divorced several years ago, after she'd been gone for the appropriate length of time."

"She just disappeared?" Michael asked.

"Yes, just left without a word to anyone except for a note and having taken several hundred thousand dollars from her account, so the police assumed she left him and moved away. The empty bank account was used as proof, plus her vehicle was seen on an interstate near Florida. She was Hispanic and much younger than him, so he was keeping with tradition of underage or younger women as partners. We thought she was one of his maids, actually, so maybe she went back to Florida where she was from."

"The police didn't think it was suspicious?" Michael asked. "Her up and leaving with no word other than a hand-written note and an empty bank account? There was no family to ask about it?"

"I guess not," John said. "Her family was in Florida, or so her note said. That seemed to be enough for them to close the case.

"That's two wives who have either died or gone missing," Tana said, holding her cup up. "If I were his new wife, I'd be nervous."

"And you say you tried to get your daughter's case reopened several times, but had no luck?"

Tana shook her head. "No. Each time, the DA in Monterey County said that there were no grounds for reopening Louise's case. So when you called and said you were from the DA's office, we were hopeful that something changed."

Michael nodded. "I don't want to get your hopes up. I'm investigating a cold case and there appear to be links between the Stewart family and a woman who disappeared almost fifteen years ago. So, I wanted to talk to you about Louise, since when I first read about the case, I was curious. Well," he said and shrugged. "I was suspicious."

"I know! Thank you," Tana said, her eyes bright. Michael could almost sense her relief and excitement from across the coffee table. "Why weren't you in charge of the case? The police and the Sheriff all seemed to be so blasé about her death because Frank had a broken arm. Maybe he got it trying to throw her over the cliff. Why wouldn't they have at least looked into it more deeply?"

Michael smiled. "I wish I was in charge of the case, but at the time, I was in public school. I didn't join the FBI until 2012, so..." He smiled.

"You were with the FBI?"

He nodded. "Yes. I retired last year because of an injury and I'm now working with the DA's office in Seattle as an

Investigator. I'll be attending university next year to work on my PhD in Forensic Psychology. Criminal profiling."

"And what do you think about Frank Stewart? What does your gut instinct tell you about him?" John asked, leaning forward. "Or is that just in the movies that Detectives have gut instincts about suspects?"

"Understand that Frank Stewart is not a suspect of anything at the moment," Michael said, not wanting to mislead them. "I'm just trying to find out who may have been related to the woman whose remains were found and what the links were between her and the Stewart family."

"But there were links?" Tana said expectantly.

Michael nodded. "We're not sure yet how she was linked to the family, so I don't want to be premature. When I heard about the accidental death of his first wife and then the fact his second wife left him and hasn't been heard from since, I was curious. That's all."

John Connelly nodded across from Michael. "I understand. You can't say more at this time. Keep us informed, if you find anything. We think he killed Louise to get rid of her so he could move on to the young maid. It wouldn't be the first time a man killed his wife and unborn child for a lover."

"No, unfortunately it wouldn't be the first and it won't be the last."

Tana shook her head. "I knew she shouldn't have married him and should have just lived with us. We could have raised Dean on our own without Frank. Frank turned Dean against us, and we hardly see him. Things would have been so different..."

Michael felt sorry for the older couple. Louise was their only child and then to lose her and lose contact with their only grandchild.

It would be a lonely life, which made him think of his own

boys and how infrequent was their contact. It made him swear to himself that he would spend more time with them, despite the inconvenience.

He owed it to them to be in their lives.

"Thanks for speaking with me," he said and stood, putting away his notebook and pen into his jacket pocket. "I'll keep you updated on anything I find out or any developments regarding your daughter's case."

"Thank you for keeping this alive," John said and shook Michael's hand. He pointed to Tana, who remained seated. "We appreciate anything you can do."

Tana nodded to Michael. "Yes, please. Call any time if you want to talk more about Louise and the case."

John walked Michael out and watched him walk to his Jeep. When he drove off, Michael thought that Frank was probably a killer.

A serial killer. Not in the way that Eugene Kincaid was — he didn't get off killing people. Frank was probably just a serial killer who killed people who got in his way or were inconvenient to his plans.

He was rich, organized and planned well enough that his past murders appeared as accidents.

He was perhaps the most dangerous kind.

CHAPTER THIRTY

FRANK LOOKED at his cell with disdain. Dean called him using FaceTime, which Frank hated, but he nevertheless answered.

"You did *what?*"

Dean shrugged, like it was nothing. In the background, Frank could see the shops of the Sea-Tac airport, where Dean was waiting for a flight.

"Of course, I met with her. She's really sweet, Dad. I think she might be one of our blood relatives. Maybe someone on Grandma's side of the family? She has Grandma's features."

"She has no one's features," Frank said, his tone harsher than he intended, but he was starting to lose patience with all the bleeding-heart idiots in his family. "She's not family, and she's never going to be family. That's an end to it."

"We're cousins at least," Dean said. "She's related to us through your second cousin. That's how she found us."

"I don't give a rat's ass about second or third cousins. Can't you see that she's only after money? She found out we're wealthy, and now she wants in. I'd think you were smarter than that, but I guess not. You and Curtis..."

He strode to the fire, cell still held up so Dean could see him, and moved the logs with a long poker, wishing he had the bitch there with him right then and now, so he could shove the poker through her eye.

That would be satisfying and would end this whole charade.

"Curtis and I like the idea of another addition to the family, Dad. She's harmless. Poor kid's been in foster care all her life and just wants family. You know, Christmas dinner, Turkey Day, Easter. She's nice. She's smart, and she's all alone. Her mother died and they found her foot in the Salish Sea in 2012. Probably a suicide. Poor kid. I feel sorry for her."

"That's what she's counting on — rubes like you and Curtis feeling sorry. She just wants our money. That's it."

"It's always about money with you, Dad," Dean said, his tone withering.

"It's *always* about money with women," Frank shot back. "Don't you get it? I thought at least *you'd* understand."

"Understand what? Why would you think I'd agree with you? I want more family. I miss Mom and I like family get-togethers. We hardly ever see Mom's family. One day, I hope you can understand what it's been like for me, not having a mother while I was growing up."

"You had her for six years," Frank said, a little too harshly. The boy had been a mess after his mother died.

It had been a spur-of-the-moment thing — his young wife 'accidentally' falling down the cliff while on a walk along the coast hiking trail. They'd been arguing over something, and Frank had just had it with her getting pregnant again, after he'd already planned on divorcing her.

He remembered back to that day, grabbing her, and on the spur of the moment, he'd shaken her and said, "Be careful!" and then, he pushed her, and she fell. Headfirst, down the cliff face.

She wasn't quite dead when he followed her down, and checked her pulse, her eyes half-closed, blood coming out of her nose. He had to make it look like he fell as well. He picked up a rock and knocked himself with it.

Damn. That hurt like a motherfucker.

He threw himself down the last few stairs of the staircase a few feet away, and broke his arm in the process.

At least they would think he fell along with her.

He called out, weeping like it was the fucking end of the world. He was a pretty decent actor, and knew all the right words to say.

"Please, please, someone help me! My wife fell down the stairs and she's bleeding! Oh, God, please! Jesus, please send someone now!"

Then, he'd sat cradling his arm, and watched her die in front of his eyes.

It had been quite easy, all things considered.

He felt — nothing.

By the time the EMTs and police had arrived, he was completely distraught, and they found him at the bottom of the stairs. Her head was bashed in pretty badly.

They actually *believed* him.

He was questioned for hours, but there was no reason to think he'd want to kill her. She was an exceptionally beautiful young woman, the daughter of another wealthy family from back home, and they were married. *Happily.*

There was no one who could counter that claim and so it was ruled an accident.

It was almost too easy.

He was the bereaved widower, mourning his beautiful young wife's tragic accidental death. Women in the neighborhood, the local Housewives of L.A., brought him casseroles and salads, and lots of food for him and Dean. He even got a pity fuck from one of the sluttier women who lived in their gated neighborhood.

Fine with him. He cried on her shoulder as he undid her bra, and she seemed to eat it up.

"You need a good endorphin rush to get over this," she said.

Yeah. She probably needed one to get over her picture-perfect life, married to a much older guy who was head at one of the film companies that had just made its first public stock offering.

He understood women. Grifters, all of them...

CHAPTER THIRTY-ONE

THE NEXT DAY, Penny texted Tess, wanting to talk about her mother's case and the attack. She still had a bad headache and so she took a couple of Tylenols.

"My God," Tess said, her voice sounding concerned when Penny told her what happened. "Any idea who it might be? You said an old man in his seventies?"

"I'd say he was even older. He looked really old, which was strange because he was actually really strong and fast, according to the man who saw the attack."

"God, you're lucky the witness was standing in the trees smoking a joint," Tess said when Penny told her about Joe. "If he got you in that van, there's every chance you could have been dead within a couple of hours. Based on the research, when a woman is abducted, they're usually killed within several hours. Experts tell us that you should always fight as hard as possible to prevent being abducted and taken from the scene."

"That makes me feel incredibly scared," Penny replied. "If

it hadn't been for Joe, I'd be gone and probably raped and murdered."

She shook her head, the enormity of it finally sinking in. Up until then, she'd been more concerned about her head and whether she had a concussion.

"You need to take it easy for the next while. I know all about how hard it is to keep going when you've been attacked and could have been killed."

"Yes, I guess you do," Penny replied. "I read about your case in the paper and of course, in your articles, which is why I wanted to talk to you in the first place," Penny said, thankful that Tess had offered to help. "I'm waiting on some replies from my other potential cousins. The Stewart family and the Ross family are also potential DNA matches, so if you want to look into them, that would be helpful. Maybe we can meet later this afternoon? There's a coffee shop near campus, The Second Cup, and it would mean I wouldn't have to travel so far to meet you."

"Are you sure you're well enough? You were just attacked."

"No, I'm fine," Penny said, not wanting to delay. "The doc said I might have a bit of a headache, but I feel good otherwise. I want to meet you."

"Okay, if you're sure," Tess said. "This could lead to you experiencing some PTSD, so you should definitely speak to your therapist if you start to have problems sleeping or start feeling afraid to do anything. I know what that's about. It really does help to talk."

"I will get therapy," Penny said. "I have several sessions approved on my health insurance plan, so I'll use those. "Thanks for your help. I really appreciate it."

"I'm glad to help. I'll text you when I get there."

"See you."

Penny ended the call and lay back on her bed, watching the

local news. There was nothing mentioned about her assault. She supposed that it was a minor thing, really.

It was probably just some old freak who had fixated on her, developing what psychiatrists called erotomania. He probably wanted to rape her and would give up because he had almost been caught.

If she said that enough times, she might believe it.

Penny arrived at the coffee shop after getting the text from Tess, and saw that she sitting at a table near the window.

"Hey," Tess said and smiled.

Penny put her book bag down and removed her wallet. "I'll go get a coffee. What are you having?"

Tess held up a cup. "Caramel Brûlée Latte. They're delicious."

Penny smiled. "I'll get one, too."

She went to the counter and waited for the barista to prepare it, watching Tess while she did. She felt lucky to have such an important journalist helping her with her case. Tess seemed really nice, helpful and understanding.

She'd been through so much.

Penny sat down and they spent the next hour going over the names and potential links on a family tree Tess had created.

"There aren't any clear links between your grandmother and any of the Stewarts that I can see," Tess said. "If you're related, maybe it's on your father's side. Until we know who he is, it will be hard to tell."

"When Curtis puts in his DNA sample and it's processed, we may have a clearer picture."

Tess nodded and they both examined the family tree.

It was at that moment when Penny's cell chimed.

She checked her phone and saw a text from Dean. It was from a different number than before.

DEAN: *Hey, Penny. I'll be in town for a few hours waiting for a connection. I don't have enough time to go home, so I'm just staying at the hotel by the airport. Do you want to meet? I have some interesting info about my side of the family you might like to know.*

Penny read over the text and showed it to Tess. "Dean, Frank's son, wants to meet again. He says he has some interesting information on his side of the family."

"That's nice," Tess said. "He seems really helpful."

"He has been. At first, I thought he might be my father, because he was the right age for it, but he says he never even spoke with Charlene. That she just hung out with a girlfriend of his and that's the only connection."

"Do you believe him?"

Penny frowned. "Sure. He's going to submit his DNA to Ancestry, too. He wondered if it wasn't another cousin of his. Sean Stewart's son, Will. Curtis is close enough to him that we might see connections, so I'm hopeful. Plus there are a couple of others to check on."

Penny re-read the text from Dean and responded.

PENNY: *Is this your new cell number? It's different from the one you used last time we texted.*

DEAN: *Yeah, it's my new work cell. We changed providers I guess. I use it when I'm traveling. It has the special plan. Unlimited international talk and text. I know I shouldn't be using it for personal business, but it's free so why not?*

PENNY: *I understand, and I really appreciate you helping me. Where do you want to meet?*

DEAN: *How about my hotel at the airport? I know it's out of your way, but I'll be staying at the Crowne Plaza since I'll only be in town for twelve hours on a layover for a business trip* to Singapore after my latest trip to New York, and won't actually be going into Seattle.

PENNY: Sure. Where?

DEAN: Meet me in the parking lot at the Plaza, and we can compare notes. I think there's a bus that goes directly there. We could get supper.

PENNY: That sounds good. What time do you want to meet?

DEAN: How does 6:30 sound? I'll have been traveling all day and will be ready to eat by then. There's a restaurant nearby that I like. I'll pick up a rental and can take you there.

PENNY: Thanks so much.

DEAN: You're very welcome. I thought I wouldn't get a chance to meet with you again for a while because of travel, and I found some interesting things about my family that could help you find your relatives. I figured, why not help out a fellow human some more?

PENNY: You helped me a lot already but if you have more info, that would be great. It makes me feel so great to think we might all be related.

DEAN: Me, too. I'm not married, and I have no children — that I know of! So it will be nice to have more family. See you later.

PENNY: See you!

She sat and re-read the messages from Dean, glad that he was so willing to help her with her search for relatives. She hoped so much that he really meant it when he said he wanted more family.

"He wants to meet at a hotel near the airport and have dinner, so I'll have to leave right now if I have a hope of making it there on time."

Tess shook her head and gave her a frown. "You really shouldn't be traveling all over the city, considering."

"He's only in town for a while and has some new information, so I have to. I'll be fine."

"At least let me drive you," Tess said. "Taking a bus right now would be a bad idea, given traffic and given the attack. You won't make it in time."

"I could take a taxi, I guess. I don't want to put you out."

"It's no problem," Tess said. "With your head injury, you shouldn't be stressing out. I'll drive you, then I'll do some work in my car while you meet with him. I can drive you back when you're done."

"You don't have to stay. We're going to have dinner, and he's renting a car and will give me a ride home," Penny said, feeling very guilty about it. "I can take a taxi."

"You're sure this is a good idea? You don't really know Dean very well."

"I'll be fine. It's Dean Stewart. He's from one of the wealthiest families in the Pacific Northwest. He's really sweet and is going out of his way to take me for dinner. He even got a rental, so I'm going to meet him and go to a restaurant nearby. Poor man, going to all that trouble. You go home, okay? I insist. You've done enough."

"I don't know…" Tess said, and Penny could hear the doubt in her voice. "You were just attacked, Penny. Are you even sure this man is Dean?"

"Yes, of course. He knows all about my case and everything. It's him. Like I told you – he's really helpful."

"Okay, if you're sure. But I can wait and give you a ride back."

"No, I insist. You've done far too much for me already."

Tess sighed. "Make sure you call me and let me know what he told you about his family."

"I will."

Penny checked her watch. "How long will it take to get to the airport from here?"

Tess shrugged. "Twenty minutes. We can finish these and leave at six and be there a few minutes early."

Penny smiled and exhaled in relief.

Tess leaned back. "Oh, I checked into the Ross side of the family, but so far no luck with anything in public records. I'll check some more tonight."

"Thanks, Tess," Penny said. "I really appreciate it."

"Don't mention it. Your story is really compelling, and I want to help you find your family and what happened to your mother. I have a feeling she was caught up in the sex trade and so her disappearance is definitely tied into my research.

"Well, you've been really helpful. More than necessary. I recognize that."

"Thank you for contacting me. It helps me to understand what happens to young women to draw them into the sex trade, or how they get caught up in sex trafficking. Most of the cases are just on paper, historical records, cold case files. It's good to deal with real live people for a change."

When the time came to leave, Penny watched the city as Tess drove along Martin Luther King Way to the airport.

Penny was tense but it was a happy tense, she told herself. It was excitement, not anxiety. That was what her therapist told her to repeat when she had to do something that potentially made her nervous.

"Even though I've already met with him, I'm still anxious to meet with Dean and see what he has to show me. Maybe he's going to turn out to be a family member after all."

"Sometimes, anxiety feels exactly the same as excitement," Tess said. "Keep telling yourself that you're only excited, and you can talk yourself out of a panic attack. I do deep-breathing techniques to help calm myself when I feel panic coming on."

"Yes, my therapist taught me how to do deep breathing. I'll be fine. My excitement should pass in a few moments."

Penny smiled, and took in a deep breath. As they drove down the highway, she thought about Dean Stewart and how much she wished he had been her father, but if he was only a cousin, that would be great, too. All her life, she never knew anyone who was related to her. Finally, she had some blood relations who actually wanted her to be part of the family.

That thought encouraged her, and she smiled more broadly, and this time, the smile was genuine and not forced.

They arrived fifteen minutes early, and noted that it was quite well-lit in the parking lot. She glanced around but hadn't received a text message from Dean yet about where to meet him and what the rental car looked like.

"I'll go into the hotel lobby and wait for him. Thanks so much for all you're doing to help me."

"No problem. Remember to call me when you get home so we can talk about what he found."

"Okay. Thanks again."

She left Tess's car and went into the hotel lobby, glancing around to see if Dean was there.

PENNY: *I'm here a bit early. Where do you want to meet?*

She stood in the lobby by the coffee shop, and waited for him to answer.

DEAN: *Sorry, but I was a bit delayed getting the vehicle.*

PENNY: *Okay. I can meet you outside. Call me when you get here.*

DEAN: *Already here. Just come out to the parking lot behind the hotel. Believe it or not, but the only vehicle they had ready was a van. I told the clerk that I wasn't moving anything, but he said I'd have to wait another hour if I wanted a sedan so it's this or nothing. It's a white panel van. I can drive you back to your dorm after we're done.*

PENNY: *Okay. If you're sure.*

Penny put her cell away and grabbed her book bag. She went out the rear entrance to the hotel, and glanced around. Sure enough, there was a white panel van from a rental company parked off to the side of one of the large recycling bins. She smiled when she saw it and waved, then she felt silly.

She was far too excited and had to calm down. Dean was a grown man, a veteran, and was now a successful businessman. She had to act like an adult and not an excited child.

Thing was, that's how she felt. Like an excited child going to a birthday party.

When she got closer, she saw that the interior was dark and the side door was open, so she went to the driver's side, but Dean wasn't there.

"Dean?" she said hesitantly. "Dean?"

"Over here," she heard a muffled voice say. "I had a flat."

She shook her head. "You've had bad luck today," she said and went over to the side. "First, they didn't have your rental. Now a flat!" she said, trying to be cheerful.

When she came around the other side of the van, she saw a man standing there with an implement in his hand.

It wasn't Dean.

It was the old man.

Before she could react, the old man raised his arm and struck her with a wrench.

She went down, unconscious before she hit the pavement.

CHAPTER THIRTY-TWO

Killers always got caught because they left tracks that police could find and trace back to the crime scene.

Frank was smart enough to know that he couldn't do that. He had to make sure there were no tracks between him and the girl. That meant he had to be out of town when she went missing, so he had an alibi.

First, he'd make a reservation at the hotel he usually stayed at when visiting the Portland office. Then, he'd fly there, check in, and rent a car. He'd drive the rental back to Seattle, but that would take several hours, if he drove without stopping. Once in Seattle, he'd rent a second vehicle — a van — and use it to get rid of her. It would have been better if he could take his car, but he wanted it to look like he'd flown to Portland, which is what he usually did when he had to visit the area office.

He'd make a show of going into the office and take some work with him to the hotel. He'd schedule several meetings, and he'd make sure that he was there for them. Then, he'd get in the car and drive. He'd get rid of the girl and drive back. He'd take her cell and make it look like she'd decided to go on a trip to find her mother's relatives, which she found somewhere out East. He'd send her cell in a package to a PO box he rented in New York where he had sensitive materials sent. That way, her cell would ping out east instead of Seattle. There, it would sit in the PO box until Frank retrieved it and destroyed it. He'd find an excuse to do so, once he saw that the coast was clear.

Presto -- problem solved.

With the plan in place, he felt immediately better. He'd drive back after he took care of her, make a few perfunctory trips to the area office, meet with a few staff, and then he'd fly home. He'd put a lot of miles on the rental but so what? He could say he had driven around the local area a lot to check out various properties he was interested in buying.

The only problem would be the car's GPS. It would have a record of where the car had traveled. He'd have to figure out a way to either disable it, or they would be able to track its movements during the time period he used it, just in case any cop was suspicious at any time in the future.

That was the last thing he needed. While many car companies claimed they didn't track their vehicles, he didn't believe it. He knew that some dealers had hidden GPS trackers so that the bank could track the location of leased and financed vehicles just in case they had to repossess due to defaulting on the loan or payment. He'd have to find out what cars had built-in trackers and maybe, just maybe, he'd be able to get a vehicle without a tracker.

That was a necessity.

To that end, he called up his favorite car rental company and anonymously asked what cars had GPS tracker capacity. The person who answered gave him the runaround.

"We don't track the movements of our customers, Sir," the man said, affronted at the suggestion. "All we track is mileage and gas consumption. As long as your mileage is within the accepted range and you fill up the tank, we don't care how far you travel while you're leasing it."

"I was going to rent it for my teenage daughter and wanted to be able to track her while she has it, just to make sure she doesn't go too far. I wanted to know if I had to get a tracker installed while she had it so I could make sure. You know what teenage girls are like..."

"I do indeed," the salesman said with a laugh. "I have two of my own. Some models do have built in trackers. I can give you a list, if you'd like."

"That would be really helpful," Frank said. "I'll make sure to rent one that has the tracker in it and if they don't have one, I'll get one of the ones you can buy at Radio Shack."

The salesman gave Frank a couple of names of trackers that could be installed in the car to track the vehicle's movements in case he couldn't rent one with a built-in tracker. All in all, Frank felt confident that he could rent a vehicle without a tracker. He'd ask for an older vehicle, because those were less likely to have the built-in trackers.

Better safe than sorry.

He'd find out where Penny was living and take care of her while he was 'out of town.' He could either kill her outright and dispose of the body, or sell her to a buyer he knew who liked to make snuff films.

He'd decide when he got her which direction to take.

Then, he'd stay for a week in Portland and fly back.

No problem.

Of course, life didn't always cooperate.

He'd followed his plan to the letter, flying to Portland, renting a car without a tracker, driving back to Seattle. The first hurdle was an accident on Interstate 5 where Highway 97 diverged. A huge semi-truck flipped on the highway and all its contents spilled out over the dual lanes, forcing people to divert onto Highway 97. He was able to get back on Interstate 5 soon enough, but the delay was considerable. By the time he arrived in Seattle, he was exhausted.

He'd then rented a van using fake I.D. and followed her all day, and when she was alone, he almost had her in his grasp. Some young coed saw him attack her and came running out of the bushes, interrupting him in the middle of things. He'd dropped her and ran to the van, driving away, returning the van.

He made one more try the following day after driving back and forth between Portland and Seattle. This time, things went smoothly.

He texted the girl once he arrived back in Seattle, giving himself some leeway. He knew if he was rushed, he would be more likely to make a mistake, leave evidence behind, slip up.

The actual abduction was far easier than he imagined. The girl was so interested in meeting with "Dean" that she didn't even question the late meeting time, or the location where they were to meet — the parking lot behind the hotel.

That's what hope did to a person. It made them stupid.

He was able to take her down easily enough, his mask on so that she had no idea who he was, nor would anyone remember anything but a very old man driving a white panel van.

The mask he'd purchased was so lifelike, people were completely fooled by how he looked. They really thought he was an eighty-year-old man. He had to make sure he walked hunched over, his back bent, but he passed.

The mask had come in handy and was worth the price he paid to a craftsperson he knew who worked in film down in L.A.

"Make me an old man prosthetic. Something I can slip over

*top of my head, complete with hair and a mouth, holes for eyes. I
want it for a Halloween party I'm attending. I'll pay whatever
price you want."*

His friend was only too happy to comply. The man had
worked on some of the Muppet movies, crafting puppets and
was an expert. The material was a silicone rubber. With pale
wrinkled skin, wispy white hair, it covered his neck so he could
tuck the mask under his sweater or jacket. He glanced at
himself in the mirror once he arrived in Seattle, and went to a
bathroom in a gas station near the airport.

When he walked out, he made sure to crouch, and no one
was the wiser. Just a really old man shuffling along to his white
panel van. Nothing to see here, folks.

He parked the van in the lot behind the hotel, and waited,
checking his watch with impatience.

Finally, he saw her emerge from the car that dropped her
off and go into the hotel lobby.

He abducted her easily enough. He opened the side door of
the van, and she was innocent and gullible enough to come
around the side to look for Dean. She trusted Dean. She never
imagined anyone could use that trust to harm her.

He knocked her out, loaded her into the back of the van,
zip-tied her hands behind her back and then her ankles, and
stuffed a gag in her mouth so she wouldn't make any sound.

Finally, he drove to the small private boathouse where he
often stored his boat when he had business in Seattle. He
managed to carry her to the boat, then took it and her to
Whidbey Island and his cottage.

He had originally planned to get rid of her and throw her
into the middle of Puget Sound, the body weighed down with
cement blocks but that hadn't worked out very well the last
time. This time, he'd make sure she wasn't wearing any running
shoes that would float up like her mother's had.

Instead, he decided to sell her to Harvey Dunn, a client he knew of who liked to dispose of women and film the process. There was a small but very hungry and very elite group of clients who enjoyed that sort of thing. Frank wasn't a fan of snuff, but it made an otherwise routine disposal into a work of art that would keep on giving.

Frank had only used Dunn a couple of times before, when he had a particularly difficult girl to deal with. One who wouldn't cooperate with him. He figured it would make all the effort worth it and pocket him a few grand for his trouble.

It would take the girl out of the picture. She wouldn't be attending family gatherings, Christmas Dinner, Easter, or other vacations, the way that idiot Curtis hoped. She wouldn't be matching up her DNA to Curtis, when the idiot's DNA profile was added to the database.

The trip to the cottage took a short time, and then he carried her body into the basement, and threw her down on the mattress on the floor.

He could have killed her then and there and disposed of the body himself, but he was getting too old to properly cut up a body. Instead, he would rely on his client to do the dirty work. It was the guy's kink, after all. He made a lot of money off the freaks who enjoyed watching.

Frank didn't relish killing anyone. It was more a necessity than anything he enjoyed.

Someone got in his way?

He took them out. Simple.

In nature, animals ate each other and killed each other without concern. It was a struggle for survival and although humans had progressed a lot since they climbed out of the trees back in Africa, it was still a dog-eat-dog world.

Frank was not going to let this tiny girl eat him.

No fucking way.

He was not going to let her worm her way into his family and into his life, demanding money, claiming that he was her father, bringing up uncomfortable questions about her mother's disappearance.

That would just open up a can of worms that should have stayed rotting deep on the bottom of Puget Sound.

CHAPTER THIRTY-THREE

TESS LEFT PENNY WITH RELUCTANCE, but she was a grown woman. Since Penny and Dean were going to have a meal together, Tess figured that it would be quite a long time before they were done, but she was eager to find out what Dean had to tell her about their family ties.

Her cell dinged as she was pulling away from the parking lot, so she stopped to read the text.

MICHAEL: *Care to drive up to the cabin and stay there for the weekend? I feel like a few days near the water will revive me.*

TESS: *Sounds like heaven. I just dropped Penny off at the airport for a meeting with Dean Stewart who is staying there for a layover.*

MICHAEL: *She's meeting Dean Stewart?*

TESS: *Yes. He was in town for a layover and is staying at the hotel. I offered to give her a ride home after the meeting, but they're going out for a meal, so I decided to come home. The cottage sounds wonderful. If I leave now, I should be there in an hour and a half. Can you pack my things for me? My overnight bag is in the closet.*

MICHAEL: *Will do. Speaking of Dean Stewart, I have some news about the Stewart family. You'll be interested to hear it.*

TESS: *I'll be there, all ears.*

MICHAEL: *See you when you get here. Should I pick something up for us to eat? What do you feel like?*

TESS: *You'll be going by that Korean BBQ place. Get me my usual.*

MICHAEL: *Sounds good. See you soon.*

As Tess was leaving the parking lot, a white panel van drove by. There were a lot of those Sprinter vans around, since many businesses used them. She watched the van leave the parking lot, but couldn't see inside.

She drove onto the highway, eager to arrive at the cabin and spend the evening relaxing with Michael. She was especially excited to learn what he found out about the Stewart family after his discussions with Louise Connelly's parents.

Tess arrived at the cabin, nestled on a road that overlooked Skagit Bay over two hours later, due to very slow traffic on Interstate 5 going north.

When she entered the cabin, Michael was already there, and the living room smelled of something spicy — her favorite Korean Fire Beef.

Michael met her at the door and kissed her, wiping his hands on a paper towel.

"You're late and I was so hungry, I almost started without you. Dinner's ready. Have a seat."

"It took longer than I expected." Tess glanced in the dining room. The table was set and there were candles and a centerpiece of flowers.

"You really went all out," she said and smiled. Michael came up behind her and slipped his arms around her waist.

"We deserve it. Both of us have been working overtime on these cases."

"We have," she said and turned around in his arms for a kiss and a warm moment of affection.

She sat and Michael put the plate of food in front of her and then sat beside her.

"Here's to us," he said and held up a glass of beer. "Here's to a weekend of rest and relaxation."

Tess held up her own glass, and they clicked them together. She took a sip, but didn't believe for a second that either of them would take the time to relax. Instead, her mind was already working on the family tree she'd been revising on the white board in her office. Besides, Michael had visited with the Connellys, and was eager to discuss their daughter's case.

"They really think Frank Jr. killed Louise?"

"They do," he said and passed her the plate of rice. "John, Louise's father, was more circumspect about it, but Tana was determined. She said he liked young girls and probably killed Louise because he found a new lover — a young Hispanic maid from Florida, who became his second wife less than a year after Louise died. You can imagine they were livid that the DA refused to look into it after that."

"Wow. He did have an illegal relationship with Louise. I mean, she gave birth when she was eighteen, right? That means she became pregnant when she was seventeen. What was he doing seducing a seventeen-year-old girl? Especially the daughter of a business partner of his father's. That shows very bad judgement."

"It does," Michael said. "It's also very suspicious that his second wife up and left him with no trace except a single page note. The DA said that since she emptied her bank account, it meant she probably wanted to leave and didn't want to be followed or contacted."

"Still, the police should have opened a missing persons case, no?"

"Money talks. Corruptible people listen. Stewart has a lot of money. I'd like to see who he donated to or who one of his numbered companies donated to. Maybe a Sheriff? I hate to say it, but we know that people can be bought off to look the other way."

Tess shivered, wondering if they didn't have another serial killer on their hands.

"He was probably involved with Charlene," Tess said out of the blue, the idea just coming to her.

"My thoughts exactly."

"I was thinking Dean was the father, but given Frank Jr.'s penchant for young women — girls, actually — maybe it was him. I thought he might be covering up for Dean and was afraid Penny would come asking to be admitted to the family, but this is worse."

They finished eating their meal and instead of sitting in front of the fireplace and enjoying some quiet time, Tess pulled Michael to the desk and her laptop.

"Help me with this," she said and sketched a timeline on a sheet of paper, below the family tree she had drawn on it. "When Louise died, Dean was six years old. Frank stayed in California and married his maid the following year. He stayed with her for three years, and then she left. He moved to Seattle with Dean. Dean was seventeen when Penny was born in 2000. He joined up in 2002 when he was nineteen and went over to Afghanistan. Charlene would have been fourteen when Penny was born. Penny was abandoned in 2005. Charlene would have been nineteen. Frank... Frank would have been around forty-nine with a fourteen-year-old? He was with his first wife when she was seventeen. Would he go younger?"

"For some pedophiles, any age will do as long as they are under the legal age of consent. For others, they want only girls of a specific age. Mostly, pedophiles who like underage girls like to be able to dominate them. They feel inferior in some way to women their own age. They are turned on by the illicit nature of what they do — the very idea it's illegal excites them even more. It might have been simple proximity. Charlene was a neglected girl of fourteen, in an impoverished family. She was easy pickings for a sophisticated rich older man with illegal perversions. Some pedophiles like Parkinson prey on poor girls and give them money as a way to entrap them."

Tess nodded and imagined poor Charlene becoming involved with someone like Frank Stewart, who most likely killed his first wife and maybe his second.

"Frank killed Charlene."

There. She said it.

Michael nodded and took the laptop from Tess. He did a search and pointed to an image on the screen. "Based on this article, he has a boat. Probably several. He owns a cottage not far from here on Whidbey Island. It's also not really that far from where Penny was abandoned. He could have driven his boat to meet Charlene and her pimp at Redwood Bay. He could have killed them both and dumped the bodies. Charlene's foot washes up on the shores of Vancouver Island seven years later, but they have no way to ID it."

"And because no one knew the identities of Penny's parents, the foot was unidentified until Penny submitted her DNA sample," Tess said. "She's been in contact with Frank Stewart and Dean Stewart, as well as Frank's brother, Curtis.

She told me that Frank hasn't been willing to help her, but both Dean and Curtis have. Curtis even said she looked just like his mother, suggesting a close family connection."

"You should tell her to be careful around Frank," Michael said.

"I will," Tess said. "I'll text her right now."

Tess pulled out her cell from her bag and sent Penny a text.

TESS: *Hey, Michael and I were talking, and we think you should be extra careful in your contact with Frank Stewart. I know you said he wasn't helpful, but there are some questions about his past that make Michael concerned. We can talk more tomorrow. I'm staying at the cabin near Skagit Bay all weekend, but we can talk if you want.*

Tess sent the message and then waited to see if it was delivered and read. She noted that the text was delivered, but not read.

"She's probably busy," Tess said, but a sense of unease filled her about Penny.

Michael put his arm around Tess's shoulder. "She'll text you back once she gets your message."

"I hope so. Now, I'm actually worried about her. Do you really think Frank is a killer?"

"You said it first." Michael shrugged. "It's possible we're going beyond the evidence, but it wouldn't hurt to be careful, considering one of his ex-wives is dead and the other hasn't been heard from since they split. He was also in a relationship with an underage girl and got her pregnant, even if he married her."

"He sounds like a real first-rate creep." Tess took out her cell and checked once more. The message showed that it had been delivered but still not seen.

Tess frowned. "She isn't responding."

Michael peered at it. "Maybe she doesn't want to check her

phone when she's with Dean. She probably doesn't want to seem distracted."

Tess checked her watch and shook her head. "I don't know. It's pretty late. She should be home by now."

TESS: *Are you home yet? How did your meeting with Dean go?*

Again, the message showed that it had been delivered but not read, but there was no response.

"Now, I'm worried," Tess said and showed Michael. "All she would have to do is say she's okay and is at home, if she doesn't want to talk now."

"Maybe they're having a drink or something and she doesn't want to be rude."

TESS: *Hey, Penny. Please respond. I'm worried about you. Let me know you're okay.*

Tess left the cell on the desk in case Penny responded.

"Relax," Michael said. "She's probably just busy."

It was then Tess remembered seeing the panel van driving out of the parking lot. A shiver went through her.

"I've got the creeps," she said. "When I was leaving the parking lot, I saw a man driving a panel van. Now that I think about it, it made me think of the old man who attacked Penny. Now, I'm worried that the old man kidnapped her or something."

Michael reached out and squeezed her hand. "Victims of violence often have a heightened fear of bad things happening. Why don't you call the hotel and ask to speak to Dean Stewart, just to check whether Penny has already gone?"

"Good idea," Tess said and took her cell. She googled the phone number for the hotel and waited for the clerk to respond.

"I'd like to speak to Dean Stewart, a guest at your hotel. Can you connect me?"

"Just a moment, please," the clerk said. "I'm sorry. There's no Dean Stewart registered here."

"Oh, are you sure?"

"Yes, ma'am. I checked and there's no reservation for a Dean Stewart."

"Thank you," Tess said and ended the call. She turned to Michael. "I have a very bad feeling about this. There's no Dean Stewart registered at the hotel."

Michael frowned. "Maybe he used a different name to register?"

"Why would he do that?"

Michael shrugged. "I don't know. It doesn't make any sense. Why would he ask to meet at that hotel if he wasn't staying there?"

Tess shook her head. "Because it wasn't him?"

Michael rubbed his forehead. "You could try calling his number directly. Does he have a listed phone number in Seattle?"

"I'll check," she said and googled Dean Stewart. There were several D. Stewarts in the listings and only one Dean J. Stewart in Broadmoor.

She called the number. Of course it went to voice mail.

"Hello, Mr. Dean Stewart, of Stewart Shipping? Son of Frank Stewart? My name is Tess McClintock and I'm working with Penny Schafer, who you have met before. I'm helping her find her relatives. She was supposed to be with you at a restaurant at the airport tonight. I was wondering if she's still with you, because she isn't answering any texts. If you can, please call me back at this number."

Tess ended the message and turned to Michael. "I don't like this. I don't like it one bit."

"I have to agree," Michael said. "All we can do now is wait."

Tess sighed heavily, a sense of doom filling her.

If Penny wasn't with Dean, where was she? Who did she meet at the airport hotel?

CHAPTER THIRTY-FOUR

WHILE HE WAITED for Dunn to arrive, Frank stood at the picture window overlooking Puget Sound and remembered back to when Charlene had tried to blackmail him.

There was no one who cared what happened to her, her bastard child or her pimp boyfriend. He'd checked, and there wasn't a mother or father around, no sister or brother who cared about her.

No one.

Back when he'd found Charlene, she was couch surfing after her mother was having financial problems and was almost evicted. The mother had met a new man and wanted to move to Tacoma to be with him and Charlene wasn't happy about leaving her friends. Charlene was a hard luck case, needing money just to get by. He used money as leverage with her.

She was sooo very thankful.

Frank had seen her when he had attended one of Dean's games and she was hanging around with a bunch of very nubile cheerleaders Frank was thinking of recruiting, except they all had wealthy parents and wouldn't be as open to his pitch as someone like Charlene. She was a hanger-oner, trying to be friends with the rich older girls and maybe meet one of their brothers. Frank knew the type very well. He'd made the mistake of marrying one or two of them.

As for Charlene, she was such a pretty thing and so vulnerable, and so he offered her a job as a model. Charlene was easy pickings.

She'd had stars in her eyes when she met him — all the girls he took in as hopeful models did — and she had been eager to get into the modeling business, like she actually believed she was this natural beauty and could become someone like the models they all worshipped on television. She saw him like he was a celebrity, never having been around wealth before. She was damn lucky to have the chance to apprentice with someone like him, for he was much higher on the social hierarchy than her, especially given her impoverished background. The food bank was not unknown to Charlene. Hunger was not unknown to Charlene.

That was how he was able to get to her — he understood how inferior she felt, with her family's poverty. But she was so damn beautiful with that long hair and innocent face.

In fact, she was perfect, and it didn't matter how poor her family was. In his world, she had what it took to be a real money-maker. But before she made him money, she made him happy. He had his own preferences and Charlene, before she got pregnant and ruined things, was just what he liked.

He'd managed to enjoy her quite a lot until he learned she was pregnant and then he sold her. A female's body changed after giving birth. He had no interest once he learned she was pregnant. If he had to support her, all that profit would be lost, and he did not like to lose money.

Then, a few years later, she returned to blackmail him for money. At first, he was going to refuse her demands, angry as hell that she was threatening him, but when she sent him a copy of her 'testimony' that she'd prepared, filled with a sob story of how she'd been seduced by him, and could give details about the other girls he had in his stable, and could describe the cottage on Whidbey Island and all its secrets, he knew he had to do something.

He considered paying her off, but he knew that if he gave in once, she'd be after him for the rest of her life, using blackmail to fund her lifestyle.

So, he decided to fix things. Neither she nor her pimp boyfriend were well-connected. They had no one who cared what happened to them. He checked them both out and they lived like paupers, with Charlene working as Dennis's girl so that the two of them could get their meth.

"Meet me at the boat launch near Old Town. If you want your money, come at 7:00 AM. I've got a busy day and have to get an early start. Bring the kid. Just so I know she's real."

"You already know she's real."

"Bring the kid or you don't get your money."

He arrived at the boat launch near Old Town after taking his own boat out from the boathouse that fronted his house on Whidbey Island. It was a short boat ride to the isolated boat launch on the mainland, which was perfect for his purposes. Once he pulled up into the small sheltered bay, he shone his spotlight on the dark beach and there, standing like two stupid dupes that they were, were Charlene and her tweaker pimp, Dennis.

Frank glanced around, shining the spotlight on the beach on either side of the two, but didn't see the kid.

When he tied the boat up to the small wharf, he waited for Charlene and Dennis to come.

"Where's the kid?"

"The *kid* is your daughter," Charlene said, her voice shaking a bit — probably from need and maybe excitement.

"How do I know you even still have her, and Social Services hasn't taken her?"

"She's up at the motel sleeping. She's only four and a half."

"If she's only four and a half, she shouldn't be left alone."

Charlene shrugged. "You said this wouldn't take long. Where's the money?"

He hesitated. He had planned to do them all, but surely the kid would be seen as just an orphan. They'd have no way of knowing who she was. In fact, he'd go to the motel once he was done and try to find her, take her and get rid of her.

Yeah...

"Go inside," he said and gestured to the boat, figuring that it was now or never. "I want you to sign a few documents first."

"What documents?" Charlene said, frowning. "I'm not signing any damn documents..."

"No signature, no money. They're just non-disclosure agreements that are common in these kinds of transactions. Come aboard. You'll see."

She came aboard with obvious reluctance, but her greed got the better of her and Dennis was fast to follow.

Once they were on, he untied the ropes and drove off.

"Where are we going? We don't need to go anywhere."

"The money's all there. Take a look."

He'd spread out the money on the table, and the two money-grubbers were attracted to it, despite their suspicions. "We're going just around the bay. There's a chance someone could come to the boat launch and see us. We'll be only a few feet away. Relax."

He'd left some fake documents beside it with pens, to make it look like he really meant it. What they might notice was the plastic tarp that covered the boat's floor in the cabin. That was for easy cleanup afterwards. He stacked some paint cans and paint paraphernalia around the cabin so the two idiots would think the tarp was to protect the floor from paint, and not blood.

They were such idiots…

Once he drove around the bay and they were out of sight of the boat launch, he stopped the boat and went down to where Dennis and Charlene were counting the money.

He watched them for a moment, shaking his head at their eagerness and how stupid the two of them were. Did they really think they could outsmart him?

Charlene had the audacity not to bring the kid. He didn't want any loose ends, but Charlene said that the kid was back at the motel.

The bitch left the kid alone in the motel? A four-year-old kid?

She didn't deserve to be a mother and she didn't deserve the money that she demanded.

He felt justified in getting rid of the two of them. They were human scum, living off the avails of prostitution, drug addicts, low life losers. Neither of them would use the money to go back to school, like Charlene said. They'd spend every cent on drugs.

That much he knew.

Tweakers had an express ticket to the grave. He was just giving them a shortcut to their final destination. Yes, he was doing them a favor, when it came right down to it.

Why, they should be thanking him for his benevolence.

One bullet in the back of Dennis's skull did the trick, the blood spraying all over the bulkhead, that Frank had very intelligently covered with the plastic tarp. He killed Dennis first, because he would be more of a threat.

The look on Charlene's face when she realized he'd shot

Dennis, a silencer on the end of his H&K... He put one right between her eyes, and she dropped like a cow in a slaughterhouse.

That done, he retrieved the motel keys from Dennis's pocket, so he could take a trip to the Quality Motel in Old Town and find the kid.

Next, he took a little trip into the deeper part of Puget Sound, cut the two bodies up and dumped the body parts into the water, broken cement blocks in the plastic bags to weight them down.

Once he was done, he took his boat back to Whidbey Island, moored the boat, then placed the plastic tarp in the burn barrel and lit it on fire. After he was sure it was consumed, he took his car and drove to the ferry at Coupeville, took it to Port Townsend, and then drove to Old Town, to find the motel and get the kid.

Except Charlene, the bitch, was a fucking liar and the kid wasn't at the motel.

He searched everywhere, but she wasn't there. They must have brought her with them, maybe left her in the car. He collected up anything that might identify the kid and left the motel room, their papers and personal effects in hand, and drove to the boat launch.

When he arrived, he glanced at the parking lot, and was just about ready to turn in when he saw that there were two Sheriff's Deputies there.

Crap...

He switched off his turn signal and drove past, his heart starting to beat a little faster. He drove farther and found a place to park, so he could think things through.

Did they already find the kid? It had taken him nearly three hours to take the bodies out into Puget Sound and dump the parts, then drive back to Whidbey Island, get his car and drive to the motel...

Damn. He hated loose ends.

The kid was a loose end.

As he drove off back to the ferry terminal at Port Townsend, he passed the boat launch and the Sheriff's Deputies were still there, and now there was another vehicle as well.

He'd spend the next hours and days on pins and needles, hoping that there was nothing at the scene to link him to the two, or the girl.

There couldn't be...

He'd retrieved everything from the motel room. He'd disposed of the bodies. The only things remaining were the kid and the car Dennis had rented, but he had both their cell phones and wallets, so there would be nothing to ID the car's driver.

He'd have to keep watch on the news over the next few days to see what happened and plan his response if anyone found any connection to him.

If he needed to, Frank could always escape. He had enough money and ties to people who could get him a new identity.

He could slip away and start another life somewhere else, if needed.

That thought assuaged some of the anxiety he felt at the possibility he might get caught.

CHAPTER THIRTY-FIVE

Penny woke with a terrible headache and felt as if she was being suffocated. A hood covered her head, and her hands were zip-tied behind her back. Her feet were likewise restrained.

She lay on her side on a hard floor and felt a hum under the vehicle and the loud roar of some kind of engine. Yet, she had the distinct feeling that she was outside, cool air passing over her hands and blowing the hood softly. She could hear the sound of water and realized she was on a boat.

Her instinct told her to scream, but with a hood over her face and her mouth filled with something cloth-like, she could only groan. The sound elicited nothing except a kick in her ribs from her captor — the old man. She moaned in pain, tears filling her eyes. At least he hadn't killed her outright, but then she wondered what he was going to do.

Was he going to rape her and *then* kill her?

The police officer who interviewed her told her she was lucky to be alive and that most women who were abducted were killed within a few hours of the attack.

The old man attacked her again. But... she'd received a text from *Dean*. Whoever the man was who texted her, he knew all about her quest for her family.

Was this Dean's doing? Was he working with the old man to get rid of her?

Her mind fought with itself, trying to figure it all out. It couldn't be Dean... He'd been so helpful and positive, giving her names and encouraging her. Whatever the case, whether it was Dean doing this with the help of the old man, or the old man acting alone, pretending to be Dean, she was screwed.

She listened as the boat traveled through the night, until finally, it slowed and then the motor stopped. The boat bumped against something — a dock, she figured. Then, she was picked up and carried roughly off the boat and up some stairs, the man grunting heavily as he struggled to carry her.

Was it the old man carrying her? How could he? He seemed to be old and frail with wrinkles and wispy white hair.

He carried her into a house and then, she felt him descend a staircase. Was she in a basement?

Finally, she was thrown down, onto something softer than the floor. A mattress?

Immediately, she feared he was going to rape her.

"You didn't make it easy for me," the man said. "Now, what the hell am I going to do with you?"

She couldn't respond, so she lay still and waited for what was going to happen next. She heard him walking around the room, his footsteps loud on the floor like he was angry.

"You should have left things as they were," he said, his voice full of warning. "None of this would have happened, but you had to pry. You had to keep prying into our lives."

Who *was* he?

Was he one of her relatives that didn't want her to find them?

Why?

He sounded like he was trying to justify what he was doing — to her and to himself.

"Things were going so well. All these years..."

All these years?

What did that mean?

"You've got to be worth *something* for all my trouble."

That made her frown. She listened and heard a chair scrape across the floor. He was sitting down. Then, he started to talk in a quiet voice. It wasn't so quiet that she couldn't hear what he said.

"I have something for you," the man said, his voice sounding weary. "The usual fee. It's disposable. In fact, I want it gone. No traces."

That sent a shock through her. He was obviously telling someone to kill her. *No traces...*

"I don't care what you do with it. Just make it disappear when you're done and make it permanent. I don't want it found ever. Do you understand? You've been sloppy before. They found the last one. Do this one *right*."

The last one? Had he done this before?

"Don't take too long, either. I don't have time. You have twenty-four hours, max. She's at the cottage. Get here as soon as possible and bring the money. I want this taken care of tonight."

With that, she heard the chair scrape across the floor once more and footsteps. Then, the sound of a door opening and then slamming shut, a key turning in the lock.

She lay on the floor in silence for a few moments, listening for any sound that he was gone. After what she thought was maybe ten minutes, but she had no idea how long it really was, she decided she was finally alone.

At that point, her training in self-defense kicked in. While it was too late to fight back against her attacker, she could at least try to escape.

She tested the strength of the plastic zip ties that bound her hands. They were tight, and when she tried to pull them apart, the hard plastic hurt her wrists.

She had to get her hands below her rear end and then in front of her, if she hoped to escape the zip ties. That much she remembered from her self-defense course. It took a while but finally, she managed to get her hands in front of her, which was made easier because she was on the skinny side and had long arms.

Thank God for family weirdness. Maria Ross Stewart was skinny and small, according to Curtis. Penny told herself that she was like Maria and that gave her a sense of pleasure.

The first thing she did was to remove the hood from her head. When she could finally see, the room was in almost total darkness with the exception of light filtering in from a high window in the basement wall.

Once her eyes adjusted, she could see that she was in the basement that was high end but still had a rustic feel to it. The walls and floor were covered in pine. The furniture had a worn and comfortable look to it, and the fixtures and electronics in the room were top of the line.

There were cameras set up on tripods and mirrors on the ceiling above her.

Whoever owned this cottage was wealthy.

Now that her hands were in front, she could use sheer force to break the zip-ties. She had to make sure she raised her hands up high enough, but if she did, she could break the ties. If that failed, she could find something in the room that would cut them.

After a couple of attempts, when she had cut her wrists and was bleeding, she gave up and instead, decided to look around for something with a sharp edge that she could use to cut the zip ties.

She struggled to get onto her knees, and crawled awkwardly to a desk against the wall. She would have to stand up and that would take a lot of balance, given that her arms were not free, and her ankles restrained. She had to be able to break the zip ties on her feet, so she took a few moments to slam her feet against the ground, finally succeeding in breaking the zip ties with a satisfying "pop."

She stood and walked to the desk, turning on the light that sat on its surface. Then, she rummaged through a drawer to look for something she could use to cut the zip-ties. There was a pair of big black utility scissors that she used to free her hands, and her heart leapt.

She was free!

She went to the stairs and glanced up, noting that there was a door between the stairs and the main floor. She went to the top of the stairs and tried the door, but it was locked — of course. She would have to break it down, and that would be difficult. She wasn't very strong.

She went back downstairs. There was a small window near the ceiling that faced the lawn outside. She stood on her tiptoes and looked out. It was raining hard, the water running down the windows. Outside, she could see the lights of a dock shining on the water and a boat moored to the dock. The cottage was in a small bay, sheltered by tall pines.

She checked the window and saw that there was no way to open it.

If worse came to worst, she could break it and crawl out.

Her captor was wealthy. A wealthy old man who wanted to kidnap her and then sell her to someone, who was supposed to dispose of her.

At least he didn't kill her right away. Now, she had a

fighting chance. The first thing she had to do when she escaped was run to a neighbor and ask for help. Before she did, she wanted to find some information on who owned the cottage, so she could at least help the police when they asked her questions. There had to be something to identify the owner.

She went to the desk and sorted through the pile of mail on the surface.

The top envelope had a name and address.

She had to look closer, but there was no mistaking the name.

Frank Stewart...

CHAPTER THIRTY-SIX

TESS'S CELL rang a few moments later while she was standing at the corkboard, staring at the timeline. Michael glanced up from the printout of the family tree Tess had constructed and watched her grab her cell.

"Yes?" she said and raised her eyebrows at Michael.

He waited, watching her face for her response to what the caller was saying.

"Yes, Mr. Stewart. Dean. Yes. Thanks for calling back." She frowned. "You didn't?" She glanced at Michael, frowning. "She received several texts from you about a meeting at a hotel near the airport. I drove her there and dropped her off. When we checked with the hotel, they said there was no Dean Stewart registered and so we started to worry."

Michael felt a knot in his gut that something very bad had happened to Penny. He stood and went to stand beside Tess, laying his hand on her arm. He stroked her shoulder while she listened.

"She was attacked recently, and so I'm worried she was being stalked." She shrugged. "I'm not sure. Maybe by someone who didn't like her looking into her relationship with their family." She listened some more, nodding. Finally, she sighed. "Thanks for letting me know. I'll call you if I hear anything."

She ended the call and turned to face Michael. "He's in Singapore right now."

"Singapore? When did he go there?"

"Two days ago. I'm really afraid, Michael. Should we call the police?"

"We should," Michael said and took her into his arms. "I can call Jack Mitchell at the Seattle PD."

"Thanks," Tess said. "I'm really worried about her."

Michael called Mitchell, and got right through to his personal cell.

"Hey, Jack, Michael Carter here. Sorry to bother you so late, but I have a situation here and wanted to call you and get your advice."

He spent the next five minutes going over what had happened, how Penny had been lured to a hotel parking lot at the Sea-Tac Airport and wasn't responding to calls or texts. The person she was supposed to be meeting had no knowledge of the meeting and the hotel had no record of him registering. That she had been a victim of an assault the previous day, and that Tess had seen a white panel van leaving the parking lot of the hotel. The van resembled the one used by the man who attacked Penny before and now, Michael feared that she had been abducted.

"I can put out a BOLO on her," Mitchell said.

"That would be great. You might want to check on a Frank Stewart, to see if he's got an alibi for tonight."

"Frank Stewart? Not of the Stewart Shipping family?"

"Yes. The very one."

"Why?"

Michael took in a deep breath. "I have no direct evidence

that it's him, but I have a very strong suspicion about him. He may be a close relative of Penny, and in fact, may be her father. He's done everything he can to dissuade her from pursing any relationship between them. Her mother went missing when she was four, and interestingly enough, two of his former wives, who he married when they were underage, died accidentally or went missing."

"You suspect that Frank Stewart abducted this young woman to prevent her from finding out that they're related? That's pushing it, isn't it?"

"Penny's mother's foot showed up in a running shoe on the coast of Vancouver Island a few years after she went missing. We have direct links between Penny and the Stewart family. I'm saying that I think Stewart is a person of interest."

"That's a pretty outlandish story, Michael. The only reason I'm listening is because it's you telling me, and I know you have experience on the Task Force and CARD Team. I have to trust your instincts, but at this point, there's really nothing we can do except put out the BOLO."

"Could you check on the security footage of the hotel parking lot? There might be footage of Penny being taken. She said she was meeting Dean Stewart in a van. A panel van."

"I can have someone take a trip there, but it won't happen until morning."

"Come on, Jack. Someone faked being Dean Stewart, lured her to the parking lot, and now we can't get in touch with her. If that isn't enough to go on, I don't know what else to say."

"Okay," Jack said, his tone reluctant. "I'll give this to MacDonald in missing persons. He'll drive there and check the feed."

"Let me know if you see anything," Michael said.

"I'll call you as soon as I know."

Michael ended the call and turned to Tess. "I did what I could."

"Can you talk to Nick or maybe someone on the CARD Team?"

"She's technically an adult, so no to the CARD Team. I'll talk with Nick tomorrow, but unless this is linked to an ongoing case, we have no jurisdiction until that time."

Tess sighed heavily and Michael pulled her into his arms.

"We just have to wait. That's all we can do."

"What if Frank took her to silence her, prevent her from finding out that he's her father?"

Michael couldn't reply. That was his thought as well.

Tess pulled out of his arms and tried to text Penny once more. She showed Michael the text.

TESS: *Penny, please text me to let me know you're okay.*

They waited, but of course, there was no response.

"Something really bad happened to her," Tess said, her eyes imploring. "There's no way she wouldn't text me if she could. Someone has her." She didn't say anything for a moment. Then, she shook her head. "I think he has her."

"He?"

"Frank."

"I think you're right. Given his past, given the connection between Penny and his family... I have to agree."

Michael felt on edge, like he couldn't just sit by and wait until police got back to him with news about the security video near the hotel. It would take them time to get to the hotel, and then work with the security team at the hotel to review the video feed.

"Where would he take her if he had her?" Tess asked.

"Either somewhere remote, so he could kill her and dispose of her body, or somewhere safe," Michael said. "He has warehouses where the company's ships are kept, but I expect they'd have security cams and security staff watching them."

"Didn't you say he had a cottage in the area?"

"Let's check it out." Michael went to the computer and opened a browser. He searched for *Stewart family cottage Whidbey Island* and examined the results.

There was a news story on the purchase of the mansion that overlooked Puget Sound. The address was Driftwood Way Drive. "It's on Driftwood Way Drive." He frowned, for that name rang a bell somewhere in his investigator's mind. "Driftwood Way Drive," he said again. "I know that address."

He called Jack Mitchell again.

"Hey, Jack. Sorry to bother you again, but can you verify something for me? There was an address on Driftwood Way Drive in Ericsson's files, for customers, I think. Can you double check?"

Tess glanced at him frowning. He covered his cell. "I remember an address in Ericsson's files that mentioned Driftwood Way Drive."

She covered her mouth.

Jack came back on the line. "Yeah. There's a listing at 18821 Driftwood Way Drive. No name attached."

"Thanks," he said. "I appreciate the help."

"You got something for us?"

"I'll call you if I do," Michael said.

He ended the call and turned to Tess. "Care to take a drive?"

Michael showed Tess a picture from an article in the local magazine showing the Stewart family cottage on the island. It wasn't really a cottage in the typical sense of the word.

It was a mansion.

"Why would he take her there?"

He exhaled and watched her examine the image. "Here's

my theory. Frank Stewart is a killer. He's killed two of his former wives before. He impregnated Charlene and may have killed her. Penny starts digging around in the family tree, searching for her mother after Charlene's DNA from her foot turns up in a Canadian cold case search. Frank doesn't want the fact he fathered her to be found out. He kidnaps and murders her to take care of the problem. Is that crazy?"

"My thoughts, exactly. We're both crazy."

"First, let's call Frank at his home. See if he's there."

"What are you going to say if he is? Did you kidnap and murder Penny?"

Michael laughed grimly. "No. I'll hang up if he answers. This is just to see if he's home."

Michael googled Frank's telephone number. Of course it was unlisted.

"I have a few tricks up my sleeve," he said and sat down at the computer. He used his access to a police-wide database to look up the phone number and entered it on his cell. He watched Tess, who sat on the corner of the desk beside him.

"Hello, this is Investigator Michael Carter calling for Frank Stewart."

The woman who answered had an accent — Hispanic — and he assumed it was the housekeeper or servant of some kind.

"Mr. Stewart is out of town at the moment. Can I take a message?"

"No, thanks. When did he go out of town?"

"He left yesterday and should be home next week."

"Should I call the office in L.A. or San Francisco?"

"Portland," the woman replied.

"Thank you," Michael said and ended the call.

"He's apparently out of town in Portland," Michael said. "He could easily have rented a car and driven up to the airport and taken Penny. The question is, what would he do with her?"

"He'd kill her and dump the body somewhere — in Puget Sound, probably. Only this time, he'd make sure to take off her running shoes, if she's wearing them."

"He has a boathouse at the house, according to the real estate article. We could drive there and see if there's any activity at the house. I know I won't be able to sleep if I just sit here and wait."

"How long will it take us to get there?"

"Half an hour, if we leave now."

"Are you sure you want to drive all the way there at this time of night? We won't be back until midnight or later."

"Stay here and rest," Michael said and embraced Tess, kissing her on the forehead. "I can go by myself if you're too tired. It's just this itch I have to scratch. I have no idea if he's there or anything, but I can't just sit by and do nothing."

"You're not going by yourself. I'm coming with you." She pulled out of their embrace and went to grab her bag and jacket. Then, she opened the small safe provided for renters, located in the front closet. It was where they stored their handguns. "Just in case, I think we should take these." She checked hers, and then grabbed a magazine before stuffing both in her bag. Then she handed Michael his gun.

"You need yours, as well," she said, and watched while he checked his weapon.

Then, they left the cabin.

Michael figured it was a fool's errand, but at least it would tire them both out so they could sleep.

CHAPTER THIRTY-SEVEN

FRANK STEWART?

Dean's father...

Curtis Stewart's brother.

She stood in shock for a moment, her mouth open.

Frank wanted to get rid of her? Why? Dean had said he never had sex with Penny's mother. There was no way Dean was her father, as much as Penny wished it was so.

Dean could have been lying, but he seemed so willing to include her as a member of the Stewart family. If Dean *had* been her father, why would he lie? Wouldn't he just refuse to have anything to do with her?

Maybe Frank was really worried that Dean was her father but why kidnap her and then sell her to someone for disposal?

It didn't make sense.

Then, she saw something that caught her eye. The corner of a photo sticking out from inside a file on the desktop.

She pulled the photo out of the file and saw it was a young girl. She was wearing a sexy dress that was far too old for her age, which Penny thought was around twelve, based on how flat her chest was. Still, she wore garish lipstick, and her hair was styled in a fancy updo. She was posing, her lips pouting.

At first, Penny thought it was just the poorly executed attempt of a young girl to look like a grown-up woman, but then she opened the file and saw the other photos...

There could be no mistake of what they were.

Child pornography. Each photo was more explicit than the last, culminating in one which included the girl performing a sexual act on a man.

Frank was into child porn.

Something was nagging her at the back of her mind.

Frank...

He was into child porn. He liked young girls.

She rifled through the photos and then saw several photo albums on a shelf beside the desk. She pulled one out and turned the pages, her stomach turning at the photos.

All of them young girls. Twelve or thirteen. There were names beside the girls, and ages.

There were years beside the names. The one in her hand was from a decade earlier. Several girls populated each volume. He had dozens and dozens of photo albums.

Then she found the volumes for 1998.

There, in the pages, was a young girl with long dark hair and dark eyes.

The caption read, *Charlene. 12.*

Penny was afraid to look at the photos. The first were innocuous. Photos of Charlene at the football games that Dean played in, sitting with the older girls. Photos of her smiling, posing with her hand fluffing her hair. Photos of her in a bathing suit, skinny and flat-chested.

One of her naked.

That's when Penny stopped looking.

It wasn't *Dean* who was her father.

It was Frank.

Frank was the one family member who didn't want to meet with her.

Frank was her father, and he was going to sell her to someone who would kill her.

If that wasn't bad enough, another thought came to her mind. She went back to the window and looked outside. The boat had a dark roof, but she could see, when the boat rocked slightly and was in the light, that the roof was red.

She stared at the boat in shock, her body trembling as recognition hit.

Frank had killed her mother.

That morning back in 2005 when she'd waited for her mother to return with Dennis and money so they could go for breakfast at IHOP?

It was Frank on the boat.

Her mother was planning on getting money from Frank, Penny's father, and Frank had come to meet them in the boat.

Frank killed her mother and Dennis, probably dumped their bodies in the Salish Sea and the only proof was her mother's sneaker-clad foot finally coming loose from its watery grave seven years later, floating to the surface and becoming a Jane Doe cold case in the Canadian government's cold case registry.

If she didn't do something to escape, she'd be next.

She searched around and found a box-cutter inside the drawer. She grabbed it and pushed the blade out so that it extended a good two inches.

She'd use that if she had to.

She tried to remember all the ways people in television shows and movies had defeated someone who broke into their homes or apartments. They hid beside a door, out of sight, and struck when the person entered the room. You had to strike fast, once they crossed the threshold or else the attacker might see you and overwhelm you because they were bigger and stronger.

Armed with a two-inch box-cutter, Penny was dangerous to anyone who didn't see her coming.

She'd aim for the neck, because that was where the carotid artery was — that much she remembered from her anatomy and physiology class. The carotid was an artery, and that meant it brought blood directly from the heart to the brain. Sever that and a person would bleed out in moments. They would pass out when thirty-seconds had passed without blood flow to the brain.

That was her best bet, so she stood in the darkness beside the stairs, her heart beating so fast that she was afraid she'd pass out.

Frank had called someone to come and take care of her, and she knew what that meant.

Kill her.

Frank was a killer.

Her father was Frank, and he was a killer. He'd called another killer to come and get her and kill her.

She heard noises upstairs and wondered if Frank would come back down again or whether it would be the man Frank called. She heard voices and she heard footsteps.

Then, she heard the sound of the lock jiggling at the top of the stairs.

He was coming.

She tried to stop from hyperventilating, taking in a few slow deep breaths, saying a prayer for herself, asking whatever god existed to protect her and help her escape. She wasn't sure there was a God Almighty, or if He cared about someone so small and insignificant as her, but if so, she prayed to it.

Please God. Please...

Footsteps sounded on the stairs, each one creaking as the man came slowly down each step.

When he emerged fully into the room, she saw that he was a tall man with a heavy build and dark hair.

She jumped at him from behind and jammed the blade into his neck, again and again. Her ambush was so successful that all he could do was reach up and try to push her away, but she had one arm around his shoulders and her free hand stabbed again and again and again...

He groaned, but didn't scream, his voice gurgling as blood spurted out of his wound, and a fine red mist came from his mouth. He staggered and fell to the floor and Penny fell on top of him, straddling his back, stabbing again and again.

She finally stopped, her hands bloodied, a spray of red on her hands and arms from his wounds.

The man was still, his arms spread out on either side of his body, his head turned to the side, eyes half-open.

He was dead...

He was dead!

She climbed up and stood for a moment, catching her breath, then glanced at her hands. She wiped her hands on her clothes, but the blood didn't go away.

She grabbed her bag, which Frank had left on the floor beside where she'd been restrained, and then held the box-cutter in her hand at the ready, just in case she had to defend herself. Slowly, she climbed up the stairs, her heart beating fast once more.

When she got to the top, she glanced around the hallway, but saw no one nearby. The front entry was clear, so she ran to the door and went out, almost falling on the way down the steps.

From behind her, she heard footsteps, and then Frank's voice.

"You fucking bitch!"

She didn't stop, running down the driveway in the darkness.

CHAPTER THIRTY-EIGHT

WHEN THEY ARRIVED at the Stewart cottage, Michael had to park several blocks away from the driveway, which was gated and had security cameras monitoring the perimeter. He strained to look down the driveway and saw a white panel van parked near the front entrance.

"There's a white van in the driveway."

"Oh, my God. She must be in there." Tess turned to him, her eyes wide. "Do you think he has security personnel on site?"

"Probably not, although there are security cams. We can walk to the beach and go along the coast. The cottage is visible from there, based on the images I saw on the real estate page when it was first built."

They walked through the woods that bordered the beach, and came out onto sand. Above sat the cottage, which was a large two-story home with wooden siding and a rustic-looking façade.

There were lights on in the interior.

"Look," Michael said and pointed. "The kitchen light is on. Someone's there."

"You don't think they leave on a light just to make it look like someone's home?"

Before Michael could respond, a figure walked in front of the window and stopped to look outside.

Michael instinctively ducked behind some brush at the edge of the property line. "He's there. That has to be him. Who else would be there?"

"I think you're right," Tess replied. "Michael, I'm scared. He must have her. Can't you call the police and get them out here? I don't want you going there alone. You can't even shoot well with your left arm."

"I can shoot well enough if it comes to it," he said and pressed her down. "You stay here. I'm going to go up there and check it out. See if he has her there."

"Michael!" she called out, but he was already on his way along the fence that marked the property. The going was rough because many large trees hung over the fence and he had to detour along the perimeter, with only the full moon to light his way. He remembered Eugene using night vision goggles for his abductions, and wished he had a pair himself. They would have helped immensely.

When he got to the house, he saw that there was a walk-out basement with a door and small window. He climbed over the fence, which didn't seem to have any extra security measures in place and went to the window. It had some kind of blackout covering on it, so there was no way to see inside.

He went around the house and peered in a side window, taking care not to make any quick movements, his gun at his side.

At that moment, a car drove up, the headlights shining onto

the property. Michael ducked down and waited, listening as the front door opened and a man, whom he assumed was Frank Stewart, stood on the doorstep.

A man exited the car, and reached into the back seat of his vehicle to remove a duffle bag.

"She's inside," Frank said. "In the basement. You have everything you need?"

"Yes," the man said. He was wearing a jacket and ball cap, but Michael could see he was a middle-aged man with a greying beard. "It's all in here. I'll take her off your hands. Here's your money."

"I'll count while you get her. Come in."

Michael knew what that meant. Stewart had sold Penny to the man — maybe a sex trafficker or pimp. He knew he'd have to do something.

While he watched through the side window, the man with Stewart disappeared from view and Michael felt helpless. He'd just have to wait and confront them once he knew Penny was in the vehicle. He could hold them at gunpoint. He decided to call the police while he waited.

Before he could, he saw Penny come running out, throwing the front door open and almost falling down the stairs. Behind her came Frank Stewart, a few feet behind her.

"You fucking bitch!" Stewart yelled as he chased her.

Michael acted without thinking. He ran to the front of the cottage and held out his weapon.

"Stop!" he yelled. "Police! Stop or I'll shoot!"

Frank wheeled around, and when he saw Michael standing with his weapon drawn, he reached into his pocket and withdrew a dark object, which Michael recognized as a handgun.

Michael aimed and shot.

The bullet slammed into Stewart's body, and he fell back,

his own weapon firing up into the sky when he struck the ground.

Michael ran to his side and kicked the weapon out of the way, then took out his cell and dialed 9-1-1.

While the call connected, he breathed in deeply, trying to calm his rapidly beating heart.

Finally, a dispatcher answered.

"This is Investigator Michael Carter, with the Seattle DA's office. I was investigating a case and need police and an ambulance. A suspect is down."

The dispatcher took the information and when he was finished, Tess came running up to where he knelt, checking Stewart's wound.

"Michael! Are you okay?"

"I'm fine. Penny ran down the driveway. You should go to her."

On the ground, Stewart groaned. Michael kept his gun trained on the man, but he did check the wound, which was on Stewart's side just above the right hip. It looked like a clean through and through injury, but it was bleeding pretty badly.

Michael removed a wad of tissue from a pocket in his jacket and stuffed it into the wound. It wasn't much but it would help.

"Who the fuck are you?" Stewart asked, his face a grimace.

"Investigator Michael Carter with the Seattle District Attorney's office. You're lucky I'm such a bad shot or you'd be dead right now."

Tess came back, her arm round Penny, who looked pale, her eyes wide.

"Thank you," Penny managed to say, her voice shaky. "I think I killed the man inside. I stabbed him with the box-cutter. He was going to kill me."

Michael nodded, examining her, noting the blood covering

her hands and clothing. "The police are on their way. You're safe."

In the light from the open front door, Michael watched as Penny began to weep.

CHAPTER THIRTY-NINE

PENNY RAN DOWN THE DRIVEWAY, blindly, running into the trees that bordered the property.

She heard someone call out behind her. "Stop! Police! Stop or I'll shoot!"

She made it to the woods at the side of the driveway and ran inside, when she heard a shot ring out. Then another.

She turned and saw that a man was standing with his gun pointed at Frank, who lay on the ground on his back.

The man who identified himself as a police officer shot Frank.

She remained just inside the trees, watching as Tess McClintock came out from beside the house, her own weapon drawn, and spoke with the police officer.

Then, Tess came down the driveway.

"Penny?" she called out. "Penny, it's me. It's Tess McClintock. You're safe now. Michael shot Stewart."

Penny stepped out from the trees and Tess saw her and put her handgun away, then came right over, her arms open wide.

"Oh, Penny..." she said, her expression full of sympathy. "Are you okay? You're bleeding."

Penny looked down and her hands, which were in fact, bleeding. She must have cut herself when she stabbed the man in the basement.

She held up the box-cutter. "I stabbed a man in the basement. He was there to kill me."

"Oh, my God, Penny," Tess said and reached into her bag and pulled out a tissue. "Give that to me."

Penny handed Tess the box-cutter and watched as she wrapped it in tissue. Then Tess examined Penny's hands, pressing some more tissues against the cuts.

"Squeeze this," Tess said. "It will slow the bleeding." She put her arm around Penny's shoulder. "Let's go back to the house. Michael's an Investigator with the DA's office and a former FBI Special Agent. You're safe now."

Penny let Tess lead her back up the driveway to the front entrance, where Michael stood talking on his cell. At his feet lay Frank.

"Thank you," Penny said when they got to Michael. "I think I killed the man inside," she said to Michael. "I stabbed him with the box-cutter. He was going to kill me."

Michael nodded. "The police are on their way. You're safe."

Penny exhaled finally, and started to cry.

Tess put her arm around Penny and hugged her, and that made Penny feel embarrassed. Tess had been attacked by a serial killer. She was brave and strong. Penny took in a deep breath and wiped her tears with her good hand. She smiled at Tess.

"Thank you," she said. "I'm fine."

"It's okay to cry," Tess said. "You were abducted and were

going to be murdered. You had to attack someone to escape. You have every reason to cry."

"No, really. I'm good." Penny smiled, feeling almost giddy. "I'm really good."

On the ground, Frank moaned, and Penny couldn't help herself. She went over to him and looked at his face. He had a bald head, and his skin was aged, but he did resemble the man in her mother's photo from years earlier. The man her mother always said was her father.

The same brown eyes. The same chin.

The family chin. The one that he got from his mother. The one his mother had given to Curtis. The one she had, too.

"*You're* my father," she said to him. He was gritting his teeth like he was in pain.

"Fuck off," Frank replied, his hand holding his side.

"You *killed* my mother. I saw the boat that day. It had a red roof. Like the boat at the dock."

Frank did nothing but grimace, his hands holding his side.

At that moment, the distant wail of a siren sounded.

"The police are almost here," Michael said. "You and Tess should sit down on the stairs. They'll want to talk to you."

Penny nodded and then turned to Frank. "You're a pedophile," Penny said, staring at his face. "You raped my mother and got her pregnant."

"Go to hell," Frank said with a grunt.

"I saw the photos of my mother in your basement. You're a pig. I hope you bleed to death. No," she said, correcting herself, tears coming once more. "Bleeding to death is too good for a monster like you. I hope you go to jail, and the inmates kill you after raping you."

Penny felt Tess rub her shoulder, like Tess was trying to soothe her.

The flashing lights of a police car lit up the driveway as the vehicle came to a stop a few feet away from where they stood. The doors opened and two uniformed police officers came out and ran over to them.

Then, an ambulance drove up behind the police car.

Penny wiped tears from her face and listened as the police spoke with Michael, who showed them his badge.

Tess pulled Penny into her arms and gave her a hug.

She really was finally safe.

The EMT came over to where Penny stood with Tess's arm around her.

"Let me see your hands," he said, and she opened her hands gingerly, the tissue soaked with blood. "Come over to the ambulance, so I can see them in the light," he said, and Penny followed him to the back of the ambulance. The young man pulled on gloves and peeled back the soaked tissue to expose the cuts, which still oozed blood. "You need stitches. We'll take you to the local hospital E.R., where they can treat you."

Penny turned to Tess. "Can you come with me?"

Tess nodded. "Sure. Michael will follow in the Jeep once he's done talking to the police."

"Thanks," Penny said. "I hate hospitals."

"Don't mention it," Tess said and went to speak with Michael before returning. "Michael will come by later and pick us both up. He'll take us to the local police station, where you can give your statement."

"Thanks," Penny said, tears starting again because Tess and Michael were being so nice to her.

Tess rode in the ambulance with Penny, while the EMT cleaned her hands and bandaged them. When they got to the E.R., Tess checked in with her, helping with the registration and insurance, and then waited in the room with her while the E.R. doctor examined her hands.

"You need stitches," he said. "You're not going to be able to use that hand for a while."

Penny smiled. "I can type with the other hand, I guess."

The doctor gave her a shot of anesthetic, which hurt more than the actual cuts by that point, and then stitched up the main cut. When the procedure was finished, and all the blood had been washed up and the fresh bandage applied, she and Tess went to the waiting room, where Michael was sitting, reading a paper.

"All done?" he asked, placing the paper down and standing. He glanced at Penny's hands. "Looks like you're all patched up."

"I am. Are we going to the police station?"

"Yes," Michael said. "I have orders to bring you in for your statement, to help police with the case."

They followed him out to his Jeep, which was parked in the patient parking lot.

They drove through the streets to the Coupeville police station, where they met with a detective in charge of the incident.

"We'll wait for you," Tess said and gave Penny a hug. "They'll be coordinating with the police in Seattle. Right now, give your statement on what happened. We'll drive you back to your dorm when you're finished."

"Thanks," Penny said, and took in a deep breath. "I'm so glad you're here." She turned to Michael. "You saved my life. If you weren't there, he would have killed me."

"I'm glad we came to check out Stewart's cottage."

"Why did you?" Penny asked. "What made you come all the way to the Island?"

"We were already suspicious about Frank," Tess said. "His

first two wives were either dead or hadn't been heard from for years. Plus, we checked the hotel and Dean was never registered and when we called Dean, he was in Singapore, so we knew someone was trying to lure you there. When you didn't answer your texts, I was scared that someone took you. Right away, I thought maybe Frank abducted you. We wondered where Frank would take you and looked at Frank's property on Whidbey Island, not far from the cabin where we were staying. Michael remembered the address from the sex trafficking case. We decided to drive there and check it out, just in case."

"I'm alive now because you did," Penny said and wiped tears off her cheeks. "Thank you."

"We're so happy that we did."

With that, Penny followed the detective to a room in the back of the police department office building, while Tess and Michael remained in the waiting room.

Penny's hands were still shaking just a little, but she was starting to feel like everything was finally going to be okay.

CHAPTER FORTY

Both Tess and Michael were separately interviewed by Detectives at the Coupeville Police Department. When they were finished, they sat in the waiting room for Penny to come out, so they could take her back to her dorm in Seattle.

"How are you doing?" Michael asked, rubbing Tess's shoulder.

"I'm fine," she said and gave him a smile. "I'm just glad you've been practicing shooting with your left arm."

"I'm just glad I didn't kill him outright," Michael said and stretched his arm, rubbing the shoulder. "I want him to help us take down Parkinson and what's left of Ericsson's sex trafficking ring."

"You think they worked together?"

"Stewart's cottage was listed as a customer. He bought girls from Ericsson. From what Detective McCurdy said, there's a treasure trove of photos and videos in Stewart's cottage basement. Lots of evidence of previous victims, trophies, you name it. I'm hoping that we can trace back to Parkinson and Ericsson, and take the whole ring down. We have Stewart cold, for abduction and conspiracy to commit murder. Depending on what evidence we find in Stewart's cottage, we might be able to get him for dozens of child rape charges, not to mention reopening his wife's case. And of course, Charlene Schafer. He's a very bad man."

"He is," Tess said and leaned her head against Michael's shoulder. "I'm glad you suggested driving out to the cottage to check it out."

"Me, too."

They waited for another ten minutes and finally, Penny came out to the waiting room, her book bag on her shoulder.

"Thanks for waiting," she said. "I'm exhausted, but can we stop at McDonald's on the way home? I haven't eaten and I'm starving."

"Of course," Michael said and stood. "We'll get you something on the way. I'm sure there's a twenty-four-hour one open somewhere."

The three left the police department, walking out into the parking lot. The sky was still pitch black.

Michael felt lucky that the evening had a good outcome. It could have turned out much worse. They could have stayed at the cottage and Penny would have been dead. She would have become just another one of the hundreds of young girls and women missing in the Pacific Northwest.

Thank God for whims...

The three got in Michael's Jeep. Tess sat in the back with Penny, just to keep her company.

As they drove back to Seattle, they spoke about the case.

"I feel really bad for Dean, to find out that his father — *my* father — is a killer," Penny said. "I'm sure he killed Dean's mother, and he killed mine. Who knows how many other girls or women he's killed? He's a serial killer, right?"

"I don't think he's a typical serial killer, who actually likes to kill," Michael said, making eye contact in the rear-view mirror. "He killed people who got in his way or became inconvenient. He got away with it for so long, because he's smart and has good lawyers and lots of money. Plus, people give him the benefit of the doubt because he's such a wealthy man, and considered a pillar of the community. He puts on a good façade, but underneath, he's a pervert and a killer. He's a sociopath. A high functioning sociopathic killer."

Penny sat watching out the window, and Michael felt bad for her. "How are you doing, knowing that your father killed your mother?"

Penny shook her head. "I always felt sad when I thought that my father died, but that was just a story my mother told me so that I wouldn't feel like he abandoned me. If I had known he never wanted anything to do with me, it would have hurt a lot more, so maybe the story was actually a good thing. I do like Dean and Curtis. Curtis is my uncle and Dean is my half-brother." She smiled. "I hope we can both get over this and actually be a family."

Tess squeezed Penny's arm. "Give him time," she said. "Both of you need time to absorb everything and figure out how to go forward. It would help to get some counseling. Mrs. Katz will help you deal with it."

"I'll definitely talk to her," Penny said with a faint smile.

They stopped at the first McDonald's on the way, and Penny ordered a chocolate shake, a Big Mac and fries. Tess had a coffee and Michael picked a soda, so they all had something for the rest of the drive to Penny's dorm.

"Will you be okay staying by yourself?" Tess asked. "Is there a friend you could stay with tonight?"

Penny shook her head. "I'm really fine," she said and slurped her milkshake. "I feel alive. Really alive."

Michael smiled and watched Penny eat the burger with

gusto. Both he and Tess knew that feeling — the feeling you get when you realized you were finally safe.

The case against Frank Stewart would wind its way slowly through the courts over the next year or two, but mostly, Penny's part in it was over. She could focus on getting on with her life, connecting with her family, and finishing her degree. Now that she knew who her mother and father were, he hoped that she could move forward.

They dropped her off at the dorm when it was starting to get light in the distant horizon.

Tess and Penny hugged and then Michael gave Penny a quick hug before they watched her enter the dorm.

Michael put his arm around Tess. "All's well that ends well, I guess."

"I'm exhausted," Tess said. "I feel like I could sleep for twenty-four hours."

"Let's go back to the cabin," he said. "We need a few days to recover, don't you think?"

"I think."

With that, they went back to the Jeep and drove off as the first rays of sun peeked through the trees.

Later, Michael sat behind the desk at the cabin, his laptop open and a window showing the face of Nick at the DA's office.

"You had quite the night, I hear," Nick said, grinning.

Michael laughed grimly. "You might say that."

"I've been speaking with Detective McCurdy in Coupeville. They've got dozens of boxes of material from Stewart's house. It's going to keep us busy for quite a while, but I'm looking forward to it. When you get back from your days off, you can take over and provide me a summary of everything. I'm glad I hired you, Michael."

'I'm glad you did, too, although I didn't expect I'd have to discharge my weapon."

"You weren't technically on duty," Nick said with a laugh.

"Luckily, my shot missed the center of mass or Stewart would be dead instead of recovering in hospital."

"Yes. I prefer the wheels of justice to turn, even if they are slow and not always perfect. We can probably close a few cases based on the materials we recovered at his cottage. A few more links to Ericsson, that will help us get Parkinson as well. These creeps like to share their perversions, so we may be able to find a few more like Stewart and put them away."

"Hope so," Michael replied. "I'll be in on Monday. Ready and eager to get going."

"Good," Nick said. "See you then."

Michael ended the Skype session and left the room he and Tess were using as a shared office. He saw that Tess was up but was still dressed in her nightgown, robe and slippers. She was sitting at the kitchen island reading the Saturday newspaper and drinking a cup of coffee.

"You're finally up," Michael said. "I'd say good morning, but since it's almost supper time, that wouldn't be right. So good evening."

They kissed and Tess gave him a big smile. "I got a text from Penny. She's feeling good, and generally is positive about things, so that's a relief."

"She's good now, but may have a hard time later, once she starts to process things. She's still on a high based on surviving a near death experience."

"I know," Tess said. "I told her to take a few days off and just laze around. Book an appointment with her therapist."

Michael sat on a stool beside her and took a section of the paper. For the rest of the evening, they relaxed, listening to music and doing nothing more than reading the newspapers and eating take-out food delivered by one of the local delivery services.

Both of them had to decompress after the previous night and there was nothing better than the peace and quiet of the cabin overlooking Skagit Bay to accomplish that.

They drove back to Seattle on Monday morning, stopping at a local IHOP for breakfast.

"What made you want pancakes?" Michael asked after the waitress brought their orders.

"Penny's story about the day she was abandoned," Tess said, with a wistful sigh. "She was expecting to go to IHOP after her mother got money, and I can't get that image out of my mind. Poor child."

Michael nodded. "At least now she knows," he said and cut into his omelet. "She can move on with her life."

"I hope so," Tess said.

They finished their breakfasts and Michael dropped by their apartment so Tess could pick up her own car.

Then, both went to their own workplaces, each to pursue their own part of the case.

It had been quite a weekend — one neither of them would soon forget.

EPILOGUE

DEAN STEWART SAT in the booth across from Penny, playing with the food on his plate as he listened to her tell him the story of how his father kidnapped her and had planned for her death.

They'd agreed to meet at Blends, the local cafe that they'd been to the first time they met, to talk about the case and their new relationship.

"That's a horrible story, but it had a good ending. We're brother and sister," Dean said, a half-smile on his face. "Even if only half."

"We are," Penny replied. "Half is better than none. I wish it was under better circumstances."

"Me, too, but it is what it is," he replied. "I try to take a stoic view of life. Change the things I can change and accept the things I can't. I can't do anything about my father and what he did — to you or to me or my mother. I have to just accept it and move on. At least now I know the truth. I know I have a sister." He glanced up from his food and smiled at Penny. "That's worth a lot."

"It is to me too," she said and smiled back, feeling a little teary-eyed at his words. "All my life, I never had a real family. I never knew my real name."

"You're not going to call yourself Melanie Schaffer?"

Penny shook her head. "That would feel too weird. I'm going to keep Penny."

"That's good. Although I hardly know you, I know you as Penny." He sighed. "You had a hard childhood." Dean's voice filled with sympathy. "Living in foster care."

"My foster mother was wonderful, but that's not the same as having a family who's yours forever."

"That's right. We're permanent." He held out his cup of coffee and they clinked cups together. "We're family."

They ate in silence for a moment and it was a comfortable silence instead of an awkward one. Even though Dean was so much older than her, he seemed like he could be a real brother.

"How are you handling the idea that they're reopening your mother's case?"

"It makes me sad," he said, and averted his eyes. "But it has to be done. I remember when it happened, I wished my dad had died and my mother had survived, because he was never really very close to me. He was always off flying around the country, or on international trips, at conferences, and I didn't feel close to him. Then, I was stuck with him alone, with house-keepers and nannies looking after me. I felt like I was cheated out of my childhood. If someone had to die, I thought, why did it have to be my mother? She was so good. I always thought that it should have been him. I even blamed him for taking her on that hike. I blamed him for putting her in danger. Even before she died, he and I were never very close, and after even less close. So, you see, you and I are a lot more alike than you might think."

"We are," she said and reached out to take his hand. "We're both his victims. He killed both our mothers."

"He's a monster." Dean shook his head and sighed audibly. "Well, we have each other now. You're part of the family. There are some decent people in it, like Curtis. Even Sean, my other uncle, is nice. I never believed my father's lies about him and his side of the family."

"Curtis was really nice and helpful," Penny said and went back to eating her muffin. "I'm looking forward to Christmas. He already invited me to Christmas dinner at his house." She smiled.

"Good," Dean said. "Maybe I'll go this year as well. I usually tried to be out of town on holidays because my dad never made a big deal out of them. I feel bad for the girls, my step-sisters," he said and frowned. "I wonder if he did anything to them, considering he's a pedophile. He probably married Lena because she had three young girls."

He shook his head and Penny made a face of disgust.

"Our father is a monster," she said softly. "But I'm not and you aren't either. We can have good lives, regardless of what he was like."

"I'm determined to do exactly that." With that, Dean picked up his muffin and broke a piece off. "I'm not letting Frank Stewart ruin my life any more than he already has. From now, on, let's commit to only getting better. Deal?"

Penny picked up her muffin and held it up. "Deal."

She felt like she could face whatever evidence they turned up about her mother and what Frank Stewart had done to her. Michael warned her that the wheels of justice turned slowly, but at least they were turning finally.

That gave her hope and in the end, hope was what kept you alive.

END OF BOOK ONE

ABOUT THE AUTHOR

Susan Lund is an emerging author of crime thrillers and romantic suspense. She lives in a forest near the ocean with her family of humans and animals.

Join Susan Lund's newsletter to get updates on her new crime thrillers.

http://eepurl.com/dAfi6j

Printed in Great Britain
by Amazon